# Promises
## *at*
## Indigo Bay

# BOOKS BY ELLYN OAKSMITH

*Summer at Orchard House*

# ELLYN OAKSMITH
## Promises
### *at*
## Indigo Bay

bookouture

Published by Bookouture in 2020

An imprint of Storyfire Ltd.
Carmelite House
50 Victoria Embankment
London EC4Y 0DZ

www.bookouture.com

ISBN: 978-1-83888-991-3
eBook ISBN: 978-1-83888-990-6

*To Liv, my beautiful, intelligent, brave, and funny friend who hardly ever falls in rivers.*

# CHAPTER ONE

## No Surprises

What were the odds of a girl like me becoming a Pavarotti fan? Slim to zero.

"Romeo calling," Rachel sang, leaning across her client's head. Izzy, stationed at the middle chair, simply smiled. At sixty, Izzy didn't get excited about much. When a client's ex-husband once brandished his hunting rifle in the salon, Izzy famously deadpanned, "Earl Carter, put that damn thing away before you shoot off your toe."

Earl went home.

Paolo had set his ring tone on my phone to one of the most famous Italian tenors, so I'd always know it was him. I'd grown to love Pavarotti—if not exactly for his singing, for the single fact that his voice meant that the love of my life was calling.

I'd never been lucky. Far from it. I didn't grow out of my childhood; I survived it. So for me, meeting a sexy Italian wine master had been somewhat akin to winning the lottery while riding a unicorn with a leprechaun.

But better.

Because, well, Paolo.

With Paolo, you were pulled into celebrity orbit. Eventually everyone who was attracted to men, discreet or not, was going to check him out. Try describing that star quality and you'd come up short. Truth was, he made people feel good. Especially me. His laugh brightened a room. It wasn't his appearance, exactly. His Roman nose was on the majestic side. His warm brown eyes were bit close together. His curly hair, despite my best attempts, was always slightly unruly. However. When he flashed his joy-seeking grin, delighting in the tiniest thing—a good meal, a beautiful sunset, a long, relaxing swim—his true beauty showed. When Paolo smiled, you noticed the warm gold flecks in his eyes, his broad shoulders, his clear brown skin. Everything else faded away.

"You gonna get that, hon?" Izzy growled, in a voice roughened by a pack-a-day habit since birth.

The professional thing to do was to not answer. I owned Twig, a three-chair salon in Chelan. Izzy and Rachel were technically my employees, although after nine years in the trenches with Izzy and six with Rachel, the lines had blurred. We'd drunk half a lake's worth of margaritas at Señor Frog's and been through, collectively, three divorces (Izzy), countless breakups, two cheating husbands and dozens of deadbeat boyfriends. Izzy was the one person besides Carmen I'd talked to about my childhood. It pained her. She was friends with my mother and wished we were closer. Still, I needed to set a professional standard, which was harder than it sounded. When it came to Paolo, I didn't have much self-control. Life was uncertain. Enjoy it now. I'd learned that at nine years old.

Lonnie Bexbury, the woman sitting in my chair, studied me in the mirror with raised, perfectly groomed eyebrows. I had to stop myself from running to the phone like a lovesick teenager. There was a sharp line in my life. Before Paolo, I'd been hemmed in by the two square miles of this town. It was Saturday nights at Señor Frog's, getting just buzzed enough to pretend that one of the men at the bar was interesting enough to talk to. It was getting all the ladies in town gussied up to look their best while wishing I had someplace nice to go.

It was a good enough life.

But then.

When Paolo smiled at me that first time, it was like a giant switch went on after a power outage. He adored my freckles, my wild reddish auburn hair, the way my skin took a while to accept the sun, forcing me to wear sunscreen until I had a tan. Most sporty men wanted a woman to join them or wait, like dogs, while they completed their paddle, swim, or half marathon. This man appreciated my curves. Paolo didn't need us to be a matched set. If I sprawled like a cat in the sun with my mess of magazines and a cooler, he stayed and chatted. Eventually, he'd venture out in his kayak, after asking what time he needed to be back for dinner. He didn't want a fitness freak Barbie to his Euro Ken.

He had not asked a million questions about my family history. It was a relief, not being with someone from Chelan who knew me as That Girl. With Paolo, I was perfectly normal.

So yes, although I knew I should not be checking my phone during work hours, I couldn't help it. For once in my life, I had something more important than a client. I had a boyfriend.

Not just any old boyfriend.

Paolo.

Lonnie Bexbury wasn't a woman used to waiting. She was one of those high-maintenance blondes whose life revolved around looking good. Yoga. Pilates. Eating clean. Regular facials and skin peels. She'd made a big deal of explaining to me what her stylist in Seattle did to get her hair looking so fabulous. She'd described a balayage as if Lake Chelan wasn't stuffed with women just like her, terrified that a local hairstylist was going to butcher her expensively highlighted mane and turn it into an over-processed mullet. (So, so, so tempting.) She'd stated she was a taking a "huge risk" with me, but Taylor in Madison Park couldn't fit her in before the Seattle Tennis Club's fall luncheon. She was taking her life in her hands, sitting in my chair.

Summer people were like that. Living on the edge. Words like "luncheon" were said with a straight face. They were disappointed when I wasn't impressed that they belonged to the Seattle Tennis Club.

Nope.

Yes, I did know what it meant.

Lady, if I cared less, I'd be dead.

I gave Lonnie a "one sec," holding out my finger, green eyes wide, trying for apologetic. Lonnie would close up her summer house and disappear from my life for nine months. She could wait two minutes.

Izzy gave me an amused grin. Attitude was her middle name.

"*Ciao, bella* Stella, I am just leaving work." Paolo's voice always knocked me out. If someone had told me a year ago that listening to my boyfriend on the phone would turn my brain into mush, I would have said, "Yeah. Not that girl." He'd lived in the United States for a little under a year. His voice made me feel like crawling into my phone, pinging off a satellite and launching myself at him like a heat-seeking missile. I was so entranced by the melody of his accent, it took a while for the actual meaning of his words to filter through. "The lake is bountiful."

I cradled the phone on my shoulder, turning to glance outside at the ridiculously blue sky. It was an Indian summer. The kind that made me want to ditch Lonnie, run to my car, change into my bikini and sit on the dock, watching Paolo swim. Paolo swimming was a piece of performance art.

I didn't want anyone to see the goofy grin on my face. "You mean beautiful." Paolo, whose English was very good, occasionally messed up, just to make me smile. "She cuts the hairs," he said, when asked about my business.

"No, bountiful. The sun, the grapes, the wine. It's like gold." I pictured him shifting on the hot leather Jeep seats, driving from the Hollister Estate, anticipating a mind-clearing dive into the deep blue of Lake Chelan. Work. Home. Dive. Cook. The man was a living, breathing miracle. "I have a surprise."

"Yay. What are you cooking?" When he had time, Paolo surprised me with meals from his native Lombardy region. Fresh fish, berries baked into lemon-soaked pastries and, always, pasta. We would eat on the dock until it grew chilly. September was a glorious month in Lake Chelan. The August heat had faded, leaving the lake warm, clear and turquoise blue. Crimson aspen leaves rippled in the hills. Tourists packed up.

"Not a meal. Something else," he said.

"I can't cook."

"True."

"I'm still working." I turned to face Lonnie, who impatiently tapped her limited-edition gold Apple Watch.

Paolo groaned with frustration. "Ah, I forgot the late night. Come home at seven. No stops, *per favore.*"

Lonnie gave me the stink eye. She still needed a trim, but wait up—a what? "A surprise? Wait, what's the surprise?"

"Meet me at the dock."

It was probably a kite board. The man was an overgrown teenager when it came to water sports. "Okay."

"*Sì. Ti amo. Ciao.*"

"*Ciao.*"

When I apologized, Lonnie took it like a sulky summer person: a subtle *I forgive you* mixed with *don't ever let it happen again.* She eyed me with curiosity, as I trimmed the fringe framing her tan face. "You know Italian?"

I'd seen this look a thousand times. Summer people expected locals to stick to a certain script. Sailing little boats, fine. Crewing a sailboat team? No. We were small-town people and should act as such.

"I know one Italian. My boyfriend." What an idiot, still thrilled by saying *Italian* and *boyfriend* in the same sentence. "And he's got a surprise." I sang it, a tinge of excitement blossoming.

Lonnie's face lit up as she played with a glittery diamond sandwiched between two elegant pavé bands. "Oh my, that sounds promising."

My face flushed. "Uh, no. It's probably another kayak."

The ring sparkled on her manicured hand. "How long have you been dating?"

*None of your business.* "A while."

My fingers trembled slightly. Could I skirt this conversation as skillfully as I danced around Paolo's questions about my childhood? With him, it was easier. He wasn't a busybody. He didn't pry.

"Aren't you two coming up on one year?" Rachel chirped, turning to Lonnie with breathless enthusiasm. "He's just crazy about her. Sometimes he packs her lunch and it looks like something you'd get in a really fancy restaurant."

Lonnie's Botoxed brow struggled to lift. "Oh my! What kind of a ring do you want?"

In the last year, I'd discovered that Paolo's father had taught him everything about making Italian wine. He'd grown up with long family meals. A bookish sister, Emilia. Chickens, dogs, outdoor cats, and plenty of love. My throat tightened whenever he asked, gently, about my family. "You know, usual family stuff," I'd say, employing a bag of tricks I'd learned in grade school when a teacher had asked, with great concern, how I was doing.

Distraction. Question. Subterfuge.

Lie.

I hadn't lied outright to Paolo. Not intentionally.

I'd just never told him the truth about my family.

That marriage, for me, was a bond that pulled you both under when you were sinking. Ties that bound until you couldn't breathe. Love? Yes. Forever? Maybe "till death do us part" worked for some but for me? Too dangerous. Loved ones could slip away and leave you forever. I wouldn't risk it. Couldn't.

Suddenly, the thought of Paolo's surprise seemed less promising. A ring? A proposal? Not now. Eventually.

People like me didn't do therapy. We freaked out. *Thanks for nothing, Lonnie Bexbury, because I'm pretty sure I'm exhibiting three out of five symptoms of a panic attack right now. Which I'm going to google after I finish your stupid haircut.*

Picking distraction, I steadied my shaking hand. "How long do you want your bangs?"

"What the hell?" Lonnie Bexbury shot daggers at me, furiously blinking.

Oh no. I'd accidentally snipped one of her lash extensions. Her eyelids dragged the half-snipped extensions up and down, tiny black crow feathers. Izzy was trying not to bust up laughing. Rachel asked if I wanted any help.

My hand was over my mouth. "Oh. Sorry," I blurted.

That was a first.

Lonnie Bexbury would not be a repeat customer.


Paolo and I had been together nearly a year, living together for close to two months. The first week after moving in with him, I'd left my salon exactly as I'd done for the previous nine years. I'd locked the door, tossed the keys in my purse and crossed the street, passing Local Myth Pizza with its line of people already outside, waiting for one of the twelve tables, salivating at the aroma coming from the wood-fired ovens. I'd continued across the bridge which spanned the tail end of Lake Chelan, where it turned into a lazy green-tinted river. Busy thinking about nothing, I'd ignored the paddle boarders, the tourists eating ice cream in the riverside park. I'd gotten as far as the garden gate, when I saw my former landlady grinning at me in the garden, asking me, with obvious delight, if I was moving back in.

Mrs. Fennelly, a widow with a gap-toothed grin whose dentures clicked as she talked, missed me. Said she'd kick out the current tenants if I wanted. I'd felt compelled to stay for a glass of lemonade, explaining to Mrs. Fennelly that no, I'd just been absentminded. It made her feel better, seeing a girl my age forgetting something as important as where I lived.

Today, I couldn't forget. Ever since the phone call with Paolo, my mind had been spinning on itself like a wind sculpture. I'd shooed Lonnie Bexbury out of the salon with her flapping eyelashes, not charging her a cent, even though the cost of the balayage and cut exceeded what she'd spent on her lash extensions.

I needed time to think.

On the drive home, I pulled into the parking lot of the Red Apple market and bought myself a tall can of Arizona iced tea, heading to the city park. Across an expanse of ridiculously green grass going dry in straw-colored patches. I found a bench near the lake and watched some kids throwing French fries at seagulls big enough to knock the littlest kid over. I called Carmen. My lifeline.

I'd say Carmen was like a sister to me, except that most women who came into the salon complained about their sisters. A lot. There were a whole lot of, "You know, I love my sister, but—"

Yes, Carmen was occasionally annoying. Since she'd moved back from Seattle and begun working for the family winery, she'd become even more of a workaholic. She couldn't help it. The girl had stayed up all night in fourth grade making sure her Alexander Hamilton diorama was so perfect that Mrs. Marsden had accused her of hiring it out. But I knew that if I was stranded on a rock in the middle of the Pacific, surrounded by circling sharks, she'd swim to me if she had to. Everyone needs a person like that in their lives.

When she answered, I was shocked. Carmen usually let everything go right to voicemail, so I didn't waste a second. The winery always needed her immediately. I launched right in. "Car, he's got a surprise and he sounded very excited about it. It worries me. I googled the signs of a panic attack. I have three of them. Maybe four, although this iced tea has a lot of caffeine, so maybe that's why my heart is racing."

"You're not having a panic attack," Carmen said.

"How do you know?"

"If you were having a panic attack, you wouldn't admit it. You'd be like, me? Have a panic attack? No way. In the middle of a panic attack. That's how I know. Remember in high school when your foot was pointing in the wrong direction and I said your leg is broken? And you insisted that feet just do that sometimes?"

"Oh. You're right."

"Also, you do like surprises and by he, you mean Paolo?"

The seagull made a run for the littlest kid. He started screaming bloody murder, then tripped. The seagull made its move on the French fries.

I strolled down to the water. "I like fun surprises, like spontaneous day drinking and picnics, and that helicopter ride was amazing, but this feels scarier."

"Scarier than a helicopter ride? What are you worried about?"

I crossed the lawn, slightly crisp with fall approaching. Late season campers strolled around the Chelan City camping ground to the north, lighting their barbecues. The scents of lighter fluid and charcoal wafted in the cooling air. Shimmering in the late day sun, the lake was a deep turquoise ribbon, running the length of the sage foothills of the North Cascades. "You know what I'm worried about."

Carmen sighed impatiently. "You're being ridiculous."

"In the immortal words of Bobby Brown, that's my prerogative."

"Bobbi Brown, the make-up artist?"

"The singer. You know the song." I sang a few bars, trying to capture the singer's disco dance beat, shimmying a bit. Teenagers on the deck of the Lakeside Drive Thru shook their heads. At their age, I would also have thought a thirty-something dancing on her own in a park was epically tragic. I would have told Carmen, "Please shoot me dead if I ever do that." What I found tragic now, though, was my best friend forgetting a great song.

Carmen was silent, patiently waiting for my solo to end. My voice left a lot to be desired. Tone. Pitch. Melody. "I don't get you," she said, when I'd finished. "You fell for him so hard. So fast. What was it, a month after laying eyes on him, you dropped the 'L' word? I've never seen you like this. Ever."

"I know. Most guys make me wish I was the other 'L' word." Living with Paolo this summer had been like inhabiting someone else's glamorous Instagram feed. He'd come home from work, drop his bag in the hallway, disappear into the bedroom and reappear seconds later in his swim trunks. Paolo in swim trunks was something to behold. Like a professional soccer player, without the tattoos and side-shaved haircut. Arms muscled from all the kayaking and paddle boarding. Every single time he walked toward me down the narrow hallway, I thought, *This has to be someone else's life.*

After kissing me, he'd open the sliding glass door, stroll barefoot down the dock and dive. Never paused, just threw himself into the lake. That was Paolo, no hesitation. Pure movement. The same way he'd come across an ad for a winery manager in an international online trade journal, googled Lake Chelan and immediately called Evan Hollister.

Paolo had a talent for taking the plunge.

With long, sure strokes, he'd swim down the length of lake until I couldn't spot him. I'd either hang out on the dock and relax in an Adirondack chair or go inside and take a shower. Half an hour or so later he'd emerge, wrap himself a towel, shake the water from his dark curls and tell me what he had planned for dinner.

It was the perfect life.

He was going to mess it up.

Reaching the end of the park, I spun around on the path. Sun glimmered on the rippling lake like a shattered mirror.

"But Paolo? Every day I wake up, look over at him and think, Stella Gallagher, this is your life. Can you believe it?"

"And?" Carmen's impatience was palpable.

"And we're in a serious relationship. Serious. A word normally associated with heart attacks and cancer. I don't do serious."

A mother duck and her babies paddled past, churning their tiny feet furiously in the waves. A visible reminder that while the rest of the world paired up, produced offspring, I did not. The party wasn't over. Not yet. I paced the water's edge, keeping to the path in my wedge heels. The crying kid had been soothed. The seagulls had moved on to other victims at the Lakeside Drive Thru.

Carmen whispered to someone, "Bring another case of rosé out of the cave." Back again, she said, "He's not going to propose."

"Why not? I'm a catch."

Another heavy sigh. "Where are you? You sound out of breath."

"At the city park, avoiding emotions. It's my hobby. I'm very good at it."

"Go home, Stella. Even if he does propose, you can say no. It's a perfectly acceptable answer for a thirty-one-year-old when the love of your life pops the question."

"Thanks for nothing."

"If Evan proposed, I would not be on the phone complaining."

"You're ready. You had a happy family life. You came from a normal family."

"All right, I get it. But again, what is wrong with saying no?"

"Once a proposal is on the table, there is no going back. You aren't dating, you're the one saying 'no.' You're living in limbo."

"What's wrong with that?"

"It's a relationship killer. He'll have put his heart on the table and I'm like, nope, no thanks. I'll pass."

"You can't hide in the park forever. Go home. Stop being such a baby."

"Wow, someone's crabby."

"Hang on. I'm going outside."

I sipped the last of my iced tea as I crossed the street back to Red Apple parking lot.

"Guess who signed up for the fall wine tasting dinner at Blue Hills?" Thanks to Carmen and her sisters, the winery did a lot more than sell wine.

"Beyoncé?"

"I wish."

"Pete Carroll?"

"Who's that?"

I tossed the iced tea can into the recycling bin outside the store. "Seriously? The head coach for the Seahawks."

"Right. Evan's parents. They're in town between a safari and a Scottish golfing trip. They didn't even call Evan. Didn't say, 'Oh, hey, I heard your girlfriend has the winery next door and maybe we could have dinner sometime and meet her.' Lola saw their name on the reservation list and wondered if they were related to Evan."

"Weird."

"Right? I can't say no. They signed up. Paid a lot of money."

"If I can say no, you can. Just say no. Both of us. You don't have to meet his parents and I don't have to get married."

"You're being paranoid."

"He said we'd make beautiful babies."

"Wow. Okay. That's a new one. What did you say?"

Sliding into the seat of my car, I tossed my purse on the passenger seat. "I dropped my sandwich in the lake."

"Brilliant move."

"Prosciutto, tomato and fresh basil. He baked the bread." One of Paolo's many, many charms.

"Of course he did. Anyway, I want to meet Evan's parents. Just not while I'm working. I'm going to feel like the help."

"You want me to work at the fall wine dinner? I'm very good at drinking wine and telling people what to do."

"Yeah, 'cause that's what running a winery is all about. Listen, I have to go back inside."

"Thanks for totally not reassuring me."

"Any time. But Stell, would marrying him actually be the worst thing in the world?"

I started the car, giving myself a look in the rearview mirror. Carmen lost her mom to breast cancer when we were in tenth grade. She knew about loss. But my loss was different. My parents had so many friendships that dried up and blew away. People want an expiration date for grief. A smile. A sign of happiness. I did that. Sometimes I was genuinely at peace. But twenty-two years wasn't long enough. Not for me. "I don't want anything to change."

"Everything's gonna change, Stella. You know that, right? It's just the nature of life. I didn't think I'd be able to run this winery, but I did."

"Running a winery and getting married are totally different things."

"Are they?"

Chelan was divided into two camps. Those who lived on the waterfront and those who did not. The waterfront dwellers had homes with the best views, parties and recreational opportunities. Hill dwellers, with their sweeping views of the valley and the North Cascades, pretended that they were above it all. They thought their views made up for the sweet joy of relaxing in Adirondack chairs on the dock, listening to the waves ripple onto the shore as the sun slipped over the hills, crowning the lake in spectacular colors.

Those people were dead wrong.

We moved into Chelan from the country when I was ten. A little rambler on a dusty, no-name street. Eventually, it sagged with neglect. For fun, I'd wander down to the city park and pretend I lived in one of the pretty houses lining the lake. Every day I'd pick another one, fantasizing about how idyllic my life would be if I inhabited it. There was one with a gazebo near the water. Another had a fire pit by the dock. One had jet bikes perched on bulkhead racks. Life inside those homes, I'd think, would be happy. How could anyone not be filled with contentment while gazing out at Lake Chelan?

The home I shared now with Paolo was a squat toad between two spacious modern homes. Rough-hewn logs and river rock stones signaled their second home status. In the past few decades, since the dot com era, Lake Chelan had become an oasis to millionaires and their families. They'd bought old homes, torn them down, then replaced them with second homes larger and flashier than their primary abodes.

Ours was one of the dated holdouts. From the road, it appeared neglected. A 1960s ranch-style fishing cabin in need of a coat of paint. Scraggly bushes. Cramped gravel parking spots facing a dusty laurel hedge, which divided the narrow property from those of the neighbors. A piece of driftwood nailed to the doorframe was painted with faded looping lettering: INDIGO BAY. The inside of Indigo Bay, however, told another story. Freshly painted in creamy white, a gleaming open kitchen faced a wall of windows, showcasing the view. A neat rectangle of emerald green lawn, cropped and lush, bordered the lake. The L-shaped dock jutted into the water, set with three inviting red Adirondack chairs. A lakeside weeping willow blocked the neighbor's view into our small patio with its barbecue and fire pit.

Two weeks after moving in, I'd padded down to the dock with binoculars. I'd called Carmen, who I knew was at Hollister Estate, asking her to find Evan's binoculars and search for me on the dock. It was important, somehow, for me to see her, across the lake. When Carmen had returned to Blue Hills to help her father save the winery from the bank, I'd slogged alongside her and her sisters, hefting patio stones, painting, even playing caterer when they'd hosted weddings in an attempt to drum up revenue. Blue Hills and Orchard House had always been a part of my life, but the sweat I'd put into turning it around a year ago had made it even more mine. My place in the world would always be relative to Blue Hills Vineyard. It held a piece of my heart.

Evan's vineyard was on the lake slightly to the north, across from Wapato Resort, adjacent to Blue Hills. Carmen had been impatient at first when I'd called, but she'd been a good sport, calling me back and dutifully scanning the lake. I'd spent five minutes describing homes we'd been to in high school. No, not the one with the water slide. I kept telling her to look for the hulking willow. Finally, she found me. We waved. I felt happy.

"Now what do we do?" Carmen asked.

"Come over and have a glass of wine." It was impulsive. I already knew the answer, and Carmen confirmed it. She had to work at the family wine bar they'd opened last fall. I'd been a little disappointed, but still validated. Now that Carmen could locate me, had seen me on my new dock, that made it real.

Opening the door to Indigo Bay now, I calmed myself. Maybe Carmen was right. It could be something else. Paolo's news could be that he'd finally heard back from the State Department and his work visa had been extended. That had to be it.

"Paolo?" The smell of grilling meat drifted into the house from the neighbor's outdoor barbecue. We wouldn't eat until eight at the earliest. A night owl by nature, I had adapted easily to Paolo's European habit of late dinners. I hung my purse on the hooks lining the entry way, calling Paolo again as I slipped off my sandals. He didn't answer.

Our house had a simple layout. Small entry ending in a hallway. Immediately to the right was a galley kitchen, overlooking an open living room and dining area. To the left was a small guest room, a bathroom and a master suite facing the water. I took a right into the kitchen. Empty and sparkling clean. Freshly mopped hardwoods gleamed in the late afternoon sun. I'd forgotten about the blessed weekly event called A Visit From the Cleaning Lady. Evan Hollister had lured Paolo from Italy with the promise of a lakefront home, including a gardener and weekly cleaning lady.

When I'd learned of her existence, I'd practically levitated in joy. Paolo had asked if I minded someone else cleaning our home. "Do I mind?!" I'd laughed giddily. "On what planet does someone *not* want a cleaning lady?"

Then I'd patiently explained that, while I did like a tidy home, I did not enjoy spending my days off cleaning. I was Marie Kondo's lazy little sister. I'd drag a dust cloth around the house for ten minutes before finding something much more interesting to do.

"She changes the sheets, Car," I'd breathlessly reported to Carmen after Paolo had informed me of this miraculous creature. "While I'm at work, someone else is cleaning my toilet. It's magical."

Carmen, who'd been raised in a much more stable home environment than I had, with a mother who had done housework and forced Carmen to help, agreed wholeheartedly. A cleaning lady was the best kind of magic.

The kitchen bore traces of Paolo's after-work snack. A few Marcona almonds. Some mineral water. A green apple core.

Propped on the cutting board was a folded piece of paper. An arrow pointed to the sliding glass doors. Typically, I showered when I came home, to sluice off the hair clinging to my body. It could wait. Changing into a bikini top over my favorite frayed cut-offs, I pulled on a tank top and brushed my hair into a ponytail. A slick of ChapStick. A quick smile in the mirror, enjoying the anticipation of seeing Paolo. I did this sometimes. Looked in the mirror and thought, *Hello, you. You with the Italian boyfriend, the waterfront home and the cleaning lady. You have one hundred percent reached your destination. You're not waiting for your life to start. This is all yours.*

Then I was out the sliding glass door, across the thick grass prickling my bare feet, and down the dock, ready for my surprise. The surprise that would upend my happy world and bring it crashing down. There were two kinds of surprises. This was not the good kind.

# CHAPTER TWO

## Do I?

Paolo was at the helm of a low-slung wooden speedboat. The closer I got, the worse it appeared. The leather seats were crinkled and faded; stuffing poked out like clumps of yellow bread dough. The exterior wood was tarnished and dull.

"She's a beauty, right?" Paolo looked up with the anxious face of a boy who'd brought home a stray dog. "A 1955 Chris-Craft Capri Runabout. Very rare. Only one hundred and seventy made in two years. A classic." He kissed his bunched fingers, releasing them to convey that I was looking at a masterpiece. He'd brought home a waterborne work of art.

Tracking a gull lazily drifting above us, I took my time before dashing his dreams. A cool boat in Chelan was not a rundown heap of Popsicle sticks. It was made of high gloss fiberglass. It was fast, and preferably, if you really wanted to rub it in, a Cobalt or a Bayliner with white leather seats. This boat might have gotten my great-grandmother excited about a hundred thousand years ago, but to me, Paolo had wasted his money on proving the truism: a boat is a hole in the water that you pour your money into.

"It's wood."

"*Sì*. A classic. They gave me eight thousand off because the exterior needs refinishing. The seats need new leather."

I played innocent. "Do they?"

"I am thinking red." He scrambled onto the bow of the boat, running his fingers down the metal striping the wood. "This teak, when refinished, will shine. With the red leather seats, a true beauty. A knockout." He jumped off the boat, pointing to the stern where the words "Chris-Craft" and "Capri" were embedded in the wood in faded silver script. "Capri. It's Italian."

"I've heard of it." Italians who lived in Capri wouldn't be caught dead in this boat. Weren't Italians known for their good taste?

Paolo stuck out his lower lip. "Stella, you don't like the boat?"

A good girlfriend would lie. Clearly, Paolo had fallen hard for this old heap. He was an otherwise perfect specimen of manhood, who treated me like I'd personally invented sunshine, happiness and the male orgasm. "It's super…" I knew I should fake it. Somewhere in the good girlfriend handbook there is a chapter on pretending you approve, just to be a good sport. But here's the thing. I couldn't. "It looks like it did hard time in someone's trashy vacant lot. Where did you find it?"

"The List of Craig." Of course. Paolo's favorite place in the world for sporting equipment. The side of our house was a veritable rainbow of kayaks, paddle boards and one small sailboat.

Crossing my arms, I gazed wistfully at a gorgeous sleek white speedboat docking at the neighbor's. "Thank you, Craig."

Paolo grinned, leaping easily off the boat onto the dock, moving closer to me as if he knew his proximity made my blood pool everywhere but my brain. Wind ruffled his dark curls. His warm brown eyes crinkled at the corners. Tiny crow's feet, from years on Lake Como. "She's like the old lady. A little sad, maybe lonely in her garage, but, you give her some love, some attention and she shines."

"Baby, I'm a small-town American girl. I like fast boats and cheap beer."

Paolo frowned, suddenly serious. "She is fast. Rebuilt, 158 power of horses." He snapped his fingers. "We go for a ride. Pronto. On with the bikini."

I hooked my bikini straps with my thumbs, waggling my eyebrows. "Check." I perched on my toes, kissing him, wondering why he hadn't bought a normal boat. Surely the List of Craig had some better boats. This tinder box had probably cost as much as a brand-new fiberglass Bayliner. What if he tried to refinish it himself? Paolo knew more about wine than anyone in this valley, but he was no handyman. A light northern wind made me shiver, despite the sun. "Let me just grab a sweatshirt." I was halfway back to the house when I turned around, calling back to Paolo. "This was the surprise, right?"

Paolo didn't hear. He was testing the engine.


"You see." Paolo waved to the surrounding landscape, the sun dropping behind the hills like a neon fireball, shedding a caramel shine over the lake. "We have our own island." This was expansive Paolo, after a glass of wine. I loved him like this, when work had drained off his body and he relaxed, talked about Italy. The boat bobbed slightly in the gentle calm. "When I was a boy on Lake

Como, I'd take the boat, zip out." He slid his hand through the air. "With my *paesanos*, my friends. Instant privacy."

"The girls must have loved you." I sipped my homemade spritzer. Mineral water and rosé.

Paolo shrugged, lifting the bottle of wine from the picnic basket. "You take this beautiful, delicate Italian rosé and you destroy it with the minerals. I do not understand."

I lifted my glass (Paolo didn't drink from anything other than glass), enjoying the sight of the blush tone against the sunset hues shifting from raspberry pink to deep tangerine. "Face it, Paolo, you're dating a heathen."

He placed another delicacy on my plate. "Prosciutto with the melon."

There was a brown squiggle across it. I wrinkled my nose in distaste. "There's something on it."

"Balsamic reduction. Brings out the sweetness. Please eat."

I took a tentative bite. A sip of spritzer. Raised my eyebrows. "It's not terrible."

Paolo leaned back on the towel-covered leather seats. Thick new beach towels I'd bought at Costco, kept folded and ready in a linen basket. Was there anything better than a basket of clean beach towels? "You love it." He rubbed the sun-bleached wood of the interior. "Just like you will love this girl when she gets her facelift. Some stain and varnish to bring back the beauty to this wood. Lipstick-red leather seats."

I smoothed a hand over the leather. "How about white?"

He made a face. "Red is sexy. Like a well-aged Nebbiolo. Earthy and full bodied."

"White never goes out of style." I popped another fig in my mouth, enjoying the salty sweetness. "It's your boat."

Paolo leaned over to caress my knee. "It's *our* 1955 Capri Runabout."

I felt myself shifting. "I could get into it. Wear a 1955 retro bikini. White. Like the seats."

Paolo shook his head, leaned down to frame my face with his hands. He kissed me, playing with my lips. "Swim with me."

I pulled back. "Didn't your mother ever tell you not to swim after eating?"

Paolo shucked off his shirt, gazing down. "This isn't eating. Later, the pasta." How did the man eat constantly and keep those abs?

He stood, climbing nimbly to the stern, balancing for a moment. He dove in a gentle arc, his body a pale line under the darkening water. He slid effortlessly under the surface, his long body fluid. I used to enjoy swimming. But aged nine, I learned that lakes can be deadly. Carmen and her sisters had all been like fish, kicking off sandals, shorts and sun dresses, plunging into the lake with wild abandon. My middle school and high school years had been spent manufacturing excuses. Always on the edge of the boat or beach, promising I'd join them when I warmed up. Wading, dipping toes, avoiding submersion. I knew how to swim. I just didn't like it.

Paolo surfaced, floating on his back, searching for stars in the periwinkle sky. "Stella, Stella, please. Come in. Swim with me. The first star of the night is more beautiful with you." He loved that my name meant "star" in Italian. Took it as a sign. "Venus." He pointed. "There you are. Goddess of love."

How deep was the water beneath me? A dark unknowing crept into my throat, making it hard to breathe.

And yet.

Resisting him was impossible. My entire dating life had been a long series of disappointing moments punctuated by interesting, but ultimately unfulfilling, sex. Paolo was a beautiful marlin dropped into a very small pond of guppies. I'd captured the attention of the most fascinating creature I'd ever met in my entire life. He'd probably bought this boat for exactly this cinematic moment. He'd trawled the List of Craig hoping for a clear night, a picnic, and the two of us in Indigo Bay as the first star flicked on.

Why not make him happy?

Peeling off my tank top, I filled my lungs with air, stood on the stern and plunged in.

It was a huge mistake.

For a split second, I was Paolo's girlfriend, delighted and happy. Then I glanced down. Dark water flew at my face. Daylight disappeared as I sank, heart hammering. Water filled my mouth as I screamed, gagging on the lake. It was swallowing me whole. My brain went blank, inches from death. Submerged in the third deepest lake in the entire country. The horrifying unknown.

Looking up, I saw a shape dark against the light. Kicking with all my might, I swam toward the familiar form, bent on survival. Reaching out, I grabbed his arm, pulling him to me, bracing myself to his torso. At first, he was gentle, trying repeatedly to push me away. When that didn't work, he lifted his arms, breaking my hold before roughly dragging me to the surface. Snot, lake water and tears streamed from my face. I tried to talk to him but there wasn't time.

Paolo hushed me, pointing at the sky. "We need to get out. A storm is coming."

What is the appropriate apology for nearly killing your boyfriend? It was a tricky process, particularly when you were on a lake, in a boat, trying to outrun a storm.

"I'm sorry, I'm so, so sorry." Shivering in my damp towel, I groaned as Paolo tried his best to berth the boat. Whitecaps slapped the rocking boat. Paolo couldn't listen. He was too busy trying to navigate toward our dock in the growing dark. He'd flipped on the running lights. They glowed across the dark water. Paolo navigated by the hulking shape of the willow tree, guiding us home.

"It's nothing. I have to concentrate, please." Paolo was having a hard time bringing us in. A northern wind had kicked up. Waves crashed against the dock. The first gusts had arrived shortly after we'd gotten out of the water. Shaking his head in frustration after multiple attempts, Paolo spun the rudder, piloting us to leeward side.

Paolo had a reassuring confidence navigating the rough weather. Jumping onto the dock, he looped lines around cleats with neat half hitches. He offered me his hand, pulling me out of the boat as rain sprinkled the newly slick wood. The air smelled of sweet, pungent ozone, charged with tension. Clouds rolled over the hills.

Paolo gently rubbed my back, covered by the soggy towel. "Go in the house. Get warm."

Feeling slightly guilty, I hurried down toward the lawn, leaving him to gather the glasses, picnic basket and wet towels. Snapping the boat cover on would be easier with two people, but he'd insisted, I rationalized, shivering uncontrollably.

After a warm shower, rinsing the lake from my hair and body, letting the black thoughts wash down the drain, I could finally face him. In our cozy bedroom, I wrapped myself in a white terry cloth bathrobe, my hair damp, smelling of the Aveda shampoo from the salon. As I toweled it dry, the rosemary mint fragrance calmed me, reminding me of what I loved about Twig. The predictable neatness, fresh towels, scented candles, glasses of wine for evening clients and wedding parties. Making people feel beautiful was deeply satisfying. The opposite of what had happened out on the lake.

Paolo was in the living room, lounging on the overstuffed sectional, staring thoughtfully at the lights across the lake, glimmering through the rain. A dim glow came from the kitchen. His laptop was open, ignored.

I curled up in the corner of the sectional, resting my head on one of the woven indigo pillows. He caressed my leg, waving at his computer. "Enough thinking of the pinot grigio. Evan says cut back; I say we double production. Who knows, right? He listened to me on the sparkling wine. Maybe some pasta?"

I closed my eyes tightly, unable to look at him. "I'm sorry I almost drowned you."

"Is that what you think happened?"

"You were floating on your back looking at stars, having this peaceful moment and I dragged you down like a lake monster."

Paolo couldn't stop laughing. He threw back his head on a pillow, nearly toppling his laptop, his teeth white against his brown skin.

I glared at him. "What?"

Paolo snorted, trying to stop. "You think you can kill me that easily?"

"You could have swallowed lake water. It takes sixty seconds." I snapped my fingers. "Like that. Over. Lights out." Every year, things happened on the lake. Some of them predictable, some sharp reminders that even shallow water isn't safe. I knew.

Paolo winced. "Poor thing. Nothing happened. You hugged me. You say 'let's go back to the boat.' We go back to the boat."

"I had a panic attack." My brain reverted to that of a terrified nine-year-old.

He turned his head, keeping his brown eyes, full of warmth, on me. "No. Even people who swim perfectly get scared. You aren't used to jumping off the boats. It's different. Scarier."

I sighed. Maybe he was right. "Okay. Maybe not. But I wrecked your romantic evening."

Paolo nodded, bending to look at the time on his laptop. "Impossible. No. I'm with you." He tapped his temple as he rose. "I will always remember tonight." He bent to kiss my forehead, heading for the kitchen. "A little pasta, some candles. We talk about the time you tried to kill me."

"The first time." It was easier to believe it was nothing. To slide back into our cozy life. Joining him in the kitchen, I grabbed a knife from the wall magnet. "I need practice."

Paolo placed a blue bowl of fragrant tomatoes on the oak chopping board. "Here you go, *bellissima*. Murder them."


Something was off. At dinner Paolo seemed distracted, or tired. I made a big deal about how delicious the dinner was because, honestly, every meal Paolo made was a work of art. Even when it seemed there was nothing in the refrigerator, he'd get out a can of beans, a stick of butter, snip some herbs in the garden and make us a beautiful pasta dish that tasted like it had been simmering all day. He used the simplest ingredients: homegrown tomatoes, basil, garlic, lemons, olive oil and pasta. A little butter on the noodles before the sauce, a handful of Parmigiano-Reggiano (the look of horror on Paolo's face when he'd asked for Parmesan and I'd brought out my green can of powdered cheese), and some homemade rustic bread. Every evening, I sat down to the best meals of my life. For a girl raised on canned ravioli and frozen vegetables, it was a revelation.

Our ritual was that he'd go for a swim while I showered after work. We'd meet in the kitchen, where he'd pour me a glass of wine. He'd long given up on asking me for tasting notes ("It takes like wine") although slowly, through osmosis, I was learning more. Lombardy, the wine region where he'd been raised, bordered the Italian Alps. Colder weather made the grapes less fruity, more earthy. These were the things he shared as I sat like a lump at the counter, completely enthralled by this exotic creature in the kitchen. He'd throw a kitchen towel over his shoulder, roll up his sleeves (which was somehow incredibly sexy), and chop, dice, sauté, all the while sharing stories about his day. A red blend that soured for no understandable reason. The new chardonnay, redolent of lemon and papaya, that was one of the best wines he'd ever produced. A surprise.

Sometimes he would share something his sister Emilia had said about one of her two boys, who were holy terrors. They were seven and nine, constantly being called into the principal's office of their Catholic school in Rome for releasing lizards in class or literally climbing the side of the school to peer into windows. Their father, Roman, thought that boys would be boys. Emilia wanted them punished. It was a nonstop fight between the couple. Emilia called Paolo to blow off steam, which was adorable.

If I cooked, which was rarely, I needed absolute silence and a recipe which I referred to a hundred times, checking and rechecking. Paolo was of the school of a dash of this and a handful of that. He could chatter away, barely glancing at his hands as he handled sharp knives or simmering pans. Every night it was a magic show for one.

Tonight, though, he was subdued. Maybe he'd genuinely been scared when I'd grabbed him underwater and was protecting me out of kindness. What if he knew that I was terrified of the lake? One of those, "Hey, my girl almost killed me, but it was an accident" kind of things. He usually embraced my eccentricities. In Italy he'd dated girls who came from the same kind of well-bred families who traveled in packs, went to the same schools and married within their class. Girls who knew how to tie scarves and order in French. Girls whose lives revolved around shopping in Milan, skiing in Switzerland and marrying someone appropriate, like Paolo.

Although things felt off tonight, we were both so tired, I was convinced we'd stick to our routine. Clear the table. I'd wash up because he'd cooked. Maybe watch a little television or read. The usual.

But Paolo looked like he'd made his mind up about something. His spine straightened as he reached across the table. "*Bella*, come into the living room. I have something to ask you. Something very important."

I thought I knew what was coming. Our lovely domestic routine meant more to me than he could possibly imagine. I just wanted another night.

I thought I knew what was coming. A proposal.

If only it had been that simple.

# CHAPTER THREE

## Yes. No. Maybe.

The living room faded from burnished gold to crisp magic hour shadows. Sliding glass windows reflected us, a cozy pair. One of those couples that makes sense. Particularly in this setting. Nestled into a waterfront rental with a cream leather sectional. Behind us was the simple wooden dining table and the open, modern kitchen. We had quartz counter tops, for crying out loud. And a cleaning lady.

I'd never wanted to be anybody else. But right now, I wanted to be a woman who could say, wholeheartedly, yes.

Instead my heart stuttered, my vision blurred and my throat cinched shut at the thought of Paolo proposing.

I babbled. As if a steady stream of words could stop fate. "Is this about the boat? You know, I'm not a huge fan. Fiberglass is a lot less maintenance, and who is going to refinish it? If you think I'm going to help, lemme just say right now that's not an option. I've got zero interest in spending my Sundays with a sander. I love you, Paolo, but not that much. Refinishing a boat together is above and beyond."

Paolo waited patiently for my verbal torrent to dry up. "It's not about the boat."

My jaw dropped, then snapped shut. "Am I going to need more wine? This feels like I will." His face fell, just a little, but I noticed. Leaning toward him, I touched his knee. "Okay. I'm done. Go ahead."

Paolo grinned nervously, exposing his one slightly crooked tooth. One of those imperfections that added beauty. "*Bella* Stella. I hated Chelan when I first moved here. I thought I'd made a terrible mistake." He shook his head, frowning in concentration. His English fell apart when he was emotional. The look on his face meant he was composing in Italian, mentally translating. "But then, we met and it was like the sun coming out."

I felt a fuzz of panic. We were getting closer and closer to a precipice from which there was no coming back. That was the problem with a proposal. Once the offer was on the table, you couldn't go back to dating. I jumped up. "Do you want some ice cream?" He shook his head. "Affogato?" It was his favorite. Espresso poured over a scoop of vanilla ice cream. "Are you sure?"

He sighed impatiently. "Please, Stella, let me talk."

"Okay." I lowered myself gingerly, sitting on the edge of the couch, giving him my attention.

He took my hand. "*Stellita*, I have wondered, many times, how to tell you this." He sighed. "There is no easy way. I have to leave in two weeks. Back to Italy. The extension on my visa was denied."

For the second time that night, my lungs went on strike. Game over, while I gasped like a beached dolphin. *What the what?* Someone needed to hit me on the back. Reboot my brain. "But Evan said—" I gulped. "He said it wouldn't be a big deal."

Paolo ran his hands through his hair. "He was wrong. Things have changed."

I stood up, opening the sliding glass door, gulping in the night air. "When did you find out?"

"Two days ago." He hung his head, unable to meet my eyes. He held up his fingers. "I'm sorry. Four."

"Four days? And you didn't think to tell me?"

"I had to think. It was very hard. I feel terrible."

"Paolo, we live together." I slipped out of the crack in the sliding glass door, went outside onto the patio. Time to think. That's what I needed. A million crickets chirped away. Stars blasted from a storm-cleaned black sky. The lake was calm, having finished its tantrum. Our willow was a dark giant, weeping into the lake. I felt insignificant, puny and furious. I strode back into the living room, where Paolo was holding his head in his hands. He looked up.

"Four days of eating together every night. Talking about our plans for this winter. Our trip to Whistler. Why did you even bother?" Paolo tried to speak, but I talked over him. "I can't believe you kept this from me."

He shrugged. "I know."

"You've had almost a hundred hours to think about this, and you just spring it on me?" I pointed to the lake. "I should have drowned you out there." Crying, I furiously swiped at my tears. He approached. I held him off. "No, no. You don't get to comfort me. I'm angry and sad and—"

Paolo opened his arms, as if to hold me. "Marry me, Stella. Please."

My eyes widened. Now this? "What?"

"I didn't want to tell you until I knew for sure that this was right. I know if we marry, we might stay here, and leaving Italy is a big thing for me. For you, I would do anything. Spend the rest of your life with me. Grow old with me. In Italy or Chelan. I want to make my life with you. Become a family. When I left home, I needed a break from, well, everything, even my family. One year, and I'd go home and settle down. Then I met you and everything changed." He stopped to breathe. "Marry me. I want you more than I've wanted anything in my entire life. We cannot be separated."

It was the tsunami after the earthquake. Ground shifted beneath my feet. I clenched and unclenched my fists, staring at him before turning to the window. "I can't think with you looking at me."

"Evan's immigration attorney told me that if we marry, I can apply for the green card the same day." Paolo made a move as if to kiss my cheek, but I shook my head. "You think, okay?" He nodded, walking down the dark hall to our bedroom, his hands buried deep in his pockets. He stopped in the hallway. "Take your time, Stella." He exhaled. "The ring I want to give you is in Italy. My *nonna* gave it to me. It's very old and beautiful. I called my mother to send it."

My deep and abiding love for all things sparkly raised its head and screamed: *Stella! Italian heirloom on your finger! At least look at it.* I sniffed, slightly mollified. "What did she say?"

Paolo flushed, running his hand down the wall. "She, uh…"

"Paolo, what did she say?"

He looked up at the ceiling. "She was so very happy for me. She wants to bring the ring in person and meet you."

I pointed to the floor. "She's coming here?"

Paolo nodded. "It's great, no?"

Would the bombs ever stop? Would he tell me about his love child next? I felt faint with anger. "No, not great."

He winced. "I know. It's too much. I told her not to come, but she's too excited. She can't ship a ring so valuable. You know…"

"Your mother is coming here with an engagement ring?"

Paolo did this thing when he was uncomfortable. This whole body twitch. His eyes avoided me like a dog's, he rubbed his hands together, he tapped his toe. It was as though his body physically revolted at the thought of confrontation. "Uhhhh…"

"What? Tell me."

"She is on her way."

"You mean like…" I made my hand into an airplane. "Right now?"

He looked so miserable. "I tried to talk her out of it. She was so excited."

"Do you even realize what you've just dumped on me?"

"Yes."

"Your visa, a proposal and your mother?!" I hated when people did this, pointed out the obvious as if the other person wasn't right there.

"I did not handle this well. This is all very hard for me, too."

"You had all the information, Paolo."

"I know."

My hands flew around, gesticulating. Paolo and I were alike in this way. When we got emotional, our hands moved on their own. "This is too much. I'm going out. I need to talk to Carmen."

Paolo shook his head. "I know. I know."

"But you don't know. You've planned out the rest of my life without even asking. You know I love you, Paolo, but I can't give you an answer just because your mother doesn't trust Federal Express."

Paolo's little empathetic nods were getting annoying. "Can you stop doing that?"

"What?"

"The nodding. You don't understand. You've had four days to process this and you spring it on me. Marriage. Your mother, and the United States government interfering with my love life. It's just a lot."

"I know."

"No. You don't. That's the whole point."

"*Bella*, look. You can take the time. All the time."

I rubbed my face. "Two weeks? You call two weeks all the time?"

"Or I can go back to Italy?"

That was when I burst into tears.


"Ma'am, can I see your license and registration?"

The bridge was just after Campbell's Resort. Blue flashing lights had woken me from my angry stupor. I'd pulled into the Seashore Hotel parking lot with a Chelan County Sheriff's car lighting up one side of the five-story hotel. Blue, white, blue, white.

I handed over the requested items. "Gary, what's with calling me ma'am? You know damn well who I am."

Gary Hartley and I had known each other since first grade. In second grade, Gary had started wearing his Superman Halloween costume to school every day. A year and half later, it fell apart. The man loved uniforms. "What's with the bathrobe, Stella?"

I looked down. Oh no. My fuzzy white robe. "None of your business."

Gary examined my license as if it was holy scripture. "You going to see Carmen?"

"Why'd you pull me over, Gary?"

"You ran a stop sign."

"I'm upset. Okay. Sorry. Can I just go now?" *If you give me a ticket I'll ball it up and throw it in your stupid face. Also, shut off those obnoxious lights.*

He leaned down toward me, arm resting on my car, giving me a whiff of his garlicky breath. "What you upset for?"

"Seriously?"

Gary blushed. "I just thought…" His ears stuck out tragically from his Smokey the Bear hat. I was not proud that I'd contributed to the list of his ear-themed nicknames in grade school. He looked down bashfully. "I just thought with our history, you could, you know, talk to me."

Gary had badgered me relentlessly for so long that one night, a couple years ago, in a moment of drunken stupidity, I'd agreed to a date. One night of dinner and dancing at Señor Frog's that had lasted approximately five years. Loads of drinks hadn't sped up anything. Throwing up in his car hadn't prevented him from poking his head into the salon, telling me what a great time he'd had. Now this. Gary wasn't going to let me go until I told him. "My boyfriend is going to be deported."

His face lit up as if he'd swallowed firecrackers. "That's too bad."

"Can I go now?"

"Sure, Stella. When's he supposed to leave?"

"Why, so you can give him a ride to the airport?"

"Do you think he needs one?"

I started the car. "Goodnight, Gary." You big dork.

"Goodnight, Stella. Watch out for deer."


"Have you seen Carmen?"

Octovio Font, the dishwasher at Orchard House, gawked at me over a sink of soapy wineglasses. My bathrobe was throwing him off. "I left the house in a hurry. Where's Carmen?"

Octovio pointed to the wine bar. I still hadn't gotten used to Orchard House being a restaurant. Carmen and Lola had taken out a business loan to remodel the main floor, carving out what used to be the master bedroom into a small wine bar that opened onto the patio. Their kitchen had been upgraded to commercial grade. The tile-topped counter where I'd once perched on a stool after school was now a stainless plating station. Appetizers and salad for the lunch crowd. Cheese plates and artisanal pizzas at night. Carmen, Lola and their father Juan slept on the spacious second floor, using half the main floor for living. The arrangement seemed to be working for everyone but me. Orchard House had been my refuge. Now I hardly recognized it. Worst of all, I hardly got to see my best friend.

The only reason Carmen had agreed to slip out of the wine bar tonight was that I'd begged, hinting at dire consequences if we couldn't talk.

Carmen wasn't a bad friend. When she'd moved back from Seattle a year ago to help save the business, Blue Hills Vineyard had been mired in debt, badly neglected and close to foreclosure. Thanks to Carmen and Lola, they'd dug themselves out of trouble. Adella, their oldest sister who lived an hour away, helped when she could. Carmen was still struggling to keep the winery afloat while managing the wine bar, though. It was a lot.

Orchard House was more than my second home. It had been my refuge while my own home crumbled. My parents had slipped into their own worlds, leaving me adrift. Mrs. Alvarez had taken me to get my hair cut, made sure I had enough clothes, pulled me into her family like another daughter. The Alvarez family hadn't just offered me a warm place to land: they'd offered me a lifeline.

I poked my head into the wine bar. Carmen was at the long oak bar across the room, perusing the evening receipts. I watched her for a moment. She quietly worked while the wait staff set up for the next day, placing fresh flowers on the round café tables, laying out silverware and napkins. When was the last time we'd gone out, just the two of us? Months ago.

"Psssst!" I motioned, not wanting to enter the room.

Carmen looked up, grinned. "Nice outfit."

"We need to talk."

She lifted a finger, returning to her receipts. "One sec."

My mouth dropped. I reached into my pocket, extracting my cell phone, hitting Carmen's number. She glanced down at her cell phone and frowned.

"What?" She was looking right at me, a tiny crease between her eyes that she got when she was annoyed.

"If wearing a bathrobe into a bar isn't a cry for help, then what is?"

"I said I'd be right there. If I stop now, I'll have to start over. I'll meet you in the living room."

"Paolo proposed."

Carmen tucked away her phone, dropped her pen, found a waiter and whispered something. She rushed over to me.

"You should have led with that." We went to the open-beamed living room. She plopped down onto the couch with a sigh.

"I thought the bathrobe would work." In my anxiety, I checked my phone. Nine-thirty. "Do you always work this late?"

Carmen simply nodded, familiar with my diversion tactics. "Talk to me."

"I said I'd think about it. He wants to get married in two weeks."

"Two weeks!? What's the problem?"

"His work visa is about to expire. Marrying me would solve that problem, which in a world where I was a typical female, would be hunky dory. But, marriage, as you know, is not my jam. Vows with death in them. Till death do we part. My grammy lived to be a hundred and three. No contract needs to be that long."

"Do you believe him?"

"Yes. He's in love with me for all the right reasons. Even I can see that. But his mother is flying over here with the engagement ring. I feel like I can't breathe. The idea of walking down the aisle is like a vice around my neck. I feel faint and scared and—no, wait, not scared, what's the word I'm looking for? Terrified. Like I'm that girl in the horror movie and there's an axe murderer hiding behind the door. And I'm going in there, like an idiot."

Carmen lifted a finger, tilting her head like a curious bird. "Hold up. His mother is flying over from Italy?"

I nodded miserably. "With the ring." I showed Carmen the image that Paolo had texted me while Gary had been playing Officer

Friendly. Together, we examined the tiny picture. An art deco style wide band, with an inset starburst of small diamonds nestled between two deep blue sapphires. The box said "Bulgari."

"Geez. I'll marry him."

"Right?" It dazzled with artistry, not karats. The kind of glittering bauble you'd expect on the hand of Carole Lombard, Vivien Leigh or some other long-forgotten Hollywood starlet. "What's wrong with me? Paolo is all that and a bag of chips, but when I think about getting married, it feels like…" How to tell her about grabbing him underwater? Words could never quite explain my fears. Excuses about not swimming piled up between us. High school graduation, birthday parties and life revolved around water. So did my lies.

Shutting my eyes, I wrapped my hands around my throat, head tilting.

My eyes popped open as Carmen threw an arm around my shoulder. "There's not one thing wrong with you. We'll figure this out."

"His mother will be here in two days. I can barely face Paolo, let alone his mother."

"How long will she be here?"

"One week."

Carmen pointed upstairs. "Move in here. Give her some space. She stays with Paolo. You plan a bunch of things together to make sure she has a good time. She falls in love with you and you've got more time to think about what you're going to do."

"Go on a charm offensive with Paolo's mother?"

"If you marry Paolo, you're going to have to get along with this woman. If you don't marry Paolo…"

"I'll never see her again."

"In the meantime, move in here. Chill for a while." Carmen got up from the couch. "I'm sorry, Stell, I have to go finish the receipts before I drop. Do you want to stay here tonight?"

I couldn't imagine facing Paolo. "Can I?"

"Absolutely. Make him sweat a little."

I wouldn't sleep a wink beside him. I wouldn't sleep here either, but at least I wouldn't have to stare at the back of his head. Paolo could sleep through an earthquake. "Thank you."

"Tomorrow we'll come up with an itinerary for his mother. It'll be good. With a son like Paolo, she's probably really nice."

"Did I tell you she hates Americans?"

Carmen smiled. "Good thing there's none of them around here." She gave me a hug. "I'll see you upstairs." She pulled away. "I know I've been checked out since we renovated. This will give us more time together."

My favorite place in Orchard House was the living room. In the winter, Carmen and I had roasted marshmallows in the two-story river rock fireplace for off-season s'mores. Large windows overlooked the orchard where Mrs. Alvarez had once paid us to gather apples. Later, I had realized this had been her way of giving me pocket money. Although they had a big old house in constant need of repair, a growing business and family to feed, Mrs. Alvarez had taken care of me.

Taking out my phone, I texted Paolo: *Staying here tonight*. Heart emoji.

Seconds later, the bubble of his typing appeared: *Miss you*. A heart emoji and a bottle of champagne.

\*

"But Stella, this is your home." Paolo trailed me as I gathered things from the bathroom and bedroom, pleading and arguing for me to stay.

Arms full of hair products, I dropped my shampoo. He bumped into me as I picked it up. "Can you just let it go?"

He nuzzled close, placing his chin on my shoulder. "How can I let you go?"

We looked at each other through the mirror over my narrow dresser. "How could you not tell me that you were being deported?"

Dejected, he sat on the bed beside my open suitcase, delaying his early morning departure for Seattle. His mother's flight would land in less than six hours. "She can stay in a hotel."

"Paolo, we have been over this. I need some space." I closed the suitcase onto the giant lump of clothing. It bulged like an overstuffed clam. No way was the thing going to zip, but I'd be damned if I'd ask Paolo for help.

Trying not to smile at my struggle with the suitcase zipper, he bit his lip. "You're still mad."

Pushing the hair off my flushed face, I stood up. "Who wouldn't be? You should have told me about the visa."

He nodded. "Yes. I know. Please. Stay here." Spoken like a man used to getting his way. Used to his looks, his charm and his enormous charisma bulldozing lesser mortals.

This mortal was moving across the lake. Once I got my suitcase closed. The suitcase was an old soft-sided monstrosity I'd bought at Walmart for a vacation with the Alvarez family in high school.

A suitcase would not defeat me. Sitting astride it, I bent over to do further battle with the zipper. "We. Both. Need. Some. Space." I huffed with each pull.

"I do not need the space. I need you."

Defeated by the stupid bag, I dragged it onto the floor, turning to him, red-faced. "You're really not going to help me with this, are you?"

He put his hands together in supplication. "Let's talk. Please?"

Pointing out the window at the lake, I shook my head. "I will literally be half a mile away. You work next door."

"This is your home."

"Paolo, I do love you. Honestly. But here's the thing. You lied. You knew something really important that was going to change both our lives and you kept it to yourself. Yes, you needed time to think. What about me? Did you not think for one minute that you were taking valuable time away from me? No. You thought about how it impacted you. On top of it all, you invited your mother to come to visit without even asking me."

"I didn't invite her. She decided."

My arms flew out. "What? That's even worse!"

"I have reservations at Wapato Resort. She can stay there."

"Paolo, all I need right now is for you to help me zip this stupid suitcase." I lifted my index finger. "One thing. That's it."

Paolo joined me on the floor, pressed one hand down and effortlessly zipped it shut. He sat back, trying not to grin.

"Don't you dare. This isn't funny."

He pinched his fingers together. "A little bit."

"Not even." I mock-glared at him. "First you make me fall in love with you. Then you tell me you have to leave. Paolo, I was happy with the way things were."

His face went sad. "Me too." He sighed, his face close to mine, the hazel flecks in his eyes darkening. He smelled of wine tannins, clean cotton and fresh herbs. "Don't go."

I stood. The weight of the suitcase nearly tipped me over. "I'll be across the lake."

"Yes, but you pack your bag, walk out the door." He circled his hand in the air, including the dock, the garden, and the house. "Here. This is home."

Hunched over, I dragged my suitcase down the hallway. "Spend time with your mother. It's only a week."

Following, he shook his head, waving his hands. "I don't need space. I want to come home and see you, not my mother."

The wheels on my suitcase might have been scratching the hardwoods but I resisted the urge to check. "Maybe you shouldn't have invited her to come here without asking me."

Paolo tried to help but I wouldn't let him. "When I'm at work, I'll come over and see you."

We'd reached the front door. Standing, I massaged the small of my back. "I'll be at work, then I'm going to clear my calendar to do something with your mother."

Paolo rubbed his forehead. "Maybe I should be there."

"Maybe it's not up to you."

"But Stella—"

I cut him off. "Can you put this in the car?"

Paolo grabbed my suitcase, carrying it outside. "So heavy."

"I packed my weights."

"The ones that sit in the corner. The ones I never see you lifting?"

I nodded. "I might try."

He threw the suitcase into the open trunk of my car and turned to me, wrapping me in his arms. We kissed and I wished we could rewind. Yesterday. No surprises. Just life. "Don't go. I will miss us too much."

"Go get your mother. You're late."

He nodded. "She will love you."

"You said she hates Americans."

"For you, she'll make an exception."

Before I got into the car, Paolo grabbed me, giving me a long, passionate kiss, gazing into my eyes as he spoke. "I will miss you."

We were the perfect height ratio. Our bodies fit together. Dazzled by this kiss, I weakened. "If, and this is a big if, we get married, we'll do something very simple on the weekend before your visa expires… But I'm a long way from being okay with all this right now."

The joy on his face made me ache. More than anything, I wanted to be the girl who said yes. His features grew somber. "If, in the very unlikely scenario that you forgive me, and we do get married, this is not something we do for the visa problem. This is something we do for love."

I nodded. "For love."

That's how we left it as I drove away. His mother was en route. *Thanks for the heads up, Paolo, you big dope.*

As exceptional as Paolo was, he was the same as every other man I'd dated. In high school, when Rob Ballinger's very conservative mother had accidentally-on-purpose spilled coffee on the crotch of my micro-mini skirt, giving me her prairie skirt as a suitable replacement, I'd learned a valuable lesson. All men were utterly clueless when it came to their mothers.

# CHAPTER FOUR

## That Sinking Feeling

"Hold that thought." Carmen dashed off to seat a group of people. Left stranded like a ditched date, I nursed a glass of water at the bar. Two waiters were available, but Carmen threw herself into the fray as if nobody else was capable of delivering a glass of pinot noir. This morning I had been ignored as Lola and Carmen spent breakfast discussing a food order for the wine bar and last-minute details of the fall wine dinner. Lola had hugged me, said she was "amped" I was staying with them, just like the old days, before continuing to bicker with Carmen. They ran the winery together, but it was a constant power struggle. Lola was creative and impetuous. The opposite of Carmen. Lola wanted the ageing residential part of the house updated. Carmen said no, too much money. Lola asked about rotating shows in the wine bar with local artists. Carmen said it was too much trouble. Carmen was born type A, treating her little sis as the forgetful art school dropout, although Lola had changed significantly since she'd moved home.

Tonight, it was futile trying to have a conversation with Carmen. She felt compelled to personally greet every guest as though they'd just opened. Although the wine bar hadn't yet been open a year, already it was a huge success. Fabulous for the Alvarez family, and not, I ruefully noted, as Carmen flitted about, so great for me.

Carmen and I had driven to Montana last September to purchase the bar's pièce de résistance—a long, turn-of-the-century polished oak bar and matching barback inlaid with marble, formerly housed in a cowboy bar. It was a gorgeous piece whose journey had been featured in Lola's Blue Hills Vineyard blog. Carmen had thought the blog was another of Lola's passing fancies, but the entry had been picked up by the Seattle press, including photos of the long, crackled mirror over the bar, reflecting the lake view. Curious vacationers who had seen the photographs came for a drink and enjoyed the stunning vistas, farm fresh menu, simple but elegant natural linen and wild flowers. The Blue Hills wine bar was a roaring success.

My guest room, where I'd often slept as a child, was directly above the bar. Last night, when I'd opened my window, the restaurant noise had floated up from the patio below. It even drifted up through the floor. Until now, I'd never realized how hard Carmen and Lola worked. Daytime was devoted to winery business. At four o'clock, the tasting room opened for service. The family ate dinner with Juan at around seven o'clock, scarfing down their food in fifteen minutes. Then it was back to the wine bar to give the wait staff dinner breaks. I'd felt guilty today, coming home from work at six and sneaking upstairs to rest. Juan was the only one with free time, but he was hard to find, puttering about the winery, the fields and Orchard House.

It was hard, processing my feelings about Paolo alone. An hour ago, Carmen had been happy to see me. She'd set me up with a pineapple and soda, settling down to listen, perfectly focused with her elbows propped on the bar. Five minutes later, the door had opened. That first, "One sec," had felt okay. She was busy. But ever since we'd had a fragmented, frustrating conversation.

Carmen returned again, resuming her spot behind the bar, pouring three glasses of red wine. "Oh my gosh. Was that two sauvignons and one..." She squeezed her eyes shut. "Okay, got it." She finished pouring the three glasses, lifting a finger to me. "I know. I know. I know. I will be right back. Things should slow down. It's nearly closing."

She went off to deliver the wine, leaving me to stew. Why wasn't I happier? I'd received a proposal from a wonderful man. I should be planning my bachelorette party and a quickie wedding to stop him from being deported. *Deported.* What an ugly word. It didn't belong in the same sentence with *wedding.*

Mixing hair color earlier that day, I'd let my mind drift to wedding scenarios and boom, my pulse had started racing as if I'd just run down the street, screaming. Which is what I felt like doing when I looked across the street at St. Andrew's Episcopal Church. This had happened approximately nine billion times that day.

Carmen leaned her elbows on the bar. "I'm back. Where were we?"

"I'm meeting his mom tomorrow for lunch."

Her brows shot up. "Yikes."

"Thanks, Car. That's super reassuring."

Carmen kept one eye on her guests. "Does she know how you feel about marriage?"

"I don't know what Paolo's told her. We're not talking. He's called me about fifty-five times since I left."

"Hold up. You mean *you're* not talking. I feel sorry for him."

"Don't. Here's a little refresher. He knew for four days that he was going to be deported. He came home and said nothing. Nada. Zilch. Niente."

Carmen shook her head. "I got it."

I lifted a finger. "I'm not done."

"Be done."

It was fun, teasing her. "Nul, null, nola."

She grinned. "I kind of hate you right now."

A gaggle of red-cheeked girls in their twenties clattered in the door, laughing hysterically. One of them wore a white veil and a sash that said "Bride."

Carmen frowned. "I'll make them leave." She went to the girls. "I'm sorry, it's too close to closing time."

"Puleaaaaaaze! I'm getting married tomorrow. A nightcap?" the pretty bride begged, her fresh skin nutmeg against the snowy veil. Her friends joined in a chorus of pleading. They had an Uber. It was safe. On and on. On another planet, this should have been me. Carmen and I should have been barging into some winery with friends from high school who'd seem fun, initially, and grow increasingly annoying with each drink. I was torn between hating these girls and feeling a certain solidarity.

The conversation with Carmen wasn't going to happen. I might as well let these girls have their fun. That was how it worked when you loved someone. You got engaged and forced all your friends to send you off in a haze of champagne and giggles. For one day, no matter how much of a wallflower you were, you were the center of the universe.

Sliding off my bar stool, I went to the door and placed my hand on Carmen's shoulder. "Go ahead. I was headed outside anyway. We'll talk later."

The scent of fragrant roses from Mrs. Alvarez's garden drifted from the private patio. It was portioned off with a lattice fence and faced the sloping vineyard hill. It was the perfect quiet place to watch the night creep across the hills. At the table was the one person at Blue Hills who had time to listen. The man who had built this vineyard out of nothing. Juan Alvarez.

Mr. Alvarez enjoyed his nightly glass of red wine alone. His profile was craggy in the dim light. Thick salt and pepper hair waved over his broad forehead. He was an institution in Chelan County. A role model for wine growers of every background who admired Juan's work ethic, his success and his family. He looked so peaceful, I hated to disturb him. Mineral-rich aromas from the irrigated vineyard filled the air over the dusty bite of wild sage that covered the surrounding hill. Two deer grazed under an apple tree near the driveway. I watched the lights from the Hollister Estate winery lose the battle with the brilliant blanket of stars overhead. Crickets chirped. Crushed apple scent wafted from the orchard.

Juan turned at the sound of my footsteps on the gravel. His weathered face broke into a grin. "*Stellita*. Come." He reached over to pull out a metal chair, patting the surface. "Have some wine. I'll get you a glass."

"No thanks, Mr. Alvarez. I'm fine." Settling down beside him, I squeezed his shoulder. Juan was like a father to me. When my family had faded, I'd latched onto the Alvarez family and held on for dear life. Mercedes and Juan had carried on as if adding one more chair to the table, one more girl in the car, was as natural as breathing. Although the entire town had chattered about what happened to my family, the Alvarezes hadn't forced a conversation about it. That was the beauty of the arrangement. I'd melted into the Alvarez family; they'd absorbed me without a ripple. They'd acted as though a girl who didn't spend any time in her own home was normal. I went to church with them, had Sunday dinner at their table, and was held up as an example.

"Stella doesn't squabble over who gets the drumstick. Stella doesn't push her way to the front of the line. I bet Stella doesn't shove people off the dock at the beach."

They'd spoiled me. Claimed me as their own.

Which was what I'd longed for. To be normal.

"Where's Carmen?" Juan asked, after bringing me a glass of water, insisting that I drink something.

"Working. In the wine bar."

Juan nodded. "*Sí*. Yes." He tapped his head. "I forgot. Sometimes I come downstairs and wonder what all these people are doing in our kitchen." He smiled ruefully. "Then I remember. We have a restaurant. In our house. It's crazy, no?"

I drank some water. "It's doing really well."

Juan nodded, looking slightly put out. As if missing family dinners that were longer than breaks. "*Sí*. It's good. Carmen thinks of everything." He lifted a finger. "But she works all the time now."

I nodded. "She does."

"I worry about that one. She needs to slow down." He sighed. "Lucky me, I get to be the one to see you." Juan had a talent for making the awkward comfortable. He could talk to the CEO of a huge winery or a migrant picker and maintain the same friendly warmth.

"Thank you for letting me stay here."

Juan nodded, although I wasn't sure if he'd remembered I was staying. He'd grown adept at covering his Alzheimer's, pretending he knew details that had randomly disappeared. "Don't you have an apartment in town?"

"I used to. I'm living with Paolo across the lake now, but his mother is visiting from Italy. I'm giving them some space."

Juan took a sip of his wine. "I shouldn't say this, but the best visit from *mi suegra*, my mother-in-law, was the one where she missed the plane."

I grinned. "Actually, Paolo asked me to marry him."

"That's wonderful."

"I'm not sure. His work visa expires soon, and I don't want to get married just because Paolo fell in love with the United States."

Juan surprised me by nodding. "Mercedes didn't want to marry me. Not at first."

Not what I'd expected. Mrs. Alvarez died when I was fifteen, but I'd never seen such a happy married couple. They'd been like teenagers. Mr. Alvarez would come to the kitchen door, making a big production of entering the back door in his dirty work clothes. Mrs. Alvarez would flap her dish towel, chasing him out of the kitchen, telling him to enter by the side door when he came home from working in the fields. He'd always take one step further into the kitchen to the delight of the girls, tapping his cheek as he winked at them. "I'm not leaving without a kiss, *mi amor*."

"You think I'm going to kiss a man in dirty work clothes? Go wash up and then maybe I'll look at you."

Sometimes he'd chase her around the kitchen, flirting in Spanish while the girls squealed with laughter. Moments like these had made me feel simultaneously happy to share in the laughter, and sad that my own parents were so different. They'd flirted happily when I was younger but by the time I was ten, they'd retreated to separate sides of our small house. They didn't share much except me, and they weren't particularly interested in me. Or in anything.

When Mrs. Alvarez died of cancer, an unseen hand had flicked off the lights in the Alvarez household. Mrs. Alvarez's prayer group ebbed and flowed, bringing fragrant casseroles and baked goods. Every time I visited, there was a stack of washed Pyrex by the kitchen door, waiting to be reclaimed. For a brief time, the Alvarez home resembled my own. Everyone struggling under the weight of their grief, trying to find their way forward, and failing.

Six months after the funeral, Juan had come out of the fog. He'd started cooking, driven the girls around the lake, learned their schedules and planned family outings. Made sure they went to church and ate home-cooked dinners together every night. Sometimes the only conversation at dinner was, "Pass the rolls," but eventually, they'd found their way.

A few yards away now, the door to the wine bar opened and drifted shut. Alert deer lifted their heads, eyeing guests crunching down the gravel driveway to the parking lot below the house, above the orchard. I waited patiently for Juan to continue.

He lifted the wine bottle. "Are you sure you don't want any?"

I shook my head. "I have an early morning at the salon. Tell me about Mrs. Alvarez."

"Oh. *Sí*, where was I?"

"She didn't want to marry you."

He nodded. "*Bueno*. Mercedes told me that even though she needed her job as a grocery checker in the United States to support herself, she came from a prominent Mexico City family. Her father was a politician and his opponents came into power. There was an attempt on his life. At night, the compound where the entire family lived was raided. Most of the family's money was seized. Things were getting very unstable. They had family in Argentina, but Mercedes didn't want to go to South America, so she struck out on her own." He pointed to the north. *"Los Estados Unidos."* He shook his head with wonder. "She had a childhood friend that had moved to Washington State. Mercedes took some money she'd saved. Enough for junior college. She worked in the Safeway to get by. She lived with a few girls in a rented house. Very nice girls and probably six cats. So many funny little cats. They slept in the garden in the afternoon and I'd go back there and try to count all of them." He smiled, counting off on his fingers in Spanish. "I used to take her to dances that the church put on in Manson. They wouldn't let the Mexicans into the hotels, back then. We had to find our own fun. I told Mercedes that I loved her, and proposed. Down on one knee. So worried about what she would say. She told me her family would never let her marry a *temporero*, a field worker. That's what I was. I picked grapes during the harvest season, but I also picked apples, cherries, asparagus. Whatever there was, I picked. I was saving my money to buy my vineyard. But my family was from a very poor, small town in Baja. They fished and always had enough to eat, but you know, we had one pair of shoes. We didn't own any land or have money in the bank. They were *los aldeanos*. Villagers. Mercedes' family would have looked down on us. Anyone from Mexico City who didn't live in a slum looked down on everyone else. That's just how it was. If Mercedes had married me, they would have never spoken to her again."

A coyote howled in the distance. Juan pointed in the direction of the sound. "He's lonely. I hear him, looking for his mate." He took a small sip of wine. "Mercedes felt very uncomfortable with the final decision. She missed her family very much and wrote them every Sunday. But we had no choice. If I could not marry her, somebody else would and my heart would break. Crack. Like that." He sighed. "Everybody was in love with Mercedes Castillo." He smiled at the memory. "A Spanish name. Castillo."

"Mr. Alvarez, don't leave me hanging."

Juan grinned mischievously. "We lied. Mercedes wrote that she was marrying the owner of a small vineyard. A landowner. She said we couldn't come back for a wedding because the harvest schedule didn't permit me to travel. In truth, I was illegal. No papers. If I had traveled to Mexico, I wouldn't have been allowed back. Of course, she couldn't tell them that either, so we used the excuse of work. We had a very big wedding. Every Mexican in the valley came, as well as some big shots that hired me to pick and taught me how to run a vineyard. You know, it was a real fiesta." He looked wistfully happy. "We were so young."

"How long did you lie to her family?"

Juan shrugged. "We never told them the truth. I bought my first piece of land three years after we married. Then it wasn't a lie. Her family came to visit after we bought this house. They thought I'd owned it for decades. We worked liked dogs to get it ready for their visit. It was in terrible shape. Pieces of the roof missing. Graffiti. People built campfires in the living room. We worked so hard. Mercedes was pregnant and we only stopped to sleep."

"But she always knew she wanted to marry you?"

Juan tilted his head. "I don't know. She might have used her family as the excuse to slow things down. I was at her door every day, gifts in my hand. A bottle of wine. Some flowers. Candy. One time I arrived and there was another young man, freshly showered with his hair slicked back, waiting at the front door. I almost punched him. He was there for another girl."

He grinned. "I was very impatient. I wanted a ring on her finger. She walked down the street and people looked. Maybe she didn't know. But the first time she smiled at me, I knew she had to be my wife or I would die." His eyes focused on me as he returned. "*Mija*, do you feel the same way?"

"By the time you're my age you should feel ready for marriage, but every time I think about it, I can't breathe. What if I end up like my mom and dad?"

Juan's forehead creased as if trying to remember. "Your parents?"

I shook my head to chase away the memories. Let Juan forget. Why remind him? "You know how when Mrs. Alvarez died, you picked up the pieces and you kept going?"

Juan nodded. "*Sí.*"

"Well, when my sister died, they didn't."

*

I'd just stepped from the church lobby. Walking down the aisle of St. Andrew's as beams of jewel-toned light filtered through the stained-glass windows. As the organ played, congregants shifted in the pews to watch me walk. Paolo, dashing in a navy-blue linen suit, waited at the altar. To my right was the Alvarez family in their finest attire: Juan dapper in a suit, Lola, Adella and her three beautiful children. Many of my clients had brought their dogs. I waved happily at Grace Mercer, who'd decorated her standard poodle Louis with a brilliant purple bow. Carmen was a few steps ahead of me in a pretty satin slip dress. She was lifting the sides of her mouth with her fingertips, reminding me to smile. Reminding me that this was the happiest day of my life.

It didn't feel like it.

Instead of feeling joy, I felt a creeping anxiety. While the rest of the church was on solid ground, I was on water. Unfathomably deep, dark water, undetectable to anyone else. My dress hem was soaked. Water climbed up the fabric, dampening my knees. Propriety kept me from screaming. My friends couldn't do anything. Not even Paolo. I would drown in front of everyone I knew, every person I'd ever loved.

Paolo's wide grin glowed with warmth and confidence. I was alone. Everyone was there. Friends I'd grown up with, sneaked cigarettes with behind the high school gym, families I'd babysat for, women whose hair I'd striped orange when I was a fledgling stylist. The pharmacist who'd caught me stealing nail polish in junior high and made me work for free instead of reporting me. My former landlady. Stupid Gary and his ridiculous hat, who'd be happy when he found out that marriage to someone else ended badly for me. Half the town gazed expectantly, hoping this ceremony would lead me to happiness. They were all wrong.

I'd drown. Something was pulling me under, deeper and deeper.

My phone rang, waking me up. My sheets were damp as I gasped for air.

It took a moment to realize I was in the guest bedroom at Orchard House, tucked under a faded quilt. I found my phone, still in the grip of the terrible dream. The nightmare.

It was Paolo, again. Irritated with myself for not turning off the ringer, I answered. "What? You've called me a hundred times. I'm not ready to talk, Paolo, please."

"*Bella*, I'm sorry. Let me come to lunch. You don't know my mother."

"That's the point. That's why we're going out."

He was sipping coffee. The clink of the cup on the counter. He was an early riser. Had likely already gone for a paddle as the sun rose. "I should be there."

Throwing off the light covers, I moved to the window. Deer moved through the misty orchard, reaching for the small hard apples. Three, then a fourth, daintily stepped out from behind a tree. The lake below was still, illuminated by a haze of pale sun. "I thought you had to work."

"I still think I should be there."

"You don't usually worry about this kind of stuff. What's changed? You were fine with this before."

"She thinks you have said yes."

Opening the window further, it creaked. Deer lifted their heads, frozen, ready for flight. After a moment they relaxed, returning to graze. "Didn't you tell her?"

"What? That you can't make up your mind?"

"You said that you're fine with it."

"I am. But my mother is my mother."

I could almost see him shrug as he rinsed his coffee cup. "What is that supposed to mean?"

"An Italian mother thinks any woman is lucky to have her son."

"Especially an American."

"Exactly."

What difference did it make if Rosalia thought I was going to marry her son? I certainly didn't want to discuss my reservations with Paolo's mother. Winning her over was the goal. Charming her. I'd always done well with parents. Of course, I'd never met an Italian mother. "Did she bring the ring?"

"Yes."

"Great. I can't wait to get a look at it." I sounded like a greedy five-year-old.

"She will meet you at the restaurant."

"Okay." I softened my voice. "Paolo, listen. We have too many things going on to care what other people think, even your mother." I ended the call and slipped back into bed, staring up at the dark beams criss-crossing the ceiling, listening to the early birds chirping in the orchard, wishing I could fall back asleep, get another hour of sleep. But I was wide awake with an unsettling, irrational, anxiety with no solution.

What if Paolo's mother hated me?

# CHAPTER FIVE

## Mrs. Macbeth

At precisely eleven o'clock in the morning, the bell on the salon door rang. I was with Lola, checking a highlight foil crimped onto her dark hair. The burnished chestnut highlights were the perfect hue, ready to rinse.

Izzy swept up from her last client, walking the short distance into the tiny waiting area. "Hello. Can I help you?"

"No." The unusually sharp reply made me look up.

"Okaaaay." Izzy rolled her eyes at me as she resumed sweeping. "Vampire lady is all yours," she whispered.

Sitting on the lemon-yellow thrift store velvet couch, under a watercolor of a chihuahua in sunglasses, was an impeccably chic woman. She looked ripped from the kind of magazine where women had charities instead of jobs. Her dark bob was so precise, each hair obeyed strict orders. Her flax linen suit was toned down by a fitted black T-shirt. A thick gold chain with one link encrusted in gems rested on her prominent collarbones. Fawn sandals in buttery soft leather competed the ensemble. Gucci sunglasses rested on her head over perfectly arched brows and a strong nose. She peered around the salon with sharp, hooded eyes, taking her sweet time until she landed on me. The disappointment was evident.

"Hey, welcome, I'll be right with you." I patted Lola's shoulder. "Your color looks great. Meet me at the shampoo bowl."

Lola dragged her feet, stopping to gawk at the woman.

As I approached, the woman cringed at the painting, shedding hate vibes like a virus. Instead of wafts of Aveda mint and rosemary shampoo, she seemed to be smelling skunk. "Hi, can I help you?"

"No, I am fine." She shrugged, dangling her fingers to shoo me. Volumes were contained in that gesture. It said, *you are so far beneath me that we're in different hemispheres.* "I will wait." She picked up a magazine, flicking through it aggressively. I'd been dismissed from my own salon.

I fumed. Izzy's eyes did a loop. Rachel, mid-haircut, did this thing where she stared from her mirror to the customer in the waiting area like she couldn't be seen. We'd told her a thousand times that it was obvious. Subtlety wasn't Rachel's strength.

Lola broke the tension, hollering from the back room. "Hey, Stella! Can you sell me some of this Aveda conditioner at cost? I just want to smear it all over my body and lie in the bathtub. Or eat it. I bet it's edible, right?"

There was no playbook for this situation. Did I introduce myself? Wait until lunch? Slap her across the face and walk out? I chose option D. Hide in the back room. "Excuse me."

Rosalia—because this woman couldn't be anybody but Paolo's mom—nodded. "Fine." Again, she dismissed me.

I stomped to the back of the salon. I'd never met anyone so entitled, so horrifyingly larger than life. Like an empress had taken up residence. Paolo had said his mother was strong, but he hadn't said she was imperial. He hadn't mentioned that she didn't enter a room, she conquered it. I'd never run into anyone remotely similar. I wanted to pin her down and examine every article of clothing on her body. Before slapping that superior look off her face.

With great effort, I kept my chill until I was safely behind the partition, then dashed to the shampoo station.

Lola had removed the foils, dropping them into the basket. "It's about time."

I pushed her head back, running water while I whispered, "That's Paolo's mom."

"Does she eat children for breakfast?" I sprayed water on Lola's head. She howled in pain. "Hot! Hot! *Qué caliente*!"

I clamped a hand over Lola's mouth, turning off the faucet. "Shhhh."

Lola's eyes watered. "My head was on fire."

"Sorry, I'm distracted."

She touched her head. "Don't take it out on me."

I tested the water until it was lukewarm, then carefully rinsed Lola's hair. "She's an hour early."

"She probably ran out of kittens to drown," Lola quipped in a loud voice.

"Shhhhhh!" I turned off the water. "She can hear you."

"Do we care?"

I pumped shampoo into my hand, lathering Lola's head. "Let's just say we do."

"I wouldn't marry into that family if I were you."

"Lola, shut up!"

"Why do you think she got here so early?"

I rinsed out the shampoo. "To intimidate me." I leaned down to whisper. "To throw me off my game."

"Owwww!" Lola howled. "She's doing a pretty good job. You got shampoo in my eye. Maybe highlights are enough for today."

I massaged conditioner into Lola's damp hair, hissing, "No way. We're sticking to the schedule. I know what she's up to and I'm not playing. She might be Paolo's mom, but I'm his girlfriend."

"Dang, girl. You've got this."

I stood up straight, pushing my hair off my face. "Damn straight I do."


I wasn't so much fixing myself up for lunch, as going to battle. Meeting anyone but Mrs. Macbeth (best part of high school English), I'd just run a brush through my hair and apply ChapStick. Today, only blood-red lipstick would do. Studying my reflection in the dingy mirror, I tried to calm myself. Lola's haircut had not gone well. Rosalia's ringtone had burst into the silence, startling me. I'd turned, nicking Lola. Blood had streamed from the poor girl's ear. Never one to miss an opportunity to create a scene, she'd hollered like a banshee while I grabbed Kleenex. In a low voice, so Rosalia couldn't hear, I'd told her to stop being such a baby. It was only a little cut.

"I'm going to need a transfusion."

"Good Lord, Lola, chill."

I'd dabbed at her ear, shocked that a tiny cut could draw so much. Who knew that the human ear could bleed like this?

Rosalia appeared to be describing the scene, babbling away in Italian while I dug through my first aid kit. Lola held the Kleenex to her ear—"Look, I'm Van Gogh"—and wondered aloud if anyone had ever bled to death from an ear wound.

"It's not a wound, Lola. It's a nick."

"I think I need stitches."

Finally, I'd gotten the bleeding under control and Lola had left without bothering to pay.

In the back room now, I finished applying lipstick, blowing underneath my armpits. A hot, sticky mess. Ever since high school, when going beyond my comfort level, I'd looked at myself in the mirror. Given myself a pep talk. I'd learned as a kid that there was exactly one person in the world I could count on. She would always be there for me. She got me through everything. She'd worked long hours after school, doing foils and perms on old ladies and snotty teens at Mabel's Cut and Curl in Manson. She'd shopped for food with her own money at Safeway when there was nothing to eat at home. She'd found this salon when it had been a spider-infested dust bin. Smoothed every lick of paint and dragged these sinks from a fire sale in Yakima. As much as Carmen and her family had looked out for me, there was only one person who could help me face the woman sitting in my salon. I took a deep breath and went out to meet Rosalia.


"No." Rosalia's hair barely moved as she shook her head. "I saw the other little place. It's called Grazie. We eat at Grazie." She pivoted in the opposite direction but I stood my ground, arms crossed.

"I have a reservation at Campbell's." We were on the sidewalk in front of Twig. It was a test. We both knew it. Might as well have it out right now.

Rosalia slowly turned on her heels, then lowered her sunglasses, peering curiously. "How long did you have to wait to get the reservation at this bastion of culinary excellence? How many Michelin stars would I be missing?"

"I don't know what you mean by stars, but I have a reservation and that's where we're going." Grazie was a minimalist café done up in white and beige, with waiters in long black aprons. Thirty-dollar plates of hand-rolled pasta and twenty-dollar glasses of wine.

"I walked around your town. Grazie is much better." Her tone was aggravated. Rosalia clearly wasn't accustomed to being questioned.

"Rosalia, I know the best restaurant in town. We can stand here all day and argue about it, but Campbell's is where I am going for lunch. Are you coming?"

I could practically see the mental math in Rosalia's head. She was sizing me up, realizing that I would, no doubt, stroll down the street and eat lunch by myself rather than be bullied. No wonder Paolo was so easygoing. It was a survival tactic.

"Fine," she huffed.


We were seated at a small table on the porch with a view of the lake. Speedboats sliced the turquoise water, some towing wakeboarders. Triangles of white sails dotted the surface. Rosalia took a small sip of her wine. "This place is very touristy."

I nodded. "Yes, this is a tourist town. It's what we do. We have a lake, thus the tourists."

Rosalia sniffed. "Lake Como has a different kind of tourist." She waved her manicured fingers around. "I knew, of course, that Paolo needed to, how do you say? Spread his wings. And maybe I am too much involved in the business. But I never thought he would choose to come this far. It's what we'd call..." She frowned. "Provincial."

I sipped my water. "He's happy."

Her eyes narrowed. "How long have you known Paolo?"

"About a year." This felt like some weird kind of job interview. Hobbies? Sleeping with foreign men and avoiding their mothers.

"Only a year?"

What did she expect me to say? A decade? She could do the math. If I could harness the waves of disapproval emanating from her side of the table, I could power Grand Coulee Dam. Why on earth hadn't I ordered something stronger than an iced tea? "I've known Paolo long enough."

Rosalia pursed her lips, shaking her glossy hair. "Not long enough." A waitress brought our food and I fought the urge to order wine. This lunch might go faster with a slight buzz, but I could hardly stay drunk for a week. Or could I? Anyway, I had a long afternoon of clients to squeeze in. I'd drawn enough blood for one day.

"Not long enough to what? Fall in love?"

Rosalia took a bite of her pasta, a look of nausea passing across her face. With visible difficulty, she choked it down. "No. Falling in love is not the problem. The visa is the problem."

"Tell me about it."

"Okay, I will tell you. My son thinks he wants to stay here. With you. In a town so small, you can spit across it. He may love you now, but he will never be happy here."

"He's pretty happy right now."

Rosalia shook her head dismissively. "While the bloom is on the rose. But this…" She waved her hand around, indicating our one main street which would fold up in winter. "In Italy, we have a wine industry that is hundreds of years old. To work at that level is to achieve artistry. The wine industry here is in the infancy stage. Do you think that he will be satisfied, working and living in a place that is so primitive?"

"You make it sound like we're living in tents. We might not be Columbia Gorge, but Lake Chelan AVA is growing." Holy cow, I was learning a lot from Paolo and Carmen! Who knew? AVA meant American Viticultural Area: a designated wine grape-growing region.

Instead of asking more, like a person who cared one iota about this place, Rosalia tilted her head. "You must put it in perspective, culturally. The United States does many things well. I don't dispute that. But this region is not the right place for my son."

"Don't you think that's up to Paolo?"

She placed a napkin over her food, as if the very sight of it turned her stomach. "When Paolo was a boy, he decided he would be a veterinarian. He found a rabbit with a broken leg, a bird fallen out of the nest, a mouse attacked by crows. He nursed them back to health. One by one. Tended them every day as if they were his children. Next, he wanted to be a DJ. He learned everything there was to know about music. Played at all the parties and made a great deal of money. Next, it was a water taxi company. All the time he was working for his Uncle Riccardo in the vineyard. Learning his actual trade." She smoothed the tablecloth, pushing off imaginary crumbs. "All these things interested him, but he didn't know what was best. His father was gone. Riccardo, his uncle, and I said, 'You see, Paolo, all these other things are distractions. Winemaking is in your blood.' And you know, we were right."

"He's a winemaker here. Evan Hollister gives him free rein."

Rosalia peered out at the glassy lake. "Does he talk about Lake Como, the Gentillo Vineyard?"

I shook my head. "No. Not really."

Rosalia pursed her lips. "Don't you find that a little strange?"

"No." Okay, yes, maybe.

"The Gentillo Vineyard was started in 1820. Some of the vines are two hundred years old. Our wine is sold everywhere. Some is in the shops. Some in the House of Windsor. Places like that. Paolo knows this life. He is comfortable there." She sighed theatrically, lifting her hands, palms up. "How quickly a man like Paolo can change his mind."

The waitress appeared, asking if everything was all right.

"Can I get a glass of wine?" Clients or not, I needed wine. "Like, now."

"Sure." The waitress rushed to the bar.

"So, to recap: Chelan isn't good enough for your son."

"It is not bad or good. It is a matter of belonging."

"What if he belongs here, with me?"

Rosalia nodded. "Back home, he has a business, he has family and a life. This is a last distraction. To show he is an independent man. This is all good. But when a man wants to settle down, he always returns home. To the familiar."

"Talk to your son."

Rosalia took another sip of wine before opening her purse. She extracted a check, sliding it across the table. "This is for you. To help you make the decision for Paolo."

*What?* This kind of thing actually happened? "You're paying me to break up with him? Like a bribe?"

Rosalia shook her head vehemently. "Not a bribe."

The wine arrived. Taking a fortifying sip, I flipped the check. "Ten thousand dollars. Wow. That's quite a payout."

Rosalia looked pleased.

"Does Paolo know about this?"

Rosalia frowned. "No. Of course not."

I took a deep breath. "Let's not tell him, okay? Let's pretend this never happened. It's beneath us. Rosalia, I know you don't like Americans. You think American small towns are petri dishes of ignorance. My salon is probably the tackiest place you've ever seen in your entire life. Nobody has ever accused me of being classy. But your son is the best thing that's ever happened to me. He doesn't want me to be anything other than a small-town girl who happens to like paintings of dogs in sunglasses. He thinks it's funny that I like ice in my wine." Rosalia winced, which made me kind of happy. "Paolo wants to get married and spend the rest of his life with me. Here's what's going to happen."

Taking a bigger sip of wine (probably a gulp), I ticked off points with my fingers. "First, you're going to get to know me. The only thing you understand about me at the moment is that I'm an obstacle to your goal. Second, we're going to experience Chelan together. I have some things planned." I slid the check back across the table. "You should know exactly what you're asking him to give up."

Rosalia lifted her glass. "May the best woman win."

If Rosalia believed this to be a contest, fine. I clinked glasses with hers, taking a sip. Rosalia's eyes flashed. She'd come ready for a fight. Enjoyed it.

Neither of us expected to lose.

"How was the lunch?" Paolo strode down the gravel path of the Hollister Estate winery, glancing at me. His usual loose-limbed exuberance was muted, as if someone had turned the dimmer down a notch.

"Great."

He kissed me on the cheek, whispering, "Really?" As if surprised his mother and I had gotten along.

"Yes. It was… fun." I was happy to be out of the car. Rosalia had brooded the whole way, probably plotting her next move. I couldn't wait to drop her off and get back to the salon to finish my afternoon appointments.

The Hollister Estate winery sat on a triangular piece of property facing north, toward the lake. From the Mediterranean-style house, you could see up the water, toward the North Cascade mountain range. In winter, snow-capped peaks fringed the horizon. In summer, a green stretch of foothills met the snaking fifty-five-mile lake in a haze of blue and green.

Rosalia's personality transformed around her son. She spun around enthusiastically, hand perched over her sunglasses. I half-expected her to start singing "The Sound of Music."

"Paolo, this view is glorious. No wonder you wanted to come here. The mountains, the lake. Looks a little like Lake Como, no?"

Paolo's wince was nearly imperceptible, but I saw it. "No." He chuckled. "Not even a little bit, Mamma." He bent down to kiss her cheek. *"Ti è piaciuto il pranzo?"*

"A very nice lunch." She plastered a phony smile on her face. "Right, Stella?"

"I told you. It was great." Two could play this game. Apparently, the game was called Fooling Paolo.

Paolo glanced between us as if he knew. Rosalia and I sported inane grins. As if someone had said: *look happy or I'll kill you*. The tension was palpable.

"We had a fabulous time!" I insisted.

Rosalia strolled to the Hollister Estate patio, gazing up at the vineyards. *"Bellissima."* Barry, Evan's dog, bounded out of the door, wagging his tail. Rosalia bent to pet him, cooing affectionately. She loved the dog.

Paolo whispered, "How awful was she?"

My smile didn't slip. "We're going to Stehekin tomorrow."

He rubbed his forehead. "I have three meetings with buyers tomorrow and Evan is gone. I can't make it."

"You're not invited." Rosalia kept at a polite distance, but I made a point of catching her eye, smiling warmly.

He tilted his head. "Are you going by boat? Isn't that an all-day trip?" The town of Chelan was at the southern end of Lake Chelan. Stehekin was a tiny outpost at the northern end.

Barry ran after a rabbit. Rosalia dusted dog hair off her hands, moving closer. "We can take a seaplane, if you want, Rosalia," I said. "You'd miss a lot of the lake but it's much faster."

Rosalia raised her eyebrows. "I wouldn't want to miss a thing. This way, we can spend more time together." She was a very good actress.

"I'm going to take the entire day off work. Great. It's settled."

Rosalia motioned at the sloping hill as Barry chased the rabbit, looking as if she couldn't wait to hike. "Paolo, give me a tour of your splendid winery." Surely she wouldn't step in the dirt with those immaculate sandals?

*"Mamma, un minuto."*

Paolo took me aside, hugging me. "Are you sure you want to do the trip tomorrow? A whole day. You'd miss work. You don't have to."

I kissed him. "Honey, chill. It's fine."

If he hadn't been so stressed, he might have noticed my misstep. Known something was wrong. Instead, he climbed the hill beside his mother, who was wearing sandals that probably cost more than my old monthly rent.

What Paolo would have remembered in normal circumstances, was that I never called him honey.


"She's a horrible old battleaxe." The wine bar of the Blue Hills Vineyard was the perfect place to nurse a wine spritzer. All I had to do afterwards was climb upstairs and pass out from fatigue. After returning to Twig, I'd done four haircuts, back to back. Thankfully, there had been no more sliced ears.

The bar was quiet. The windows opened onto the patio, where a few couples soaked in the early evening warmth. Pine cones from the nearby ponderosa lay scattered at their feet. Chubby bees drifted through the lavender that edged the patio. A slight chill signaled fall.

Inside, Lola perched next to me while Carmen manned the bar, keeping an eye on the door.

"Like Granny Worther?" Carmen asked. Granny Worther was an old biddy who ran Friday night bingo at the Elk's Club. Every morning she'd go to the Safeway bakery for coffee and a roll, plop herself on a chair outside, and critique, loudly, any passing youth. Her fault-finding was creative. Beards, bikinis, and tattoos were some of her pet peeves. If she saw someone with a leg or arm covered in tattoos, she demanded they stop and explain why on earth they'd submit themselves to such pain. Occasionally, she hollered for no reason. Every young person in Chelan expected, at some point, to be chastised by the lonely woman. She was a timeless fixture.

"Not at all," I said. "Not even a little."

"Carmen, she looks like… Oh, what is that actress's name? Sophia Loren!" Lola said. "Without the big boobs."

I laid my head down on my arms. "She's one part chic and two parts terror. And I volunteered to spend all day tomorrow with her. Paolo knows she's a lot, but I don't think he'd ever believe how serious she is. She hates me. I mean, really and truly. If we go hiking, I'm pretty sure she'd have no problem pushing me off a cliff."

"Why does she hate you so much?" Lola asked.

I lifted my head up from the bar, incredulous. "Seriously?"

"Lola, think about it!" Carmen said. "She heard her son is getting married and she rushes over here on the first flight to stop it."

"But I thought she brought the ring?"

"That was the excuse," Carmen explained. "We need to make her see that Chelan isn't such a bad place to live. Tomorrow is a good start."

"Well, maybe you *should* take her hiking," Lola suggested. Always the nature girl.

I sighed. Chelan was known as the gateway to the North Cascades. We had some of the best hiking in the country. And guess what? I hated hiking. The idea of spending an afternoon in nature made me ill. Throw in Paolo's mother, and I'd prefer the company of a hungry boa constrictor. But if today was any indication, the way Rosalia had sacrificed her lovely shoes to explore the vineyard, she'd love hiking. She could probably run up a mountainside without breathing hard. "I can think of nothing worse."

Carmen patted my arm. "I'll go with you." Things were looking up. "Yes, let's go in a couple of days. I need to get away. We need to spend time together."

I nearly cried in gratitude. "Thank you, Car."

She squeezed my arm. "It'll be fun."

Right. Wait till she met her. But with Carmen, it would be a lot more bearable.

"And how about a winery tour? I can arrange a tour of some wineries in the area," Carmen said.

"She'll hate all the wine," I said.

Carmen shrugged. "Who cares? It will kill time. You'll have done your best and then she goes home."

I texted Paolo: *Does your mom like hiking?*

He replied instantly: *She loves it.*

Of course she did.

# CHAPTER SIX

## What a Mother Does

The first hurdle was the highest. The Stehekin trip started on the *Lady Express* at 8.30 a.m. and ended back in Chelan at 3.00 p.m. The fine weather held. The pale blue sky warmed above a placid lake as I waited on the sidewalk in front of the Lady of the Lake dock. Paolo was dropping off Rosalia on his way to work. His Jeep pulled off to the side. Rosalia climbed out, dressed as if we were going on a safari: jeans, white linen shirt and a canvas jacket covered in pockets. Gucci shades kept her eyes hidden.

Paolo kissed me on the cheek, murmuring that he missed me, thanking me for taking Rosalia for the day. His smell of fresh bread and coffee reminded me of our lazy Sundays together. I felt a sudden urge to push Rosalia off the dock and drag Paolo back home.

"Is that the boat?" Rosalia called out, pointing to the double-decked wooden 1900s beauty, *Lady of the Lake*, which had retired in 1990.

"No, that one." I pointed to the stubbier modern version. Powerful, but ugly. At least it wasn't loaded to the gills with sunburned tourists. Just a few late-in-the-season hikers.

Examining both boats, Rosalia's face revealed everything. The new boat, with its powerful engines and short delivery, was efficient but loud. American. The old boat was clearly Italian. "I am looking forward to our little cruise, Stella," Rosalia said, turning to Paolo.

"I'll pick you up here, Mamma," Paolo said. "Enjoy!" After giving his mother a hug, Paolo bent down to give me a kiss. "Thank you. She's really looking forward to this. She is happiest out on the water."

"Even American water?"

Paolo grinned mischievously. "Lake Como is better."

"Obviously."

"I hope you have fun."

"Me too."


The *Lady Express* sliced a neat wake down the middle of the narrow lake. On the deck, I gazed at the Hollister Estate as we chugged past. It spread over the landscape, neat lines of grapes climbing the hill, with the mansion on a crest overlooking the lake. I'd be forever grateful to Evan for bringing Paolo here. Paolo had sparked something inside me. Woken parts of me that I'd never known existed. Before him, I'd been Carmen's sidekick. The wisecracking BFF to the pretty girl. I'd made the pretty girl beautiful. Carmen had been destined for someone like Evan. Rich, handsome and successful. She'd always been fierce, leaving Chelan for Seattle with a fearlessness I'd admired.

While she'd been in college and starting her career in Seattle, I'd opened my salon and dated a string of unimpressive local boys. My twenties had ended, but I'd never thought of marriage. I'd never thought I'd end up with someone like Paolo. I'd figured that eventually, someone would identify himself from the pack, step forward and announce himself. I'd never even said "I love you" to anyone. I'd certainly never stared deep into someone's eyes and seen the best version of myself. A Stella that was smarter, funnier and sexier. That's who I was with Paolo.

Better.

Beneath me, the boat's massive engines reverberated reassuringly. The town of Chelan grew smaller as the scenery became more rugged. The original one-hundred-and-thirteen-foot *Lady of the Lake* had been built in the early 1900s and transported to Chelan from another Columbia River lake in 1946. Although I lived two blocks from the dock, I'd only been onboard once. Our senior high school graduation party had been the last one on the *Lady*. Without asking if my parents had bought a hundred-dollar ticket for the evening or applied for a scholarship for a free ticket (they hadn't), Mr. Alvarez had paid for mine. A graduation present.

Before our first stop at 9.20, at Field's Point Landing, Rosalia's phone rang. Hikers left the boat and we sailed on. She chattered away in Italian through the next two dockings at Prince Creek and Lucerne, eyeing the scenery from a sun-warmed bench. We passed rustic waterfront homes, lodges built from rough-hewn logs. Dogs ran down from their houses to bark at us from the docks, wagging their tails with excitement. The sun beat down on my face and I began to relax. Maybe this trip could be the beginning of something. Rosalia didn't have to love me. She didn't even have to like me. But maybe, if I played my cards right, she could accept me. Because even if I didn't marry her son, I wasn't going to leave him without a fight.

We arrived at 11.00 for a ninety-minute layover. Only accessible by boat, hiking or seaplane, Stehekin was at the foot of the North Cascades National Park. It was a tiny dot of a community on the north end of Lake Chelan, with a lodge, a smattering of cabins and a dirt road that ran half a mile before turning into hiking trails. The water was crystal blue, clear and shaded by the towering mountains. We disembarked to a dock that emptied onto a grassy clearing. A large wooden lodge run by the National Park Service took up most of the clearing. The long Red Bus waited to take passengers sightseeing to the High Bridge, including a stop for lunch at the famous Stehekin Pastry Company. I'd rather eat at the bakery, which Paolo and I had visited last summer. The blackberry tart and raspberry cake we'd shared still lingered in my mind as one of the most delectable treats of my life. But I was fairly certain that Rosalia wouldn't enjoy dining amongst the smelly backpackers who'd swing down from the trail for a baked treat. We'd eat in the Cascades Lodge dining room. The food wouldn't be nearly as good, but it was a safer bet for an Italian accustomed to eating a formal meal for lunch. Paolo still abhorred the American habit of grabbing a sandwich, treating the noon meal as something to be gobbled down as quickly as possible before returning to work.

Rosalia and I disembarked, strolling around grassy Stehekin, gravitating to the edge of the glassy water. Rosalia took a deep breath. "It's beautiful."

I tossed a rock into the lake. We watched the rings in the water expand. "Paolo loves it here."

Rosalia got a sour look on her face as if I'd just ruined it for her. She turned and strode up the dirt road, toward the bakery bus. The driver waited, thinking she was making a run for it. "Come, we'll go for a hike."

I caught up with her, panting. "Tomorrow. We're going hiking tomorrow."

She glared at me through her sunglasses, picking up her pace. "It's possible to hike two days in a row."

The Red Bus driver gave me an impatient look as Rosalia continued. Lifting my finger at him to wait, I called to her. "Okay, fine. We can eat at the bakery instead of the dining room. Come on."

"We hike there."

"If you want to walk fast, go ahead. I'll meet you there." I climbed on the bus.

From the bus window, I saw Rosalia nod and wave, sprinting up the trail. How in the hell could she be in such good shape? She was twice my age. I'd be sweating to keep up with her. The driver executed a three-part turn on the paved road, churning into gear up the hill. The road gave way to gravel. We never passed Rosalia. When the bus doors opened at the bakery, she was waiting.

The Stehekin Pastry Company was at the center of a grassy garden ringed by towering trees. Climbing vines reached for the low roof. Rosalia ignored the sunning hikers, their faces upturned, packs resting beside their Adirondack chairs. She skipped up the bakery steps without missing a beat. "Paolo, he never liked the rules. In Italy, the rules for the winemaking are very strict. You can only make certain kinds of wine with certain grapes. You cannot add sugar to the wine. He always found that limiting. He wanted to experiment."

Entering the bakery, we studied the wide pastry case crammed with oversized cinnamon rolls, cheese and herb stuffed biscuits and fresh fruit tarts. "What's wrong with experimenting?"

Rosalia frowned at the chalk menu hanging from the ceiling. Friendly girls in homemade aprons waited for our order. "Nothing, if you are working in a young industry with few controls." She glanced at me sideways. "Why is everything so big?"

"You mean the Red Bus?"

She waved her hand at the pastry case. "This food is for giants."

I smiled at the waiting girl. "I'll have the pistachio chicken salad please."

"Pita, whole-grain or white?" She grinned. "All baked here."

"Enormous." Rosalia studied the loaves of bread as big as heads as I stubbornly ordered the white, knowing she'd get the whole-grain.

The second waitress nodded. "People get hungry hiking."

Rosalia sniffed toward me. "She took the bus."

Accepting my sandwich, which was truly colossal, I nodded. "Rosalia, would you like half?"

She examined my plate, which also had fresh fruit and a bag of chips. Pursing her lips, she turned to the second waitress. "Mushroom sorrel soup and salad please. Do you have fish?"

The girl frowned. "No. We're a bakery."

"You have soup."

"Yes. For our soup and sandwich specials."

"A sandwich is not lunch," Rosalia pointed out.

The rather pungent bearded hiker behind Rosalia grew exasperated. "My team is waiting at the trailhead. I texted our order yesterday."

Rosalia studied him from the tips of his dirt-encrusted hiking boots to the wild curls crowning his head. She sniffed the air and I worried she'd comment on his eau de hiker body odor that was beginning to overpower the delicious bakery aromas.

The girl took a deep breath. "Ma'am, I can sell you some slices of deli meat and cheese, if you'd like."

Rosalia dipped her head in a queenly manner. "Cheese. Havarti. Only fresh. One tomato. A roll and some fresh butter."

Basically, a sandwich.

The first waitress bagged up the hiker's large order, handing it over. The second waitress argued with Rosalia about selling her an entire tomato.


We ate lunch in the sun at the wooden picnic table furthest from the bakery. The Red Bus lumbered down the road, returning from Rainbow Falls, disgorging tourists and hikers. They ambled toward the bakery while the bus waited. Green ferns and glossy salal sprung from the shade, covering the ground. Squirrels dashed through the blackberry bushes on urgent errands, swerving to avoid us. Birds warbled and sang. I treated myself to dessert, which, of course, Rosalia declined with a raised brow.

It was surprisingly relaxing, even with Rosalia. She stared into her espresso as if wondering what she was drinking. "On the boat,

I talked to my brother. You know, he had the heart attack a few months ago. It's too much for him, working at the winery. He's not coming back."

"I'm sorry he had a heart attack." Rosalia watched me eat my large éclair without comment. A dog ran off the bakery porch, wagging its tail, sniffing us. I let him lick my fingers.

Rosalia shook her head. "His retirement is very bad. Of course he must look after his health but he's the wine master. One of the best in the region. You know, he trained Paolo."

"Paolo's talked about him." The dog jumped up, snatching the box containing the remains of my chicken sandwich, and wolfed it down in two seconds.

Rosalia stopped suddenly. "I knew he'd do that."

The dog raced around, delighted, as I picked up the cardboard remains. His owner called him and he dashed off. "Why didn't you say something?"

"He's a dog. He was licking your fingers to smell the chicken."

"I've never had a dog. How was I supposed to know?"

She wiped her hands, shoving the napkin in her coffee cup. "Common sense."

"Maybe for someone who has been around dogs."

Rosalia swept the remaining waste off the table, marching over to the bear-proof garbage can. "It's like this." She grasped the two-fold pinching mechanism with one hand, opening it easily. "Completely foreign, yet understandable."

"What are we talking about here, Rosalia? Dogs or mothers-in-law?"

The comment made her grin. "Either." She sprinted toward the line forming at the Red Bus, swinging her arms, as if the hot sun had no effect. "This air. Is magnificent? No?"

Joining her in the shuffling line, I loudly burped. Looking back, I pretended it was someone else. I was the last one in the line. The sandwich and éclair bubbled in my gut. "No." Following her up the bus stairs, I plopped myself beside her. She studied me, amused, as I panted from the five-step climb. "All right. Yes. It's nice air. I'm not much of a nature girl."

She peered at me over her sunglasses. "Paolo loves swimming in the lake, skiing, kayaking. What do you do while he does all these things?"

The Red Bus rumbled to life, starting off down the hill. "I sit on the dock."

Rosalia gazed out the bus window as we passed glossy clusters of blackberry bushes, tilting under the weight of their fruit. They pushed onto the road, ripening in the sun. "And you read?"

"Sometimes. Sometimes I just watch him swim. Look, Rosalia, if you're trying to point out that Paolo and I are very different, I'm fully aware."

We sat in silence until we reached the dock where the *Lady Express* waited, ramp down, loading passengers and supplies. We exited the bus. Tourists dashed to the lodge to buy souvenirs.

Rosalia idly watched them. "Do you want…?"

Pushing my hair off my face, I felt hot and tired, sick of this. "What, Rosalia? To admit that Paolo and I are a terrible match? No, I don't."

She shook her head. "Water." She pointed to a bench near the dock. "Sit. I'll bring it to you."

Rosalia handed me two large bottles of water. "Drink. You have a sunburn."

I downed one, and felt instantly better. "Thank you," I said. Pressing my cheek, I sighed. "Don't you want this one?"

She shook her head, leading the way to the boat ramp. We boarded, and stood at the railing as the ferry pulled away from the dock. Rosalia turned to me. "I admire your spirit."

She paused. The boat made a slow turn around the lake, ploughing through the glassy water, breaking up the reflection of the mountains. An eagle soared overhead in the afternoon sun. To the north, the Cascades shot up jagged into the sky, tipped with snow.

"I know you think I am harsh. A meddling old woman who thinks she knows everything. I can't explain our life. Like all families, it's complicated. Paolo's father, Niccolò, died when Paolo was nineteen. Lung cancer. Before he died, he did everything for the family. He made sure the winery business was handed over. That we understood every aspect. I will not pretend that we had a perfect marriage. But Niccolò was a good man. He trusted me to carry on the winery and to do the right thing for the family, even though I was not a Gentillo by birth. His dying wish was that Paolo would take over the vineyard. Did he tell you that?"

"No." Turned out we'd both hidden a lot from each other.

She nodded, as if this was to be expected. "He doesn't talk about the past. What Paolo doesn't understand is that you cannot run from the past. No matter how far you go, you cannot run from who you truly are."

The boat was running south now, passing entire forests lit up greenish gold with the sun creeping toward the western mountains. Up on the rocky ridge, a herd of mountain goats stood out from the slate grey rock. "That's not true."

"Family is everything to Italians. We live together, fight passionately together, eat together. The most common kind of business in Italy is owned by families. The largest businesses. But the wineries in Italy are always, always run by families. If we don't have tradition, then it means nothing. I cannot run Gentillo Vineyard alone."

"What about Emilia?"

Ahead of us, a speedboat sliced the lake, towing a water-skier. A rooster spray of white water shot up from the ski, creating a misty rainbow. Waves from the speedboat rippled, sending silky undulations to the shore. Rosalia shook her head. "Emilia drinks the wine, but she doesn't like to make it. She went to the University of Rome, fell in love with another student. He became a professor. She is a city girl now. Paolo is the one who fell in love with the family business."

Pulling my hair from my face, I turned to her. "Do you really think your entire business would crash and burn if a family member weren't running it?"

Rosalia lifted her glasses so I could see her eyes. "You have no idea what you're asking. You run a hair salon. I run a two-hundred-year-old winery. Where is your family? I ask Paolo if he's met your parents. He says no. If you are so serious about my son, then why has he not met your parents?"

My spine tingled. Paolo had asked the same question. Many times. "They live in Arizona."

"You don't see your parents?"

"What's your point, Rosalia? That I can't possibly understand what it's like to be in your shoes because my family isn't close?"

"Exactly."

We studied each other for a long moment. "You're not going to bribe me or scare me or eject me from Paolo's life."

She crossed her arms, letting the wind whip her glossy hair. "Perhaps. Or maybe I can convince you to think beyond yourself and do what's best for Paolo." She stalked to the stern of the boat, turning a corner until she was out of sight.

It was going to be a long trip back to Chelan.


Rosalia didn't reappear until the *Lady Express* had reached Chelan and was a few hundred feet from shore. The late afternoon sun slipped behind the hills. A few jet skis buzzed around, catching the waves from the ferry as they bounced off the shore. Paolo was waiting on the dock. He waved as Rosalia joined me on the bow, leaning against the metal railing. She waved back. "Go ahead, wave. Let him think that we had a wonderful time."

My head pounded, despite the two bottles of water I'd gulped earlier. My T-shirt felt sticky and clingy. I couldn't wait to get off this boat and into a shower. Following Rosalia's instructions felt wrong, but I waved. Not for her. For Paolo. He didn't need to know what a disaster this trip had been. "You didn't have a good time?"

Rosalia pursed her lips. "The scenery was beautiful and the company fascinating. Of course I had a nice time. We are getting to know one another."

The engines churned as the boat slid seamlessly to the dock. Teenagers on the dock took lines, wrapping them around metal cleats. The ramp descended. "And I'm getting bribed with fat checks."

Rosalia shook her head, cleaning her sunglasses. "No, no, no. What you don't understand is that is a small price to pay to keep Paolo from throwing away his life. I would cut the heart out of anyone who tried to hurt my son."

"That's dramatic."

"You will understand, some day. A mother does anything to ensure her children's happiness. If Paolo moves home, he will assume control of a winery that will bring him professional and personal success. He will become the man he was born to be. That is true happiness."

Paolo gazed at me as he waited for us to disembark. He tilted his head, as if wondering what we were saying.

"Since you know the future, Rosalia, tell me, what happens if he stays here?"

She squinted at the reflection off the water. "He gets you. What he loses is the estate. The ability to make Italian wine. The home he grew up in. He will always be welcome, but he will not own any property in Italy. I will disinherit him."

My heart sank. "That's horrible."

She shrugged. "It's for his own good. Paolo has Italian wine running through his veins. If you pluck him from Italian soil…"

She let my imagination finish her thought. "You think there is some mystical connection between your son and the land?"

She lowered her Gucci sunglasses to emphasize her point. "My darling girl. If you are not willing to leave your homeland, how can you possibly ask my son to do the same?"

"Rosalia, what you don't understand is that I never asked him. Staying here was his idea."

"Paolo has always been tenderhearted. He would do anything for love, including destroying his future."

# CHAPTER SEVEN

## He Gets You

"He gets you?" Carmen asked, peering at her iPad with a checklist at her elbow. We were in the kitchen of Orchard House with Lola. As usual, Carmen was working, going over the inventory for the upcoming fall wine tasting dinner, giving me half of her attention. Or less. It was getting tiresome. Particularly after the day I'd had with Rosalia.

I'd taken a shower and dressed for the evening. The last thing Paolo had said to me was, "See you at dinner," in such a cheery voice, I hadn't had the heart to make an excuse. To tell him that I'd rather throw myself off the dock than spend one more second with his mother. The woman who had threatened to cut out my heart.

Instead, I was in the Orchard House kitchen, trying to get the attention of my best friend, who was way more concerned with just about anything except my boyfriend's mother and her not-so-veiled threats.

"That's what she said. 'He gets you.' Instead of two hundred years of history and a winery with an estate that includes the massive Mediterranean villa where Paolo was raised. I looked it up. The place looks like it's been there since Caesar was in diapers. Her husband's family had lived in the hills since they were apes, apparently. It's way up on the hill, with a village at the foot of it. I bet the villagers used to be the serfs. She's throwing all that history at me, telling me that Paolo will lose his entire inheritance if he doesn't come run the vineyard. Hundreds of years of history and tradition. All that versus me. And his mother will never talk to him again. She's a one-woman mafia."

Lola's eyes went huge. "Seriously? She's mafia?"

Carmen rolled her eyes without once looking up. "Of course she's not mafia, Lola. Come on. So she'll disinherit him?" Carmen studied me for a half a second before returning to her computer.

"Sounds like she's talked to an attorney."

"Criminy, she makes Evan's parents sound amazing." Carmen made a check mark on her list. "I'm so nervous about them coming here. Everything has to be perfect."

"Did you just say criminy?"

Carmen looked up. "I did. Sounds weird, right?"

"Not if you're in a 1940s melodrama. Next thing we know, you'll be saying gadzooks."

"Gadzooks!" Carmen said. "I like the sound of that. I guess I've been picking it up from Mama's prayer group. They come in every week for lunch."

"They pray at a bar?" I asked.

"Something like that. More wine than actual praying." Carmen's phone rang. "I'm sorry, it's the chef for the wine tasting dinner. We have to go over the final menu. Can we talk later?"

"Carmen, can't *he* wait?" I was getting sick of this.

"Just one second." She spoke into the phone. "Can I call you right back?" She hung up, giving me an annoyed look. "What? I have to finalize the order for the dinner."

I tossed up my hands. "You know what? Go ahead."

"You *just* made me hang up."

I patted my chest. "I didn't make you do anything."

"What is so important that it can't wait? Seriously? I have sixty people coming for dinner, a chef that has to wake up at four in the morning to cook, and a best friend who is freaking out because a handsome, eligible man wants to marry her. A man that she loves. I don't see what the problem is, Stella!"

"I don't want to get married!"

"Change your mind. People do all the time. Isn't that the song you were singing to me? 'My Prerogative?'"

"You know what, forget it: just go." What was the point? Had every conversation we'd had since we were fifteen left her brain? Is that what growing up was? Forgetting?

"Fine." Carmen spun on her heels.

"You're still coming on the hike tomorrow with Rosalia and me, right?"

Carmen gave me an absentminded nod as she scrolled through her phone, walking into the living room.

Lola and I were left alone in the quiet kitchen. "What's her problem?" I asked. Carmen's dismissiveness was more than annoying; it stung.

She twisted her lips. "She doesn't have time for anybody. She's convinced if this wine tasting dinner isn't the best thing we've ever done, Evan's parents aren't going to like her. She's taken her type A personality and amped it up to a fifteen."

"I'm getting tired of it. This whole second banana to everything in Carmen's life is getting old."

"I'm third banana." Lola put her finger on her chin. "I don't even think I qualify as fruit. I'm the white stringy stuff you peel off the banana. If I ask her anything that's not winery-related she stares like I'm speaking in tongues."

I hopped off the kitchen barstool. "Wish me luck. I'm going to have dinner with Lady Macbeth."

"If she offers you the check again, take it."

"And leave Paolo?"

Lola winked. "No. Cash it and stay with him. She'll get over it eventually."

"Trust me, she won't." In the little time I'd known her, I'd learned that Rosalia wasn't a woman who forgave.

Driving to my own house as a dinner guest was surreal. Should I stop for a bottle of wine or flowers? It would be weird to show up with a hostess gift for Paolo. When I arrived, I sat in the car, staring at the same dusty laurel hedge I'd parked in front of a hundred times, steeling myself for the dinner. What kind of tricks did Rosalia have up her sleeve? At the front door, I paused. Should I knock? Another of life's questions that I couldn't seem to answer. What was the protocol when visiting your own home? Finally, I opened the door and walked in, hoping the evening wouldn't be too awful.

For one beautiful second, I imagined discovering the last few days had been a bad dream. Paolo's visa was approved. Dinner was cooking. Life would continue in a blissful haze, Rosalia would be safely in her winery, casting spells on children, turning villagers into toads, or whatever she did with her free time.

But no.

"Stella, welcome! So glad you could come!" Rosalia stepped out of the kitchen wearing an apron Paolo had given me as a joke. Hair slightly damp, smelling of lemons, she kissed me on both cheeks.

Seeing her in the apron I'd never worn, at home in my kitchen, made me wish I'd bought a can of wine so I could chug the entire thing this second. There was no way I was getting through this evening without alcohol. "Thank you?" The weirdness made me question the appropriate response.

Of course I could come. This was my house. I lived here, most of the time. Unless it was being invaded by overzealous Italian mothers with boundary issues.

"I hope you're hungry!" This was a different version of the woman I'd seen today. The woman that Paolo knew. Rosalia two point zero. Who wasn't a psychopath bent on eliminating me from the picture.

I peered down the hallway toward our bedroom. Was he showering after his swim? "Where's Paolo?"

"Outside. At the barbecue. We went out on his boat. It's a beautiful boat, no?"

Where on earth did the woman find the energy? All day in the sun and wind. I could crawl onto the couch and sleep for hours. "Sure."

"Paolo has the most beautiful boat on Lake Como. He and his girlfriend would spend hours on that boat, sunbathing and cruising on the lake." She did her famous shrug. "Too bad you don't like boats. Paolo is a big boater."

I had to admire the skill it took to both mention an old girlfriend in a way that would have me imaging Paolo with a bikini-clad vixen, while also focusing on our personality differences.

Refusing the bait, I found an open bottle of wine and poured myself a glass nearly to the rim. Rosalia's eyebrows shot up.

I lifted the glass slowly so as not to spill a drop. "Cheers."

"Indeed."

After a healthy slug, I went outside. Paolo was facing the barbecue in jeans and a rumpled shirt, brushing oil over the grilling meat. My shoulders relaxed at the sight of him. "Hey!"

His face brightened. The sun had just passed the hills, spreading a deep pink across the sky. He enveloped me in a hug, kissing my hair and lips. He smelled of lake and the familiar spicy scent of his skin. He was solid and real. Soon Rosalia would board her broom and we'd face the visa issue together.

Over my shoulder, I could see the pinched look on Rosalia's face through the sliding glass door.

"The food is ready. Perfect timing. I am so happy to see you. All my mother wants to talk about is wine. Italian wine." He pulled back to look into my eyes. "Are you still mad at me?"

"Yes."

"I was hoping to talk you into moving back."

Why bother pretending? "With your mother here?" I waved at her through the window. "No chance in hell."

"She loves you." Paolo frowned.

I stepped back, studying his face. "Paolo, seriously?"

He offered me a sliver of the roast meat. Lightly charred on the edges, seasoned with rosemary and garlic. "She thinks we are very different of course, but she likes you. She says you have the strong personality."

Ha! "You are such an optimist."

He piled two platters with roasted meat and perfectly charred vegetables. We carried them into the dining room. Rosalia had set the table. She took the place across from Paolo, where I usually sat. They were so comfortable in their domestic routine. Their quick bursts of energy were identical. It made me slightly jealous. When Paolo pulled out my chair, gently rubbing my shoulders, her eyes flickered with something I couldn't quite read.

Paolo topped up my wineglass and poured his mother more before lifting his own. "To the two women in my life. *Salud!*"

"To *my* beautiful son," Rosalia said. "And his American syrah. As good as this country can possibly get."

Paolo shook his head. *"Mamma, non stiamo parlando di vino."*

Rosalia grimaced. *"Sì."* Her eyes flashed as she translated. "You don't want to talk about wine?"

Paolo patted his chest. "I don't want to." He turned to me. "Mamma said you had lunch at the Stehekin bakery?" Paolo grinned. "With a dog."

"A cute dog," I said. "I took the Red Bus. It would be fun to go all the way up to Rainbow Falls sometime."

Paolo nodded enthusiastically. Rosalia cut her meat, waving the knife. "I think Stella is not a nature girl, no?"

"I like nature. "An utterly ridiculous, overly defensive statement that caused Paolo to snort. No, I was not a rock-climbing, zero-body-fat Terminator, but Rosalia thought I was some Cheeto-fingered, cheap-wine-guzzling sloth.

"You like nature if you can watch it from afar. Preferably with snacks," Paolo teased.

"In Italy, Paolo and his friends would hike every weekend," Rosalia said, serving some pasta to her son. "Do you want any pasta?"

I frowned. "Yes."

She gave me a tiny serving. Scarcely more than ten noodles. When I kept my plate up, she raised her eyebrows. "I just thought you'd be watching your figure."

"No." I waited until she'd loaded a double serving.

Paolo didn't seem to hear, busy watching the lake with the studied look of concentration that meant drinking wine had given him an idea. He was making notes in his head.

Rosalia's eyes narrowed. "It's okay, tomorrow we hike. If you are not too tired from today."

"No, not at all," I lied. My head ached at the thought of more sun. "I'm looking forward to it." With any luck, Rosalia would get eaten by a bear.

For dessert, we had affogato. Paolo thought he was doing me favor, but it annoyed me. Why share our special dessert with his mother? Why ruin the memory of the first time he served it to me at sunset, running with the dishes to the end of the dock where I waited, wrapped in a blanket? He hadn't wanted the ice cream to melt before I'd tried it.

I was being petty. I'd been naive enough to sign up for back-to-back days with Rosalia and was feeling slightly sorry for myself.

While Rosalia and Paolo made the espresso and scooped the vanilla ice cream, I went to the bathroom. Our master bathroom.

Paolo's razor and shaving cream were neatly lined up on the counter. His toothbrush in the glass. He was a neat person and had made me tidier. My salon had always been pristine, but not my apartment. Now, I hung my clothes up every time I undressed. Never left my cereal bowl in the sink. We had slid into such an easy domestic routine; it had been surprising. Every day in this little house had been fun. For the first time in my adult life, I had a real home. A place of love and warmth and sharing. Bad memories didn't follow me around like sharks, waiting to consume me if I slowed down.

How different my life would be if he left.

When he left.

No more lake house. No more laundry nights, piling clean clothes on the couch and watching TV while we folded. No more sipping hot chocolate with the lights off, enjoying the snowfall while Paolo nuzzled me, making me laugh by explaining, yet again, that despite the sore muscles, the inevitable injuries and waiting in chairlift lines in the freezing cold, skiing is a wonderful sport.

No more watching Paolo outside, snipping fragrant herbs, holding them to my face, inviting me to smell their perfume, explaining that some of these were tasting notes in his wine. No more counting the stars from the dock as they emerged from the deep violet sky. No more sitting in the Adirondack chairs under blankets in the fall, with my hands wrapped around a mug of tea.

Up until this point, I hadn't faced reality.

Leaving the bathroom, I had the overwhelming desire to fall face-first onto the bed. To smell Paolo in the sheets and forget, for a blissful moment, everything. With a ragged sigh, I shuffled down the hallway, wishing the night was already over.

At the table, there was a small box next to my place mat. A jewelry box.

"What's this?" I asked. I knew damn well what was inside.

Rosalia was studying me with those intelligent, hooded eyes. Behind them, untold calculations.

"Open it," Paolo said.

So I did.

# CHAPTER EIGHT

## Shiny Object

"You don't have to wear it," Rosalia said, as I slipped on the ring.

On my hand, the diamonds gathered light, sparkling brilliantly. I'd never seen such a glamorous creation. Sapphires shone deep, velvety blue.

"It's gorgeous," I whispered. I'd fight Rosalia if she tried to take it off my hand.

"Keep it on," said Paolo quietly. "See how it feels."

I fluttered my fingers, admiring how the gems caught the light. I felt myself getting teary-eyed at Paolo's tenderness. Why didn't I jump up and scream yes to marrying him? What was wrong with me? I could make this all go away if I could stop being such a big baby. Bonus: it would piss off Rosalia. I was genuinely surprised at the surge of emotions, the desire to make Paolo happy, to embrace the hopefulness of marriage. My entire being felt poised, on my tiptoes, wishing I could move forward with Paolo.

Paolo took my hand. "You see, it fits."

"It looks a little tight to me," Rosalia said, craning her neck.

"Nope," I said, truthfully. I had not been prepared for this reaction.

"It's not insured for this." Rosalia looked like she'd swallowed lemon juice.

Paolo didn't even look at her. "It doesn't matter. It belongs on her hand."

"Paolo, you can't be serious," Rosalia snapped. "It's only insured in Italy."

"It's fine. You brought it. *Va bene.*"

The tendons in Rosalia's slender neck strained as she shook her head. "It's an heirloom. We should bring it back to Italy."

Paolo shook his head. "Mamma, it's my ring. It belongs on Stella's hand." He squeezed my hand. "Wear it. I'll sort out the insurance."

I held out my hand, mesmerized. I was such a sucker for sparkly things. I needed this beautiful thing on my finger. Even if it was on loan. What if I felt the weight of it for a little while? "Just for tonight."

Paolo's grin expanded, reaching his eyes. Hazel flecks dancing. "Good. Okay."

Rosalia got up abruptly from the table. "That is irreplaceable."

"I'll bring it back tomorrow," I promised.

"Stella, it belongs to you," Paolo said.

I wished with all my heart I could believe him.

Paolo joined me near my car after dessert. Gravel crunched under our feet. When I dug in my bag, I couldn't locate the keys. Growing increasingly frustrated, I cussed under my breath.

"*Fai fare a me.* Let me," he said softly, taking my purse. He dipped his hand into my bag, immediately locating the keys.

"What's wrong?" he asked gently.

"Oh Paolo, what isn't?" I looked up at the darkening sky. Venus twinkled over the lake to the south. Rosalia's cigarette smoke drifted from the front patio, where she'd gone after dinner. Ostensibly to give us some privacy, but I knew she just wanted a smoke.

"Not an answer."

I took a deep breath to steady myself. "Your mother is going to disinherit you if you leave Italy and marry me."

Paolo looked at me for a very long time before speaking. "She said that?"

I nodded.

Paolo pursed his lips, his face growing cloudy and then, like a storm settling in, he became furious. He spun on his heels, racing into the house, yelling in Italian. Rosalia answered back from the front patio. Ducking through the obstacle course of paddleboards, kayaks and canoes, I snuck around the side of the house, but stopped. I didn't want Rosalia to see me. It was bad enough that I'd told Paolo, I didn't want to expose myself to her fury.

Paolo stepped out onto the patio, speaking at first in Italian, then switching to English after Rosalia replied.

"I don't understand. You told Stella that you'd disinherit me if I married her."

Rosalia's voice was a smooth as silk. "Oh darling. What kind of woman would I be if I disinherited you for getting married? That's absurd. Gentillo Vineyard is your birth right. She doesn't care for me, but this is a bit much."

I didn't need to hear any more. I rushed back to my car, got in and started the engine. My brain raced a million miles an hour. What a liar! What a scheming shrew! The temerity. One thing to me and another to her own son. I could barely see the road as I navigated my way to Orchard House. The only thing that was clear was that Rosalia was setting me up.

"Oh my god, she didn't!" Carmen said.

"She did. Flat-out lied about the whole thing." I replaced a piece of salami that had fallen off the platter.

We were in the Orchard House kitchen while Carmen plated charcuterie for the next day's wine tasting. Sixteen identical platters of smoked meats, cheese and pickles, covered and refrigerated for a class. In the corner, a dishwasher worked on the last few wineglasses. Servers ebbed and flowed from the kitchen, gathering linen and cutlery for the dining room.

"She's trying to make Paolo think you're lying. Classic mother-in-law move," Carmen said.

"What?"

"Oh yeah." Carmen nodded, rolling up paper-thin salami into neat batons. "Why would his mother lie? The woman who served him milk and cookies? Why would she do such a thing? Versus his girlfriend, who might feel insecure about his mother. Threatened." Carmen tapped her temple. "She's psyching you out. A complete mental game. She's a master."

I buried my head in my hands.

A dishwasher with a pencil moustache leaned away from the sink. "My mother-in-law tells my wife that she sees me in bars buying lotto tickets. Never bought one in my life."

I gave him a weak smile. "Okay." I turned to Carmen. "I'm not even sure Rosalia will still want to go with me tomorrow but if she does, you have to come."

"Tomorrow?" Carmen admired her handiwork, artfully layering prosciutto. "What's tomorrow?"

"The hike. I'll send you directions to the trailhead tonight."

"Right. Whatever happened to shopping and lunch?"

"The hike was your idea. Besides, can you see Rosalia shopping in Chelan?"

"I've never met the woman!"

"You will tomorrow."

Carmen raised her eyebrows as she sliced rolls of goat's cheese. "Great. I really want to see this creature."


By nine o'clock in the morning, it was already unseasonably hot. Rosalia and I waited at the trailhead north of Manson, watching a red-tailed hawk circle overhead in the cornflower-blue sky. Rosalia somehow managed to look both chic and sporty in black shorts, a white shirt and hiking boots. Carmen was late, leaving me to fend for myself. I kept my eyes trained on the hawk.

"Why did you lie to Paolo?"

"What are you talking about?"

"The disinheritance?"

She shook her head.

"If he marries me."

"My dear. You are young and in love and know Paolo, yes?"

I didn't say anything. If Carmen didn't show, this hike would be intolerable.

"That is a wonderful feeling. It's new. Fresh. When the difficulties happen, he will want the familiar. I'm doing you a favor." She glanced at her Apple Watch. "Your friend?"

"She's late." Also, Rosalia hadn't answered my question. Rule number one of messing with people's lives? Don't admit to being a liar.

"It's getting very hot. Maybe we should just go. I worry about you being able to make it."

I resisted the urge to throw my water bottle at her.

Our hike traversed the side of a mountain, leading to a dramatic ledge with a view of Chelan County to the south and north. Paolo loved this hike. He'd bought me hiking boots as a surprise, assuming I'd love them, because after two glasses of wine and no food, I'd professed an interest in hiking. Sheer infatuation had dragged me up the trail, rewarding me with passionate kisses at the top. Lots. With his arms wrapped around me and the lake below, it had felt like we were in a movie. It hadn't made me love hiking, but it had brought me one step closer to falling for him.

Paolo had recommended the hiking route last night during dinner. Mesmerized by the ring on my finger, I had utterly forgotten the steep incline and endless switchbacks and agreed, thinking that it would be bearable with Carmen.

Rosalia stretched her legs while I checked my phone. A blue jay screeched at us from a ponderosa pine. Still no Carmen, nor tell-tale puffs of dirt from the gravel road. I'd lost cell phone reception.

"How long do we wait?" Rosalia asked.

I had to face reality. My best friend had stood me up. Left me to face a six-mile hike with Rosalia all on my own. Thanks, Carmen. I'd sent her two texts that morning, confirming the location and time. She was more than half an hour late. "I guess she's not coming."

Rosalia gave me a shrug. "Too bad. I was looking forward to meeting this girl."

I gave her a tight smile. "Just me."

She glanced at my left hand. "Be careful with that ring."

What did she think I was going to do? Drag my hand on the ground? "Okay, let's go." Get this over with.

Rosalia started up the trail as if someone had shot off a starter's gun. Her long legs ate up the trail as if she'd trained for this for months, instead of smoking and drinking wine. "Let me know if you want me to slow down."

"No, I'm fine," I lied, cursing Carmen with each step.

My anger at Carmen kept me going for the first two miles. At some point my body realized, hey, this isn't our jam. We belong in a salon, clipping hair, listening to gossip. Our most strenuous activity of the day should be walking down the street to pick up a sandwich. Anger can only get a girl so far. Every muscle in my legs started screaming. My lungs morphed into sobbing babies, furious at this sudden change of events, begging me to stop.

Rosalia, despite the steep trail incline, hadn't broken a sweat. There wasn't the slightest hint of shine on her sculpted cheeks. Her neat bob was as sleek as a runway model's. Her shirt kept its crisp folds. Trail dust didn't dare sully her boots.

Sensing that I was lagging, she stopped. "Do you need the break?"

As much as I hated admitting it, I desperately needed to sit down. Nodding, I collapsed on a rock. Rosalia backtracked, remaining upright while I dug through my backpack for my water bottle. We were high enough to see Lake Chelan from both vantages, stretching along the valley in a slash of pristine blue. The snowy peaks of the Cascades matched their halos of wispy clouds. Velvety carpets of forest spread downward to the lake. The vegetation had grown sparse. Aspen trees fluttered below in magnificent fall color. Vivid yellow, tipped with scarlet and burnished orange. Sumacs with jagged leaves spread their furry branches. Chipmunks darted across the trails, stopping with bright eyes, standing on their hind legs before dodging into a hole or onto the top of a rock, chattering with excitement.

Rosalia took it all in, scanning the valley with her hand over her sunglasses. "The view is incredible."

"Wait until you see it from the top." My heartbeat was returning to normal.

Rosalia peered down. "Are you sure you can make it?"

I wiped the sweat from my face. "I know you think I'm a weakling, but I can do a six-mile hike." It might kill me, but I could do it.

She raised one eyebrow. "You look very tired. When you live a very sedentary life, these things can be very taxing. It's very unhealthy."

My eyes went wide. "Rosalia, you smoke!"

She was smug. "Ah yes. We all must have our contradictions, no?"

There was no winning with this woman. I stood up, slapping my tired thighs. "All right. Let's do this."

"Are you sure?"

"I have done this hike!"

"I am older than you and I can easily climb this hill. A woman who loved nature would be all over these beautiful mountains." She gestured expansively. "Racing me to the top. I don't think you've even done this hike before, have you?"

"With Paolo! It's what we were talking about last night."

She shook her head. "Okay, but if you need to wait here, I can finish the hike alone."

I shoved the water bottle back into my pack and stood. Maybe I was a little shaky. My feet, snug in barely worn hiking boots, were tender. Rosalia wouldn't intimidate me. Pushing past her, I led the way. "This is nothing. Come on, let's go."

Later on, I'd look back at this moment, wishing I could freeze the frame. That I could rewind to here and admit to Rosalia that yes, I was tired. My feet hurt. I wanted to go back.

That would have changed everything.

By the time we reached the lookout, I was ready to throw myself off the ledge to avoid having to take one more step. I'd arrived all hot and sweaty, aching in muscles I didn't even know existed. But here's the thing. The view was so jaw-droppingly gorgeous, the hike was worth it.

My interior monologue going up the trail had been something along the lines of: *Shoot me dead. I hate this. I'm never putting on these hiking boots again. This is torture. Rosalia is always going to hate me, so what's the point? Also, was that a rattlesnake?*

And then came heaven.

The trail ended abruptly on a rocky outcrop that was a ledge overlooking the valley. It brought back memories of being with Paolo, who'd lured me up with stories, songs and jokes. He was the one who'd first pulled me out onto this ledge. A higher plane of living. It was impossible not to be awed by the stunning, raw visceral beauty. I walked directly out on the rock, gazing out at the vastness of the valley as if climbing into thin air. We'd ascended so high that eagles soared below. Coasting on the drafts that hit the red canyon walls, creating ideal sailing currents. I was close enough to see each feather, unruffled by the soaring wind. Powerful wingspans of six feet, circling the valley. Below, miles of green, and the seemingly endless lake. Above the water, green hills shot upwards to peaks. The ledge thrust us into the middle, seemingly suspended in mid-air.

I ached with a deep love for Chelan. I wanted to lie on the ground and weep at the beauty. Which is what I should have done.

Instead I said, "Look at this. I mean, just look." Throwing my arms out, I spun around to look for Rosalia. She'd silently snuck up within arm's reach. My hand hit her cheek. A resounding slap that echoed across the canyon.

I'd heard the phrase "time stood still." I'd never before experienced it. Life was trapped in a surreal web. Time flies when you're having fun; it freezes to a halt when you've just slapped your boyfriend's mother.

We both stood rooted and shocked. When time picked up again, everything moved in slow motion, especially my brain, which took a particularly long time to grasp what had just happened.

Rosalia's hand went to her cheek. Under her palm, a red blotch bloomed on her cheekbone.

She began swearing in Italian. It had to be swearing. I couldn't make out what she was saying, but the look on her face was venomous.

"Oh my god, Rosalia. That was an accident. I'm so sorry. I didn't mean to—" I was babbling, practically incoherent with fear. Had this just happened? This could not be happening. "I didn't mean to do that. I didn't know you were there."

Any second, I expected her to start screaming at me, but she didn't. She kept muttering in Italian. Perhaps invoking an ancient Gentillo curse; I'd be turned into a mouse. Or a stone. Either would be preferable to living. Slowly, she raised one arm, silently pointing as her words trailed to nothing. We stood a wingspan apart, quiet. A pebble rolled down the hill. The shadow of a hawk passed. Suddenly she turned, starting down the trail so quickly she was practically running. Following, I tried to catch up, babbling apologies. She whirled around. "Don't you dare follow me!"

"It's the only way down the mountain! Let me apologize. It was an accident!"

Taking a swig from her water bottle, she shook her head. "There are no accidents in life. You are uncivilized, uncouth, ill-mannered and for your age, you are in terrible shape. Over my dead body will you marry my son!"

"It's a steep mountain, Rosalia. That can be arranged." The moment it left my mouth, I regretted it. Something had been broached. My words left us in thin air.

Rosalia straightened, suddenly regal and more than slightly terrifying. I wouldn't have been surprised if she'd sprouted wings and flown off the trail. She turned back to the mountainside, descending with such speed she left a wake of dust.

I sat down on a rock, stunned. Had I really just, whoops, attacked Paolo's mother? I looked down at my hands as if they could offer an explanation.

I was still on the rock when my phone rang. Without looking at the caller ID, I answered, gazing at my boots, numb.

"Hey, how'd the hike go? Sorry I missed it." Carmen sounded perky, not realizing that I'd recently assaulted a visiting senior citizen.

"I'm still on the trail."

"How's it going? Oh, never mind. I bet you can't talk."

"Oh no. I can. It's just me."

"Where's Rosalia?"

I stood up, carefully picking my way down the trail, oblivious of the blue jays heckling me from the ponderosas. "She left. She was kind of mad. Oh, well, let's be honest. She was hostile. Probably as mad as I've ever seen anyone in my entire life. She said, and I'm quoting here, it would be over her dead body if I were to marry her son. That sounds kind of perfect. Paolo might not be into it, but I'm game."

"Something tells me it didn't go very well."

"You could say that." I couldn't see Rosalia on any part of the switchback. She must have sprinted the entire way down.

"Stella, what happened?"

"I slapped her."

"Wait a second. You did not just say that."

"Yeah, I did. It was an accident, although, according to Rosalia, they don't exist, which is going to disappoint a lot of people. I can't even see her on the trail. With my luck, she's probably been eaten by a bear."

"Oh, this is bad," said Carmen. "This is really bad."

"Not helping."

"I really don't know how to spin this."

Oh no. This was horrible. If Carmen, the queen of strategic thinking, was out of moves, I wasn't treading water. I was sunk.

# CHAPTER NINE

## Stone-Cold Mama Bear

"I slapped her. I accidentally slapped her." I was at the salon, which I'd driven to like a scared rabbit heading for a hole. Usually the smell of shampoo, the plants and the tight, cloistered feminine atmosphere calmed me, but nothing could take away the image of Rosalia's fury.

"You slapped who?" Izzy asked.

I'd planted myself on the cheery yellow couch, gazing at the reflection of my dog painting above my head. The little chihuahua in sunglasses usually comforted me. Today, it reminded me of Rosalia's perception of me: a tacky American gold digger. "Rosalia."

Izzy laughed. "You're kidding me! That's awesome."

"No, it's not awesome. It's the opposite. She said I'd marry her son over her dead body. I amped it, saying it could be arranged."

Izzy sat on the couch next to me. "We're one scene away from a reality TV show." This from Izzy, who had once kicked open a bathroom stall in Señor Frog's and threatened to shoot the balls off a man who'd bothered her daughter.

"But I love her son."

"That broad needed punching."

I glanced over at Rachel, who reluctantly nodded. "She's right. I mean, not necessarily what I would have done, but she's got a solid point."

"There are lots of people in the world who need punching, but you can't do it."

Izzy shook her head. "Look, sister. Contrary to what the bible says, the meek do not inherit the earth. They sit around eating biscuits and gravy, waiting for the rest of us to take care of business. People like that Rosalia chick are used to getting their own way all the damn time. I bet she's got so many people cowed they just roll over when they see her coming. For Pete's sake, her own son had to leave the continent to get away. Even if it was an accident, you sent that woman a message loud and clear."

Even if I didn't agree, Izzy was making me feel better. "What message was that?"

Izzy lifted my chin, looking into my eyes like the stone-cold mama bear she was. "Don't mess with a country girl. Ever."


"You slapped my mother?" Paolo didn't waste any time. That was how he greeted me on the phone. Poor Esther, whose hair I was cutting, had heard the whole story because Izzy would not shut up. Even after I'd dragged her into the back room and hissed that the whole town didn't need to know my business, she'd gone out into the salon and said, "Yeah, I know you don't want to talk about it, honey, but maybe you need to really have it out with her."

The only thing Izzy loved more than a fight was another, bigger fight.

"Hang on one teensy second, Esther," I said, stepping away from the chair. "Paolo, I did not slap her on purpose."

"How does the slap happen then? Someone else is moving your arm?"

"I was waving my hands around, you know, like I do, and her cheek was in the way."

"Her cheek gets in the way of your hand. I know Mamma isn't the easiest woman in the world, but the slapping is just too much."

"I didn't do it on purpose. I swear to god."

"Do not swear to God for my sake." He was dead serious.

"It's a saying, Paolo. It doesn't mean that I'm actually swearing at God. What exactly did your mother tell you?"

"First, she calls me at the work. Tells me she's walking. By herself in a foreign country because you were very violent."

"And you believed her?"

He snorted with indignation. "When I come to pick her up, she's on the busy road with construction trucks. She gets in the car and I ask, 'What happened, Mamma?' I couldn't believe what she told me."

"Paolo, can you please just get to the point?"

"You slap her! I never take you for the violent person, Stella, but now I see this red mark on my mother's face and she's walking in the traffic and I'm very confused."

There is rarely traffic on the road to Manson. She probably found a construction site and camped out until Paolo came. "It was an accident."

"How can you slap my mother? She is a poor old lady."

Not poor and certainly not old. Machiavellian? Yes.

"When she called me, she was crying."

"She didn't cry at all when I slapped her."

"So you did slap her!"

"Yes, I did. But it wasn't on purpose. I don't know how many ways to tell you, Paolo, but it was an accident."

"So you say."

"Yes. Because it's the truth. If you don't believe me, we've got a much bigger problem than your mother."

I pressed end call. Izzy patted my back as I walked past, returning to Esther.

"Don't you worry, Stell. Either he's gonna calm down, or you're better off without him."


Carmen opened the salon door, carrying two grease-pocked brown paper bags. She sat beside me on the couch, immediately going in for a hug. I held onto her for all it was worth.

She handed me one bag. "Can we call this a peace offering?" Inside was a cheeseburger and fries. She handed me a shake. The waxed cup dripped with condensation.

"Yes." I shoved a few fries in my mouth. I was ravenous.

Carmen sipped her milkshake. "I'm so sorry I wasn't there."

"I don't think it would have made any difference." Across the street, two dog walkers chatted on a bench in front of St. Andrew's Church.

"It's going to be okay."

I shook my head. "I'm pretty sure people say that when you're completely screwed."

She studied me over her straw. "This is kind of bad. She doesn't seem like the forgiving type."

"She's more the vengeful type. Paolo might believe her."

"How do we feel about that?" Her voice was soft as a feather.

I took a long pull on the milkshake, getting a slight brain freeze. "Uh, let's see—really mad. I mean, how well does he know me? I always talk with my hands."

"Men never know what their mothers are like."

"Right? She's different when he's around. At dinner last night, she was Mary Poppins. He walks outside, she's Cruella de Vil."

"Maybe you'll get lucky and she'll leave early."

Putting my burger down, I wiped my lips with a napkin. "I'm so tired. I want my normal life back. A world where Paolo isn't going to be deported and his mother isn't here and we don't have to get married."

"Wait a minute. Back up. Deported?"

"I told you. His work visa wasn't renewed. He has to go back to Italy, or they'll deport him."

She frowned, shaking her head. "Right. You did."

"It's kind of a big deal, Car. The kind of thing a best friend should remember."

Carmen's eyes flashed. "I've got a few things going on myself, you know."

"People remember things when they're really listening. You've been so caught up in your own stuff. It feels like this isn't important to you."

Her lips formed a sharp line as she shook her head. "I hardly call running a business caught up in my own stuff."

"Carmen, I am living at Blue Hills and we barely see each other."

"We talk."

I snorted. "Right. I talk and you barely pay attention."

"That's not fair."

"It's true."

Carmen stared out the window for a long minute before sighing. "You're right." She kicked off her shoes, settling cross-legged onto the couch. "Okay. I'm right here. There's no wait staff, no Blue Hills employees. I'm one hundred percent listening." She ate a fry. "Was it really an accident?"

"Why does no one believe me? Yes!"

Carmen grinned. "But was it?"

"Total accident. Car, I don't know what's wrong with me."

"Nothing is wrong with you. Everyone accidentally slaps their boyfriend's mother once in a while."

"It's not even that. I'm so terrified of marriage and children. Why do I freak out every time I think about walking down the aisle in a white dress?"

She finished her burger. "Not everyone is meant to be married."

"If, and that's a big if, we can get past this, I don't see why we can't just keep going the way we're going. But he's brought up marriage. It's on the table: if we don't get married, we'll break up."

"Try the long-distance thing. Some people make it work."

"That's not what I want. I don't know what scares me more, the idea of him leaving or the idea of him staying."

"You need to stop thinking about this. You know what? Bring his mom to the fall wine dinner at Blue Hills. I'll sit her with Papi and Evan's parents. They can complain about us."

"Seriously?"

Carmen nodded, warming to her theme. "Absolutely. It's her last night in town. She'll be socializing. You won't have to worry about being around her. I'll make a space at the table."

I was in the guest bedroom at Orchard House, putting on my sandals. There was a knock at the door. "I'll be right there," I said, thinking it was Juan, who'd agreed to let me know when he was ready.

The door opened. "Can I come in?" Paolo asked.

"Be careful, I might hit you." I turned to the mirror to apply make-up, although truthfully, I was done. I just wanted to avoid looking at him.

He stepped in, so handsome I had to work at sustaining my anger. "I'm sorry."

"That's a start." I flicked on lip gloss.

Paolo glanced around the tiny room appreciatively. Dormer windows overlooked the orchard and winding lake. In the distance, snowy peaks. Something out of a fairy tale. "Very pretty room."

"Your 'I'm sorry' theme was much more on point."

He raked his hands through his hair. "Stella, you know when Emilia and I were kids and our mother would get angry at us for something, we'd say La Tempesta is on the loose. We'd hide in the cave where we stored the wine. We'd tell the foreman not to tell her, when she called. He always kept our secret." He nodded appreciatively. "Everyone knew La Tempesta was a handful. She's so much. Yesterday, when she said you hit her, I thought, of course. She's a woman who brings big feelings. And big feelings always lead to trouble." He saw my face growing cloudy and lifted his finger. "But I also know that Stella…" He paused. "That's you."

"Thank you for the clarification."

He smiled warmly, as if he'd done me a huge favor. "Yes. I also know that you, my beauty, don't lie." He raised one eyebrow rakishly. "At least not to me."

"That's true."

"Yes. So." He rubbed his hands together. "Mamma believes you hit her on purpose, but she's here tonight and leaving tomorrow. We should let hey gones be hey gones."

I spun around, grinning. "It's bygones be bygones."

He did his adorable shrug. "English is murder. You know that, right?"

I lifted my eyebrows. "The way you do it, it is."

He moved closer to me. "We'll see how you do in Italian, okay?" He took my hand, tracing the engagement ring with his finger. "Can you move past this?"

"If she can." She couldn't. Rosalia would throw herself off a cliff if she could take an enemy down with her. But. Paolo was worth putting up with her for. He'd opened up windows into the darker parts of my life. It was sometimes painful, but worth it. The man literally took my breath away. If I could've pushed him to the bed and had my way right then and there, I would have. When Juan knocked, it would be extremely awkward.

"Be my date?" Paolo jauntily crooked his arm. Could I save this moment forever? Remember him in his slightly rumpled white linen shirt, his damp curls held back with his sunglasses. His crinkling brown eyes shot through with topaz. Lingering tan and white teeth.

The look on his face as he offered his arm. If life could be lived exclusively in these moments, we wouldn't walk. We'd float.

"There's nothing I'd love more," I said truthfully.

Blue Hills Vineyard was at its best, highlighted against a purple sky. The rustle of drying grape leaves could be heard in the breeze. Below us, the lake shone from the lights of houses across the water. A crescent moon hung overhead. Bats flitted over the fields. Round tables draped in snowy linens clustered on the patio and at the end of the gravel drive. Candles flickered in hurricane lights, casting a warm glow on the guests. Lola had strung globe lights from the trees. They swung in the soft breeze. Waiters circulated, pouring wine and offering appetizers to the guests who milled about, chatting before dinner.

Paolo guided me to our table, counselling me to ignore Rosalia if she was testy. *Not a problem*, I thought, snagging a glass of wine. I could spend the rest of my life ignoring her. When we sat down, I murmured that I was sorry for the accident.

Rosalia snorted, rolling her eyes.

"This will be interesting," I murmured to Paolo, who looked like he wanted to crawl under the table. Instead he plucked the wine from my hand, insisting that the pinot gris was too sharp for my tastes. Lemony. Seconds later, he handed me a deep pink rosé. "This is you. Complex and slightly sweet."

"Slightly?"

"Europeans never add sugar." He smiled. "That's faking it."

There wasn't enough wine at Blue Hills Vineyard to drown my sorrows, so I switched to water. Tonight, I needed to keep my wits.

Paolo was seated between Rosalia and me at a table with Evan, who was to my left. Evan's parents, Estelle and Peter, were near Juan, who was dashing in a white guayabera shirt with embroidered panels down the front. Rosalia made a point of ignoring me, except to shoot daggers every time I tried to engage her. Paolo attempted to include her in our conversation about the wine, pointing out that he, Evan and Carmen were part of a movement encouraging American winemakers to stop adding sugar to their wine. She refused.

Estelle leaned toward Evan, pointing at Carmen, who was chatting with guests. "Is that one your girlfriend?"

Evan frowned. "Yes, Mom. You met her when we walked in. Can you please stop pointing?"

Estelle blinked. "Darling, it's not my fault. They all look alike."

"Who are you talking about?" Evan asked, turning bright red.

"The wait staff." Estelle was an aggressively preppy woman with a headband, cotton shift and pearls. She had tennis court skin, cured to a summery beige. The type of woman who judged by club memberships.

"She's not the wait staff, Mom. We've been over this." Evan spoke with a locked jaw. I'd never seen him so uncomfortable.

"Why isn't she sitting with us?" Estelle asked. Their exchange gave me plenty of time to study her. Nose job?

"Because she's hosting, Mom. If you wanted to talk to her, you should have asked us to have dinner with you."

Estelle peered into her wineglass, extracting a bug with her fingernail. "Darling, this *is* dinner."

Evan's father, blandly handsome in his polo shirt, looked like he belonged on a golf course. A matched set to Estelle's blonde athleticism. They had a moneyed sheen. Rolex on his wrist. One-karat diamond studs in her ears.

Carmen, a few tables away, kept pouring wine, although I could see she was listening.

"If she's not a waitress, then why is she serving wine?" asked Estelle.

"It's what winemakers do. They pour," Evan said. "It's what I do, Mom."

"She's Mexican?" Peter asked.

Evan sighed. He looked as though he'd like to ask the earth to swallow him rather than spend one more second with his parents. "She's American."

Juan leaned across the table. "She's Mexican-American. My children have Mexican passports."

Estelle looked confused. "Why would they want Mexican passports?"

Juan kept his face friendly. "They are Mexican citizens."

"I don't understand," said Estelle. "Evan just said she was American."

"Our girls were all born in the United States, but my wife and I applied for Mexican citizenship for each one. Carmen is a true Mexican-American. Dual citizenship."

Estelle wrinkled her nose, smelling a rat. "Why would you do that? Isn't American citizenship what you people came over here for?"

Evan sought Paolo's gaze, mouthing, "You people," and slapping a hand over his eyes.

Juan took a measured sip of wine. "Evan, it's okay."

Estelle seemed confused. "What's okay? I am asking a perfectly innocent question. I mean isn't that what all Mexicans want? To be Americans?"

Juan inhaled deeply, winking at me. Pride rose in my chest at his innate dignity. "Mexicans who come here and want to stay, yes, live here legally, most of them want to become American citizens. But many of us don't want to lose our Mexican heritage or citizenship. We are proud to be Mexicans. It is the country of our birth. Like many countries, we have our troubles. But it's our homeland. Which is why my wife and I wanted to make sure that our girls had their Mexican citizenship."

Peter raised his eyebrows. "Is that legal?"

"Perfectly legal." Juan got up from the table. "If you will excuse me, I'll see if my daughter needs help. Being a waitress is hard work. Even for Mexicans." On his way to the kitchen, he squeezed Evan's shoulder, as if he knew the younger man was on the verge of throwing his parents off the property.


Juan migrated back to our table during dinner, chatting with Rosalia, who had relaxed as the evening wore on. Wine loosened her. She was talking about Gentillo Vineyard. "We have so many similarities," she enthused. "The lake for one, although Lake Chelan is much less developed. It's wild in places. Beautiful. The vineyards look very similar. Your irrigation systems are more advanced. For a young wine industry, you have accomplished a great deal. The wine is a pleasant surprise."

Juan lifted his glass. "Thank you. I have owned Blue Hills for forty-two years. As you know, the best thing about winemaking:

you never stop learning. I'm blessed that my children follow in my footsteps."

Rosalia sipped her wine. "Exactly. When your children build on what you've worked for your entire life, you bring the next generation of winemakers to the table. Nothing could be more important."

Paolo stiffened as his mother spoke.

"It's everything," Juan concurred.

"It's not everything," Paolo said. "Juan's children made their own choice. That's the thing, Mamma. If, as you say, you can't run the winery on your own, maybe it's time to trust someone outside the family. I know this is very hard for you but you have always said that life is change. Maybe it's time for Gentillo to be run by someone who can bring in new blood."

Rosalia's eyes flashed. "What Juan understands is family loyalty. There is no substitution. None."

"Rosalia," Juan said. "Perhaps this isn't a question of loyalty. My daughters chose to leave their careers and return to Blue Hills. It was their decision."

"My son will not help me," Rosalia said.

"Chelan is where I've made a life," Paolo said quietly, looking at me.

Rosalia's eyes narrowed as she glanced at me. She remained quiet for a long time. "You stay with a woman who slaps your own mother?"

Paolo flushed, locking eyes with his mother, lowering his voice. "Mamma, let it go. It was an accident."

Juan shook his head with incomprehension. "I don't understand."

"She hit me," Rosalia said, pointing to me.

"Not on purpose," I said.

"You hit her?" Estelle was horrified and thrilled. "Why did you hit her?"

"An accident," I said helplessly, as everyone at the table turned to talk to one another. "I was just…" I turned away from Paolo, letting my hands fly around. "What I didn't know was that…" My hand brushed Paolo's ear.

"Nice shot!" He grinned. He glanced around the table. "You see, accidents happen."

"You weren't supposed to lean in."

He kissed my cheek, whispering, "It's okay. I did it on purpose. It's funny."

"It's not funny." Rosalia drummed her fingers on the table.

Paolo stood up, grabbing my hand. "Mamma, we are going for a walk. When we come back, you apologize to Stella."

She pressed a hand to her chest. "Me? Apologize?"

Paolo nodded. "You owe both of us an apology. This should have been a nice night. A night to enjoy the wine and our friend's hospitality. Instead you made it about a regrettable incident that should be forgotten. You act like a spoiled child. I'm sorry you disagree, but it's my life. I know you were raised to think that a son owes his life to his mother, and to the family business, but it simply isn't true."

"You are going to throw your life away and turn your back on your inheritance," Rosalia hissed.

Paolo shook his head. "Don't do this. You are the one who will suffer." He spoke heatedly for a moment in Italian before turning to me. "Would you like to go for a walk?"

I'd never felt so loved in my entire life. "Yes."

It took every ounce of willpower not to give Rosalia a triumphant look. A kid who'd faced down the mean girl and won. Instead, I took a page from Juan's playbook, willing myself to grow up. Taking Paolo's arm, I left the party a tiny bit more mature than I had been when I'd arrived.

We hiked up the hill into the Blue Hills Vineyard. Pebbles lodged in my sandals, so I left them on the driveway. Party noise drifted toward us until it grew distant and indistinct. A light wind carried the smell of apples from the orchard. Leaves rustled. Fall was in the air.

"Thank you," I said.

Paolo led the way. "For what?"

"Defending me."

Paolo snorted. "Of course. I will always defend you."

"You don't have to make your mother apologize."

"Ah, don't worry. She won't. She will pretend I never said anything. She flares hot and then, pffft, nothing. If it doesn't serve her to remember, she'll forget."

"She's very political."

Paolo nodded. "When she campaigns for something, god forgive the person in her way. One time, a neighboring vineyard tried to open a discussion of a seventy-five-year-old agricultural water rights contract with the local governing board. My mother visited each member of the board, all thirty-two, arguing her case. When the vote came, it was unanimous. My mother won."

"Impressive."

"Or frightening. Depending on whose side you're on."

We stopped to enjoy the view. A breeze kicked up the valley. Paolo wrapped his jacket around my bare shoulders. Below us, the tree lights illuminated the patio. Candles flickered on the tables as guests stretched their legs, carrying wineglasses out to enjoy the view.

Paolo pointed across the lake to the east. "You see there?"

I looked to where he was pointing. "What?"

"There is our tree."

Following his finger, I squinted in the dark. The hulking form of the willow tree, reduced to the size of a fingertip, was outlined in the dark.

"There is our house."

"There it is. I miss it. This has been a crazy week."

He squeezed my hand. "I love you, Stella."

I leaned into him. "I love you."

"When I came here, I thought I'd spend one year away, learn something about American wines, maybe travel and come home. I never thought I'd stay. Some things are more important than tradition. Like making my own life." He ran a hand through his curly hair. "I am sorry about my mother."

"It's okay."

"No, it's not. Before my father died, he ran the winery. Mamma ran the events: the concerts, the weddings, the tours. All the things that happen on a big estate. She never learned how to make wine. When my father died, she panicked. She was sure she would lose everything, even her home. My uncle came along and solved everything for a while, but she has always counted on me. We knew something would happen to Uncle Riccardo. He has always had a weak heart. His doctor has been telling him to take it easy for years. He and Mamma ignored it. Uncle Riccardo paid the price. I knew that if I was going to work at another vineyard, it had to happen soon. Before something happened to Uncle Riccardo. I couldn't count on Emilia. Emilia and my mother fight like wolves. Always have. Emilia doesn't like to see it, but they are alike, those two. They always have to be right. It would never work for them to run a business together." He grinned. "They would kill each other." He put his hand over his chest. "Until now, I was the one who could handle my mother."

"I don't want to come between you and your mother." Three or four times a year, my mom called. Messages I hoarded until I had a cluster, feeling powerful ridding myself of them: delete, delete, delete. A Christmas call I would allow, maybe. Keeping it random. Punishing. Blaming. Distancing.

"Ah, don't worry. The thing about Italian mothers is that no matter what they say, even if they say they spit on your grave, they curse you, they promise not to speak to you again—what a promise that would be, eh?—nothing ever happens. It is all words. And words get old. They are forgotten in time. A mother's love is never forgotten."

Those words split me open. I thought of my mother. Of Rosie. My twin.

Rosie had only nine years to live.

Afterwards, I was right there, still alive, but the memory of Rosie and her death sucked my mother into an undertow of grief so rough she took my father with her, leaving me stranded on the shore, watching them slowly recede into the distance. I remembered the isolation, the darkness and the unbearable sadness of being alone, dealing with the grief of losing Rosie. My nine-year-old self hadn't had the language to describe it. I had been coiling into myself when the Alvarez family lifted me from the rocky shoal, enfolding me in their love. I came in from the cold. Survived. Learned how to live without my sister. Without my parents, who'd become shadows. I kept on. Graduated. Made friends. Worked at a dusty little salon. Saved money. Opened my own business. Pushed ahead with my life, and thought I was happy.

And then.

Paolo.

If I didn't grab a hold of something, of someone, I would end up carried away. Back out to the place my parents went. If I didn't say yes to Paolo, he'd recede. He'd end it. He wasn't the kind of man to wait. Paolo was a man of action. He'd move on. Go back to Italy and stay there. Throw himself into Gentillo Vineyard, faking happiness until it became reality. I'd be stranded back in my old life, knowing I'd let a great man leave out of fear. I'd live with the consequences of my own weakness forever.

Rosie had slipped away in an instant. Maybe it was time to stop living in fear. Yes, I was tough. A survivor. I could live without Paolo, but life wouldn't be nearly as good. If I didn't grab a hold now, I'd lose too much.

I was sure of it.

"Paolo?"

"Yes?"

"Let's get married." I began tentatively, ended with conviction.

His voice was a whisper. "Stella. Stella, are you sure?"

"Positive."

"You don't have to marry me to keep me here. We can work on the visa problem. It can be solved. The immigration attorney—"

I cut him off. "Let's get married now."

He kissed me with such passion, he nearly knocked me off my feet.

"I am the happiest man alive."

I tried to ignore the tightness in my throat. The horrifying sensation that there wasn't enough air in the world to keep me alive. I shoved my doubts into a tiny dark place reserved for scary things, marching down the hill to face Rosalia. Convincing myself that everything was going to be okay. That this wasn't my only choice, just the best one.

"I'll be right back, okay?" As soon as we stepped onto the patio, Paolo disappeared, leaving me stranded on the edge of the party, nervously eyeing Rosalia. If she was angry, she didn't show it. She was completely engaged with Juan, placing her hand on his arm to emphasize a point. They were looking pretty cozy, which was encouraging. If anyone could tame the beast, it was Juan. He had a way of taking thorns from the crankiest creatures.

Inhaling deeply, I weaved my way back to the table, trying not to notice the eyes on us. Rosalia had perfected the art of not giving a hoot and kept chatting up Juan. "You'll simply have to come to Italy. I would love to show you around."

Juan nodded. "I would like that very much."

Paolo appeared with a bottle of champagne, filling everyone's wineglass at the table, forgetting his usual insistence on proper flutes. When he got to Rosalia, he kissed the side of her head. "Behave."

If looks could kill, I'd be dead.

After he'd filled my glass and his own, Paolo waited, expectantly, for quiet. It took a moment.

"Thank you. I knew there were many great things about America, but I did not know, when I came here for one year, that I would begin a new life. I came here for business and found love. There could not be a happier ending." He held up his glass. "I fear Stella is not so fortunate, but I am the luckiest man in the world. *Salute*, to my bride to be, *bella* Stella."

He toasted in the direction of Rosalia. She left her glass untouched for a very long, tense beat. Everyone at the table followed Paolo's gaze, waiting for Rosalia's response. She sat stone still, as if weighing possible reactions, studying my face without smiling. When her eyes turned to Paolo, her lips lifted at the corners. Juan's eyes followed me, and then Rosalia. Then he did something I would never forget. He picked up Rosalia's glass and handed it to her.

Rosalia graciously smiled at Juan, and took the glass. As she raised it to her son, there was a collective release of tension, as though the entire table had been holding their breath. Not once did Rosalia's eyes land on me as she said, *"Salute."*

Not congratulations, or I'm happy for you, or even I wish you the best.

Just *salute*.

But it was something.

There was a chorus of congratulations. Rosalia sipped her champagne with a sphinx-like calm, her feelings buried just beneath the surface. I decided not to care.

Juan got up to shake Paolo's hand, slapping his back with characteristic enthusiasm and warmth. "You have got yourself a wonderful woman. I have known Stella since she was this big. She'll keep you on your toes."

Paolo raised his eyebrows. "She's a troublemaker."

"Come on now, Juan, you can't tell him all my secrets," I said.

Juan's face grew tender. "She's like my daughter, you know."

Paolo nodded. "I know."

Juan's face clouded a little. "Something happened in her family. I don't remember, but she spent her time with us. We were very lucky."

Paolo gave me a curious look before returning his attention to Juan, who had drifted off.

Estelle sipped her champagne, looking confused. "Didn't she hit the woman who's going to be her mother-in-law?"

"It was an accident," Evan said.

"Still," Estelle insisted.

After kissing Paolo, I went to find Carmen, who was surrounded by a cluster of people, eagerly listening to her discuss the varietals she grew. Evan appeared at my elbow. "Good luck getting through to her. She hasn't even eaten dinner. Congratulations, by the way."

"Thank you."

"Are you two really going to stay here?"

"That's the plan."

"Where are you going to get married?"

I looked up from the text I was composing to Carmen: *Big news. Find me.* "I haven't thought that far ahead."

"You're more than welcome to get married at Hollister Estate. I assumed Paolo would want to get married in Italy. He told me that his parents got married at their vineyard."

"Oh yes, Rosalia would love that. My biggest fan."

Evan nodded, taking a sip of his wine. "You never know. Maybe if you make it her turf, get her involved, she might even get on board. You know the old saying. Keep your friends close and your enemies closer."

# CHAPTER TEN

## Wedding Belles

The day after the fall dinner, I woke up knowing something in my life had altered. But what? It was that hazy moment before the world assembled itself into something familiar. Then it hit me. I was engaged. Paolo and I were getting married.

Unearthing my hand from the tangled sheets, I gazed at the gorgeous ring. It caught the morning light streaming in the window, sparkling. I should have felt like a Disney princess, spinning around the room singing while cartoon animals got me dressed. Not waiting for a rush of happiness that never arrived, worried about destroying Paolo's future by getting him disinherited. The weight of that responsibility would crush me and, quite possibly, our relationship. Rosalia was right. Now, while we were young, it might not bother us, but what about later, when things weren't sailing along? Nobody knew better than I did that life had a way of smashing plans to pieces.

My phone rang. It was Pavarotti, "Solo Mio," so I answered. Unfortunately, it was not Paolo's voice that greeted me.

"It's Rosalia. We must meet today."

"Must we?"

"Yes. It is vital."

"But is it?" It was fun, answering everything with a question. Maybe that would be my method of communication with Rosalia from now on.

"Yes."

"Aren't you leaving for the airport soon?" Because if she wasn't, I was going to kill her. Or myself. One of us had to die. The airlines better do their job.

"Yes. But we must talk."

"Rosalia, I'm busy all day." And she needed to leave this continent.

"Just for little while. One coffee."

"This morning I have clients."

"Before the clients."

"What is this about?" Because if it was about the slap heard round the world, I was going back to bed.

"I'll see you at the Starbucks at nine o'clock." She hung up before I could protest.

Burying my head in the pillow, I threw my phone on the bed. Great.

I was drinking my coffee when Carmen came down the stairs. She went straight to the coffeepot. "Where's the half and half?"

It was my last morning at Orchard House. My packed bag sat by the back door. Juan had insisted on carrying it to my car for me, then forgot, walking right past it on his way to coffee with his cronies at the Apple Cup. Apparently, the entire Alvarez family had forgotten about my departure.

I held up the carton.

Carmen poured a dollop into her mug, glancing at her phone, spilling coffee on her white blouse. "Oh no. I'm late!" She dabbed at it with a paper towel. The stain spread.

"Hey, can we talk?" Not one word since last night. Nothing about the engagement. Zero.

She kept at her shirt. "One sec." Rushing up the stairs, she returned moments later in a different blouse. "This okay? *Seattle Magazine* wants to do some pictures."

"You should have let me cut your hair."

Carmen's hand went to her head. "Is it bad? I think my split ends have split ends."

She complied when I motioned for her to come over. I tucked the longer, face-framing strands behind her ears. "It's fine. Can we talk?"

Carmen concentrated on her phone. "Sure. How about dinner?"

"It's Thursday."

She stared at me blankly. "So?"

"My late night at the salon?" And had been for years. Seriously.

"Right. Okay. Listen, Stell, I'm really sorry, I have to go."

She dashed out the door without one word. Nothing about my engagement, my imminent departure or my request to talk. Something was going on. Or rather, nothing. That was what my friendship with Carmen Alvarez was starting to feel like.

Rosalia didn't belong in a Starbucks. Certainly not in Lake Chelan Starbucks. Her silk shirt and tailored black capris stuck out amongst the coffee-swilling Americans in cargo shorts and flip flops. A swan in a duck pond. As I arrived, she handed me coffee. "I did not know what to order. The menu is so confusing. A Frappuccino?" She shook her head sadly. "It's not a coffee place."

I settled into a chair, wondering why she'd chosen this as a meeting spot. Perhaps she considered Starbucks my kind of place. Utilitarian, generic and very American. Noise from the drive-through window added to the cacophony. "I didn't tell Paolo about you trying to buy me off."

She tilted her head as though genuinely curious. "Why not? You should be honest with the person you're marrying."

"Because he loves you. You're his only parent and I don't want to come between you."

"Very noble of you."

"No, it isn't. It's for him. I don't have a good relationship with my mother, and I don't want Paolo to suffer. I know what that feels like."

Rosalia nodded, taking a sip of her coffee before placing it on the small table between us. "I want you to know what Paolo will lose if he chooses to stay here."

"Oh, I've seen Gentillo Vineyard. Your website tells the whole story. I know very well how impressive it is."

Her glossy hair caught the light as she shook her head. "Oh my dear, you can't possibly tell what a place is like by looking at a computer. You have to smell the air. See the lake. Go inside our home. Taste the food. Our olive oil comes from our own trees. We bake our own bread. Raise our own pork. It's not a place, it's a way of life." She paused, glancing around the Starbucks, as if measuring the incalculable distance between my home and hers. "I have a proposal for you. Come to Gentillo Vineyard. You and Paolo. If you want, you can get married there. You can plan the wedding, invite the guests and come see what it is you're making him give up."

"You can't be serious?"

She blinked her hooded eyes. "My dear, I never joke about matters this important. We are talking about my son."

"Get married in Italy?"

She nodded. "Yes. A small wedding. You can make an educated decision. You can't possibly make a judgment without seeing the estate. Shall we just agree on it?"

I had to admire her boldness. Rosalia was essentially playing a game of chicken. Plan a wedding in a place that Paolo might lose. She'd seen enough of me to think she'd win. That I'd recognize that Paolo belonged with his family.

She glanced at her watch and stood, shouldering her handbag as if the matter were decided. "I'm going to be late for my flight. Paolo is driving me." She turned as if to go, but stopped. "Oh, and one more thing. I know you didn't mean to slap me."

"What?!"

She was so casual, it was maddening. "I knew you that when you slapped me, it was not on purpose. We Italians gesture with our hands too. So. I knew."

"Then why did you act like you did?"

She sniffed. "It suited my purposes. I thought it would be easier to get rid of you." She shrugged. "I was wrong. Now all I can hope is that you're smart enough to recognize what will make Paolo happy." She hiked up her purse. "You know, this is for you, too. When you get older, you'll see. In the end, people want what is familiar. Don't think I'm being entirely selfish."

She sailed out of Starbucks in a cloud of expensive perfume. It had never once occurred to her that I might say no. Maybe she was right. Perhaps I did need to see Paolo's childhood home. At the very least, I could have a wedding on an Italian vineyard.

"No. No. No. We cannot get married there."

Rosalia had left the day before. I'd moved back to our rental, spending the night alone while Paolo was in Seattle for business. After work today, I'd met him at the Hollister Estate, hiking up the short trail through the vineyard where Paolo worked. We were having a glass of wine on the patio of the cave outside his office. One of the many perks of dating a winemaker. Enjoying a glass of wine on the winery patio overlooking the estate. Evan's Mediterranean-style home was below us, edged by the garden and a pool. Further below, stretched out like a shimmering swath of silk, the lake. We were surrounded by miles of lush vineyard, rustling in the early evening breeze. Swallows swooped over the fields. Two deer nibbled apples that had fallen from the orchard trees lining the driveway.

It should have been romantic.

But it wasn't.

Paolo was agitated, throwing his arms around, pacing like a tiger. He reminded me of his mother. The same pent-up energy and focus. Both of them were accustomed to getting things done their way. They ran successful wineries. Their considerable charm and powers of persuasion wielded results. "Gentillo is everything I came here to escape. The way they do things. Ancient traditions that have nothing to do with the modern world. You've seen how my mother works. You think you can have the wedding you want, but before you know it, she'll have taken over. She'll invite a bunch of strangers. She knows everybody in Lombardy. She'll turn it into a publicity stunt for the winery. She will never take a back seat. She's genetically incapable. She'll take control." A deep breath shuddered through his agitated body, gesturing to our beautiful surroundings. "Stella, if we got married here, it would be so much simpler. Is this what you really want?"

The more he complained, the more I wanted it. What in the hell was he hiding? First we had to hurry this up, and then he didn't want to get married at his family's winery. A place made for weddings. A romantic celebration, overlooking a picturesque lake in the same place his parents had got hitched. A complete escape from my past. A new beginning. I'd had enough time to consider my options. I couldn't imagine getting married any other way. Chelan was a good place to live. Italy was a great place to make a break with the past. "Why don't you want me to go to Italy?"

He came back to the table and sat down, taking my hands. "I do. Just not now. And not for our wedding."

"I think I should see it before we get married."

"Why?"

"To see where you come from."

Paolo thought about it, gazing over the lake toward our house, hiding behind the willow tree. Another deep sigh. "Stella, does this have anything to do with my mother?"

I could tell him the truth and he'd dig in. Fight me tooth and nail. "No. I want to go to Italy."

Just like that, I lied to Paolo for the first time.

*

If you'd seen us from a distance, a couple strolling down the path of a picturesque winery during the magic hour, you would have assumed we were happy. The light was so sharp and clear the leaves were silk, the clouds plucked from Renaissance paintings. The valley was a lush bowl filled with amber light. Who wouldn't be happy in such beauty?

Except.

We weren't.

When I was nine-and-a-half years old, my aunt, my mother's sister, who lived more than two hours away in Yakima, had come to town to bring me to the county fair. We'd walked hand in hand through the agricultural displays in the barns, stopping to gaze at the squirming pink piglets with their delightfully curled tails, the silky, long-eared rabbits and the long-legged colts. My aunt had bought me a snow cone with a rainbow of flavors, encouraging me to try more. Puzzled, I'd studied her eager face, wondering how to react.

"Come on now, nobody can be unhappy at the fair," my aunt had pleaded. Up until that point I hadn't known that it was my job to reassure her that everything was okay. To convey that my household was going to soldier on, despite our devastating loss. That we were still capable of enjoying everyday pleasures. I'd squinted into the sun, biting down on the icy treat, trying to enjoy the sticky sweetness, remembering how Rosie had always asked for blue raspberry. Our dad would make silly jokes. Why were the raspberries blue? Were they sad?

That day, I'd smiled. Said thank you. Allowed my aunt to return home reassured that, despite the state of our house, the piles of dishes, unwashed clothes and unopened mail stacked on every surface when she'd arrived, that now, with a freshly cleaned house and the remaining twin given an outing, life would continue on. Normality would arrive.

It was my job to act happy. The ambassador outside of our home for a couple who could no longer navigate. From that moment on, I'd assumed the responsibility of acting happy.

I hiked down the hill now with Paolo, through the vineyard. I vaguely considered explaining that moment with my aunt to him. Its profound effect on my life. But how would that conversation work when I hadn't yet shared the death of my twin?

Paolo glanced at me from the corner of his eye, as if gauging whether to speak. He chose silence. A new and uncomfortable feeling. We weren't that couple. Were we?

We reached the Hollister Estate gravel driveway. Said goodbye at our cars. He barely looked at me as we made dinner plans. As soon as he got home, I knew he'd go for a long swim. It gave me enough time to go find Carmen. Our friendship felt like a rubber band, stretched to snapping point. Maybe she could live her life like this, but I couldn't.

Hollister Vineyard was elevated from Blue Hills Vineyard, separated by a sloping embankment. At one point, there had been a switchback trail between the two homes. Years of erosion and lack of use had erased it. Now it was a hard-pebbled slope, baked into a packed surface. Carmen and Evan sat on the back patio of Orchard House. If I was going to move this wedding forward, I'd need her help.

My progress down the hill was slow. Little pebbles came loose, skittering down the hill under my shoes, causing me to slide. My

Keds offered little traction. I kept sliding faster until I lost my balance, continuing to slip once I hit the dirt, landing unceremoniously at the foot of a rose bush.

Evan jumped up from his seat, running to my rescue. "Nice of you to drop by."

He helped me up. "Very funny." I dusted the back of my dress off, trying to salvage a little dignity whilst removing bark mulch from my posterior.

"Are you okay?"

"I'm fine. Maybe you can invest in some stairs."

"Good idea." He offered his arm, which I gratefully took until we'd stepped out of the rose bushes.

"Can I get you a glass of wine?" Evan asked.

"That sounds great."

Carmen watched me carefully as I sat down, asking me if I was okay in the most perfunctory way. I waited for her to say something about the engagement. Evan returned with the wine, rescuing us from the world's most awkward silence. We used to share comfortable silences. Now we had long gaps, filled with bitchiness. Hers.

Evan looked ready to crawl out of his skin. "I'm going to let you two talk."

"Evan, you don't have to go," Carmen said.

Evan raised his eyebrows at her. It was uncomfortable and infuriating. As if Evan was deserting her at a party, leaving her with someone best avoided. Sipping my wine, I tried to calm down. Evan kissed her on the cheek. Said he'd talk to her later.

We were left on the patio, listening to the distant noise of the guests, the clink of silverware, the conversation. Carmen fiddled with her phone, which only emphasized our silence. Frostiness fairly crackled off her. "I was just having him try the new red blend."

"You don't have to explain to me what you were doing with your boyfriend."

"I know. It's just. You know, I've been so busy."

"Wait, let me guess. You have to go." It was passive-aggressive. Childish. I couldn't help it.

Carmen sighed. "Don't be like this."

"Like what? You're my best friend, Carmen. I was staying with you and we barely talked. I have life-changing things happening and I don't know how to process them. I miss talking to you. I miss our friendship. I know you have a business to run. I get that. But I'm getting married, Carmen, and I want to do it in Italy, which, in retrospect, is more than I can handle, but I can't let it go. I need to see what Paolo might lose."

She inspected her cuticles. "When?"

"I don't know. I'm not even sure anyone can make it."

"Maybe right after Paolo arrives in Italy, before his visa expires. That way you can come back together. You've decided to do it, so why wait? Expedia has sweet deals on last-minute airfare."

"Discount airfare? That's it? I just told you that I'm getting married."

"Congratulations." There was zero inflection in her voice. As if thanking the UPS driver. Except she'd be way more excited about a package than being stuck here with me.

"You could at least fake like you were happy for me."

"I am happy for you."

"You don't act like it. I said yes last night and you didn't say one word. I chased you around all night, trying to get your attention.

This is terrifying for me and you know it. I have to plan a wedding in a foreign country."

"I'm sure you'll do great." She offered a pinched smile.

"What do you mean?"

"I mean, you'll do great. You're an organized person."

"But it's in Italy. How am I supposed to plan something in a foreign country with a woman who hates me? I thought you could help. Obviously, I want you there, but I need your help too. Please. I can't do this alone."

Carmen got up from the table, shaking her head. "I can't."

"Are you serious?"

"Just because you're getting married doesn't mean my business shuts down. I'm sorry. That's my reality."

Standing, she rushed to the back door of her house and disappeared. For about three seconds, I wallowed in self-pity. Then I decided to do something.

# CHAPTER ELEVEN

## Besties. Not.

It's unclear how long I sat on Orchard House's back patio. Could have been thirty seconds or an hour. Carmen had said she didn't want to help plan my wedding. But Blue Hills Vineyard was a destination wedding spot. Unlike me, she knew the process in detail. Now I wasn't even sure she wanted any part of my ceremony.

We'd weathered junior high, horrible haircuts, and the time Lucas Friar, the most popular boy in ninth grade, had called Carmen a spic to her face. Mrs. Alvarez had died when we were fifteen. When she'd first become ill, we'd done homemade face masks, tie-dye, embroidered our jean jackets and raided neighboring orchards for cherries that we baked into pies. I'd been a one-girl entertainment committee, dedicated to making Carmen smile. While her mother got sicker and sicker, I'd feverishly tried to drag Carmen away from the avalanche that was about to hit her family. When it hit, I felt powerless. I'd lost a sibling; I knew grief. This was my second family, and now it was happening to them, too. Mr. Alvarez turned overnight from a guitar-strumming one-man mariachi band into a ghost. Every day for a week, I brought Carmen's school assignments to Orchard House, hoping to find things a little bit better. Then Carmen came back to school, sleepwalking through her days. Bit by bit, Carmen and her family returned. One night, Mr. Alvarez invited me to stay for dinner again.

It was the beginning of the new normal. I slid back into their family life with relief. Carmen went away to college. I worked in various salons. After college, there was a brief interlude at home before Carmen left for Seattle to begin her career. The night before she'd moved, I'd talked her into letting me give her a trim. She'd ended up with a pixie cut. All that beautiful hair on the ground. Eventually, she forgave me.

What would a wedding look like without Carmen? A bat flapped over my head. The sun had slipped behind the western slope above the winery. Overhead, the sky was periwinkle. A clicking sound was followed by the steady hiss of the vineyard irrigation. Loamy soil scented the air.

The idea that Carmen could excuse herself from my life filled me with a sharp, instantaneous anger. We'd always been there for each other. If she thought she could get away with this, she had another thing coming. Friends don't let friends ghost each other.

The hell with that.

Jumping from the table, I marched into the Orchard House kitchen. I was met with a flurry of activity. Red-faced wait staff rushed in and out of the door leading to the wine bar, dumping dishes in the sink, demanding to know the location of their appetizers. Two red-cheeked young cooks worked the stove. A third plated, handing off dishes to waiters, who frowned, switched plates, then hurried off into the wine bar.

Lola bent over the counter, looking at an iPad. She glanced up. "Hey, Stella."

"Where's—"

"In the bar, but I wouldn't—"

The bar was packed with locals. Carmen was behind it, studying a drink ticket. On the bar in front of her was a line of glasses. She measured shots into a cocktail shaker.

The room was full. I stuck my head between a couple in front of me. "What in the hell was that?"

Carmen looked up, shaking her head. "Can you not?"

She moved to the far end of the bar. Chasing her, I kept an eye on her through the row of seated people. "Can I not what? Try to have a friendship with you?" Carmen returned to her drink station. The couple leaned aside, avoiding me. "Tell me, Carmen, when is a good time? When I'm living here? No, that's not a good time. When you're not working? Oh wait, you work all the time."

"It's called having your own business," Carmen growled. She shook the cocktail shaker with such ferocity I was certain it would fly out of her hands. Opening it up, she poured the frothy drink into the waiting glasses.

"I have my own business. Does that mean I'm not allowed to have any friends? Because last time I looked, there were all kinds of people running businesses and having friends. The two aren't mutually exclusive."

Carmen carried the drinks on a tray out the end of the bar near the side entrance. I rushed after her, so close I was nearly on her heels. She darted around tables, out the French doors onto the front patio, spitting words as she rushed, the drinks tilting precariously. "That isn't what this is about, and you know it. You think that because you're getting married the entire world has to stop."

We arrived at a table of women who'd been following the argument as we walked outside. "Ha! I am the last person to act that way."

Carmen placed the drinks onto the table with such force that they slopped over the glass rims. Pulling a bar rag from her apron, she mopped up the mess. "Oh no? Then why do you have to get married in Italy? Italy! As if we can afford to shell out money for last-minute tickets to Italy."

I was barely aware of where we were, let alone that every table on the patio was fixated upon us.

The same woman who'd passed out the drinks saw me glancing at her. "Italy sounds nice," she said tentatively.

"There, you see. Normal people think Italy sounds nice."

Carmen rolled her eyes, glaring at the woman. "Would you want to buy tickets to Italy right now?"

The woman looked confused. "Right now?"

"Is that what you're worried about? I'll pay for the tickets!"

She rolled her eyes. "You can't afford it!"

"I see. Is that because I am a lowly hairdresser?!"

Carmen spun around, her eyes flashing in anger. "No! It's because they're expensive. Ever since Paolo asked you to marry him, you've been freaking out." She waved her hands around wildly. "I run an entire winery. And a wine bar. Oh, also, I plan weddings in my spare time, which, in case you haven't noticed, I don't have. I am literally run off my feet twenty-four seven. Two businesses, a father who has Alzheimer's and a serious relationship. So no, I'm not going to plan your wedding for you."

"I didn't ask you to plan it! I thought you'd show a little interest! I don't know the first thing about planning weddings. Some girls have everything worked out from the minute they watch their first Disney princess movie. I never even wanted to get married."

"So don't! Don't get married. Let Paolo work it out on his own. The world will not stop spinning and everyone, including you, will be absolutely fine." Carmen spun on her heels, stalking into the dark bar without a backward glance.

Early the next morning, my phone rang while I brushed my teeth. "Stella, it's Rosalia. Sit down. We need to talk."

Pausing to rinse, I spat out water. "Rosalia, I have to get to work." Last night Paolo and I had finally come to an agreement. He'd agreed to get married in Italy. I'd compromised on a date that allowed him to return to work at Hollister Estate as quickly as possible. Before bed, he'd emailed his mother. The woman didn't waste any time.

"Your clients can wait. We have a wedding to plan."

"Can I call you back?"

"Must I remind you that you are getting married in two weeks? Do you think this comes together by magical monkeys? No. We both have to talk now. I have the best caterer in the region ready to break his contract with another family, but we need an exact time. Also, how many people are you inviting?"

"What?"

"How many guests are you inviting?" She waited for me to respond. "Darling. Did something happen since Paolo emailed me?"

"Rosalia, I'll get back to you on the guests."

"But your parents are coming."

"I haven't talked to them."

Rosalia was quiet for a moment. "My dear, you aren't acting like a girl who wants to get married."

I took a deep breath, sitting on the edge of the bath. "My best friend has been difficult. I thought she'd help."

I could hear Rosalia sucking in her breath. "I see. Carmen?"

"Yes."

"People can be horrible. My best friend got drunk at a party and slept with the best man the night before our wedding. The best man was my brother-in-law, Riccardo. His wife was pregnant. I kept her company while she cried all night. I was so tired for my own wedding I could barely see straight. It's all water under the bridge, but weddings bring out some very strange emotions. Is she coming?"

"I don't know."

"Well, should I book the caterer? He is wonderful and we'd be lucky to get him."

I felt a rush of affection for Rosalia. Why was she being so nice? Should I even trust her? "Yes. Two weeks from this Saturday. Maybe ten people can make it on my side. Maybe. I'll call my mother soon."

"Oh dear. Ten people?"

Standing, I faced the mirror. "Yes. I don't think many more than that can make it at this late notice."

"Well, you see, I've invited quite a few more than that."

"How many?"

"It doesn't matter, *mia cara*. Leave it to me." She paused. "Oh, excuse me. You don't know what *mia cara* means."

"It means 'my darling,' Rosalia. Paolo says it all the time." Now it was *mia amore*.

"*Sì*. Okay. I forget. It's so difficult, the relationships, when you don't speak the same language."

"Goodbye, Rosalia."

Putting my phone down, I unzipped my make-up bag. I thought about calling my mother. My heart beat faster until my breath was shallow and ragged. Dropping my concealer, I sat down on the bed with my head between my legs until my palpitations slowed. Why hadn't I shared the biggest thing in my past with Paolo? What was I afraid of? My life was skidding off the road, as it had twenty-two years ago, into something huge and unknowable. Something that would change things forever.

I was definitely headed on a collision course with something.

The question was: what?

# CHAPTER TWELVE

## Hi, Mom

Thankfully, my call went to messages. I'd rehearsed what I would say a thousand times. Mom's cheerful voice said she was out, please leave a message, but wait for the beep. My brain went blank. Rather than hang up, I winged it. "Hi, Mom. It's me, Stella." I gulped. Who else could it be? Why was my mouth so dry? "Just called to see how you and Dad are doing." My big bold move of sharing my news on their voicemail dwindled to a speck. "Hope you're both doing well." Really ground-breaking. I topped it with a long, awkward, "Uhhhhh. Okay. I just wanted to talk." Because we do that so much. "Anyway, we can chat later. Bye." *Chat*? I never said chat. I sounded like Mildred, the hundred-year-old who came in for perms once a month. Thus ended the world's most awkward message.

What happened to telling her? Where was the, *Hey, Mom, sorry I haven't been great about returning your phone calls. When was the last time we talked? Six months ago? A year? But anyway, I'm getting married. In another country. To a guy you've never met, in two weeks. Hope you can make it. Can't organize my way out of a paper bag when it comes to weddings. Carmen's not into it, but maybe if you don't mind running up your credit cards a bit, you can afford last-minute plane tickets. That works, right? Okay, bye.*

Why was I such a colossal chicken? Didn't other people call their mothers to share things as lightweight as, *hey, I baked cookies?* Every time she called, I stared at the voicemail on my phone until I finally deleted it, excusing myself by saying I'd call her later. But I rarely did. Why couldn't I share big, exciting news? Good news?

I sat on the bed, marinating in failure, gazing out the window at the lake, thinking about the entire world of normal mother-daughter relationships out there that I'd never know. On Mother's Day, I just sent a card. Dropped it in the mail slot. Felt empty. My parents couldn't afford Italy. What was the point in sharing this?

Outside, a light wind kicked up the waves. A small boat with full sails tilted, heading for shore. Clouds sped across the blue sky. My parents had a house in Arizona. Would I ever see it? What kind of a life did they have in the desert? They'd picked the geographic opposite of Lake Chelan.

Maybe that was the point.

There was a voice message from Carmen I hadn't noticed. "Hey, Stell, I just had the world's most awkward brunch with Evan's parents. Turns out they're friends with lots of Mexicans. Their cleaning lady, their gardener and the towel boy at their club. Great bonding experience. Anyway, I'm ready to talk. Call me."

I deleted the message. Went to heat the coffee Paolo had left on the counter. Got dressed. Fixed my face and hair.

The salon opened in an hour.

*

Ten hours later, I was the last to leave Twig, turning the deadbolt with a satisfying clunk. Today, everything had worked. Nobody had complained when their haircut didn't take off ten years or make them look like a celebrity. Gossip and jokes had flowed. Unlike her last effort, Rachel's zucchini bread had been not only edible but delicious. Sweeping leaves off my windshield, I unlocked the car. Today, I'd parked facing the lake.

At the four-way stop facing Campbell's, I should have turned right. Someone honked while I indecisively paused. Another honk. I turned left, pulling over once I'd crossed the bridge to call Paolo. Let him know I'd be late. "Okay, thank you. I'll stay at work. Dinner at eight?"

"Yes. See you then."

"Love you."

"*Ti amo.*"

I drove past Blue Hills Vineyard, heading north on the road running up the western side of the lake. My family used to live up a winding gravel road facing Chelan State Park. Deer grazed in our yard, ate apples from our three trees. Owls nested in our ponderosa pines. In winter, we'd park our car at the end of our steep drive that the snow plough couldn't reach. My parents hauled our groceries on a plastic sled.

Once a week in summer, Dad took us fishing in a rowboat before work. We'd trudge along a path in the early morning, across the road and down the sandy hill. Our boat was pulled up onto the shore. Sleepy-eyed, Rosie and I would watch the mist rise off the lake. Never a morning person, Rosie was always the grumpy one. After Dad dragged the boat into the water, he'd offer his hand, steadying it with one sure foot. The boat had an outboard motor, but he rowed. The steady plop of the oars in the water was the only sound on the glassy lake.

Rosie and I sat on the same bench, facing Dad. He'd call us his little cuties, pretending to snap pictures with his hands to show Mom. At nine, we both said he was being corny, but we let him keep going. It was fun. We'd trail our fingers, watching the V of our wake spread, rippling against the boat, marveling. Our home grew small. A dot on the landscape of limestone outcroppings and forest.

When we reached the middle of the lake, Dad would unwrap the breakfast sandwiches, joking they were what we'd requested. Sauerkraut and sardines. Lima beans and Limburger. We'd giggle. Our voices echoed off the hills: "Daddy, Daddy, Daddy! Stop. I'm hungry."

"Okay. Here you go. Pickled carrot and toothpaste sandwiches. Your favorite!"

We'd drop the crusts off the side of the boat. Silvery fish appeared, darting at crumbs until they'd vanished. Daddy handed us fishing poles, pre-baited with night crawlers purchased from the state park kiosk the night before, left outside on the deck in plastic tubs to keep cool. We'd dangle our lines into the water, watching water skeeters skate. Listening to the occasional plop of a jumping fish. Seeing rings travel across placid water.

The sun would climb. We'd shed layers. Sometimes we caught perch or trout. Sometimes nothing. Daddy always brought us back before we grew tired. Mom would be in the kitchen when we returned, enjoying a cup of coffee. We'd regale her with our adventures. The eagle that had swooped right over our heads. The speckled trout that got away. She always said the same thing. It had been far too quiet without us. As if waking to a quiet house was unendurable.

It never occurred to me until I was older that the quiet house was the point.

There wasn't a parking spot on the side of the road. I pulled off on a narrow strip of land behind a metal railing. There wasn't much space, just a few feet. An ancient Airstream had been parked there for as long as I could remember. It had a fire ring, a few ratty outdoor chairs and a rusty old barbecue. Maybe it was a grubby fishing camp. It didn't seem quite legal or comfortable, smack against the road. Granite cliffs towered across the way. Their view was undisputed. They were nearly part of the lake. Occasionally a boulder would break off from the cliff, landing a few feet from the Airstream. Eventually, they'd pay a price for their view.

I stayed in the car. The car engine made strange noises as it cooled. Air and oil escaping and settling. Across the steel lake, the poplars on Wapato Point swept the sky under fat white clouds. Such a simple landscape. Water, trees and skies. Elements of my childhood. Seasons changed, but this view would never grow old. My fingers tapped the steering wheel, thinking of what awaited me. It took so much energy to visit this spot. But I did, regularly. Often, I drove here without knowing why. It drew me in with its own power.

I got out of the car, walking to the edge of the road. To the place where it happened, twenty-two years ago.

# CHAPTER THIRTEEN

## Snowflake

Bushes had grown up over the years, but it wasn't hard to find, even in the approaching dark. A space between the limestone boulders on the edge of the road. Just big enough for a car to skid over the edge. If our car had been two feet to the north or south, we would have hit stones hefty enough to stop us. We would have continued into town to the garage, or gone home to call someone with a good story. A close call. But, of course, that's not what happened.

Cars passed by, speeding without slowing. Pebbles skittered across the road in their wake. I gazed at the lake, hands buried in my jean pockets. Rosie and I had been wearing sweaters that my aunt had knit for us. Pink for her and red for me. White hearts knit in a pattern around the shoulders, front and back. They were pretty but we hated the itchy necks, the stifling thickness. Mom occasionally made us wear them. Our aunt had gone to all the trouble to knit them, she'd insist. Wet snow made the wool stink, mixing with the aroma of my mother's coffee. She always drank out of an open mug in the car, balancing it in the holders when it didn't quite fit. Fat wet snowflakes clung to my window. They were so pretty in their crystalline delicateness. Rosie gazed out the other window, at the lake. She would have complained if she saw me open the window, so I acted fast. The back seat filled with a cold gust of wind. Rosie began yelling for me to close the window.

I would, after I caught a snowflake.

"Close the window, Stella," Mom demanded.

"Just one!" I craned my neck out the window, feeling the icy wind, the sting of cold on my cheeks.

"Stella Gallagher you listen to me right now," Mom demanded, turning her head towards me. She'd knocked her coffee onto her lap. Screamed as the liquid splashed her legs.

Then we were skidding, fishtailing as she hit the brakes, sliding over the lane, against the railing, ricocheting across the road toward the lake. I could see the water coming toward us as we flew off the embankment. There was a quiet moment where we hung in the air before hitting the surface with a jarring thud. My head snapped back. Salty blood flooded my mouth. I'd bit my tongue. Mom's head smacked against the steering wheel. A sick, solid whack. Rosie screamed hysterically, her mouth a wide O. Taking her hand, I unfastened my seatbelt with the other. Dark green water poured in my open window, climbing to our ankles, then our knees. Rosie and I looked at the dark water pouring in with growing comprehension. The car groaned as it settled deeper into the water. We were sinking. I tried to release her hand, but she crushed mine with a terrible strength. No matter how hard I tried to break free from her grasp, I couldn't. Without my left hand I couldn't unfasten her seatbelt. Dark water had reached our thighs. Sharp, cold and numbing.

"Let go of my hand, Rosie. I have to get your seatbelt off."

She shook her head. "No. No. No. No. I can't let go."

"You have to."

Her teeth chattered, her eyes glassy and huge with shock. "I can't. I'm too scared."

Water poured into the window at a faster rate, gushing louder. Our waists were submerged. We were being eaten alive by the icy lake. Rosie's eyes skittered with fear, darting frantically around the car. I wasn't sure she could hear me over the creaking car, the rushing water and her own terror so I began yelling. "Yes, you can. Let go and I'll unbuckle you. Please, Rosie!"

Mom disappeared behind the front seat, fishing around for her cell phone. She kept muttering, "Where's my phone? I can't find my phone!"

Icy water rose to our shoulders. Rosie's body shivered uncontrollably. Her hand convulsed without releasing its grip, shaking my arm. My heart raced with panic, my breath coming in jagged gulps. Panic rose, but I stuffed it down. I had to save Rosie. Pushing away the sodden wool sweater covering her body, I felt my way through the water for her seatbelt with my free hand when she released me. The water was at our chins.

Rosie's skin was bluish white and waxy. Her eyes blank with fear.

"Look at me, Rosie! At me!"

Forced to look up to keep her mouth above the water, she closed her eyes tightly. "Mommy?" she whispered to herself.

I pushed her shoulder hard, trying to make her wake up, fight for her life. "Take a deep breath, Rosie, I'm going to unbuckle you. Watch me. Do what I'm doing!" Sucking in as much oxygen as my lungs could hold, I dove under the water to find the buckle. My fingers, numb with cold, met nothing but floating wool, expanding around Rosie's small body. My hands groped in the black water and the searing cold.

Rosie's body went lax against mine. Her hand, when I grasped it, floated like seaweed. Pulling with all my might, I still couldn't free her from her seatbelt. Tiny black pinpricks floated in my field of vision. My lungs screamed for oxygen. I knew I was going to lose consciousness and we'd both be lost. I had to get out for both of us. If I could get one lungful of air, I'd go back for her. Before I blacked out, I dragged myself through the window. My sweater caught on a handle, pulling me back against the sinking car, dragging me with it, slowly down. It was hard to find the bottom of the sweater, pull it over my head as I kicked to stay upright. The heavy wool was tangled in my hair. I pushed my head to the side, shaking it frantically, smothered, unable to breathe. My hands clawed at the back of my neck, grabbing the sodden mass, pushing it off my head. Disoriented, I kicked my feet towards the light, praying that it was the surface and not the headlights of the car I was heading towards. My feet churned against the water, numb with cold.

Moments later I burst into the air, gasping painfully for oxygen as I tread water, preparing to dive back down. Fingers of pain shot into my freezing limbs. The car was so close to the surface. Snow fell onto my head as I panted, legs and arms heavy with fatigue, struggling to stay afloat. My body convulsed with shivers, making it hard to control my legs, to keep swimming.

Rosie needed me. I had to go back down. Every inch of my body ached and screamed. Before I could force myself back into the icy depths below, Mom splashed up, gasping. She screamed,

"Swim to shore! Flag someone down!" Her head disappeared under the slick water.

Although we were less than three car lengths from the shore, I panicked, thrashing my arms through the water, clawing at the lake. Rosie was the better swimmer, but I had the job. Get help, reach the shore. I screamed, forcing my legs to keep kicking, my arms to keep chopping. Lake water flooded my throat. Hair covered my eyes. What would happen if I didn't make it? What would happen to Rosie and Mom? Thrashing my way through those few yards of water felt like an eternity.

The rocks near the shore were slippery with ice and snow. I pulled off my shoes and socks. Watched them float to the bottom as I grasped at the rocks with numb fingers. After several tries, I hauled myself from the water, my hands scraped raw and bleeding. Icy snow stuck to my wet face, freezing into a crust. I wiped my clumping eyelashes to see the road. There were no cars, so I turned to watch my mother, repeatedly diving. Every time she went under her feet churned up white froth on the lake's placid surface. My feet and face were numb. My toes refused to move. My mother's faint bubbles popped on the lake's surface. The car's shape below the surface of the water was a wavering dark spot. Every time Mom surfaced, I held my breath, waiting for Rosie.

A truck skidded to a stop nearby. A man came toward me, leaving the vehicle in the middle of the road. Yellow hazard lights flashed. Words came from his mouth. My teeth chattered.

Later, I was told I argued, refused to leave the road. He picked me up, forced me in the warm cab. Said if I budged, I'd be in big trouble. The truck cab smelled of tobacco and coffee. Country music played. The truck was still running. Heat blasted my feet, but I couldn't stop shivering. Rosie was dead. The second her body went limp, I knew. Water would have flooded her lungs as she screamed.

Mom would have drowned herself trying to rescue Rosie if the man driving the truck hadn't fished her out, dragged her across the street. She was trying to escape, run back to the water…

"Hey." Carmen's voice pierced the silence, bringing me back to the present. She was standing next to me on the road in her running clothes, a thin sheen of sweat on her face. "I had a feeling you'd be here."

I turned back to the lake. "You weren't really looking for me."

"Of course I was."

"You just went for a run."

She shook out her ponytail, refastened the elastic. "Stella, I don't run. Hate it. Anyway, I needed to blow off some steam and came here, just in case."

I shrugged. "What made you think I'd be here?"

"Paolo. He said you weren't coming home right after work, but didn't say where you were headed. I know you come here when you're stressed out."

"Do I?"

She wiped her forehead with her arm. "I used to wonder if you came here to talk to your sister."

I shrugged. "Sometimes, I suppose. But not always. Sometimes it helps me remember what it was like before she died. When we lived up the lake. It was so different then, you know. It was nice. We were happy for nine years."

Carmen stepped closer. "I know."

When Carmen and I were teenagers, we'd driven out to the old house. It had been repainted. The deck had been rebuilt, stretching further to accommodate a hot tub. There were plastic kiddie toys in the driveway. Carmen had suggested we knock on the door, see if they offered to let us look around inside. We didn't. I don't know what I was expecting. It didn't feel like my home, or like the place of my memories. It was just a house. A shell. What mattered were the memories themselves.

"Look, I'm sorry, Stell. I've been a bitch."

A cool breeze lifted my hair, smelling of wet leaves. "Awwww. Well said."

She laughed. "Okay, I deserve that. It's just, ooooh, I do hate admitting this, but here it is: I'm jealous. It was fine when it was a proposal that you didn't even want, but when it got real, I kept thinking, 'What's wrong with me?' We've been dating nearly as long as you two, and you're the one wearing that incredible ring. I would die of happiness if I got a proposal. I would kill for Evan to get down on one knee, you know."

My lips twisted. "Are you talking murder or marriage?"

"Probably both, because to make matters worse, when Evan's parents were here, Evan turned into an entirely different person. I'm not kidding. They were totally... How to say this?"

"I think the word you're looking for is racist."

"A tad racist."

"Sure. A tad. We'll call it that."

"I've dealt with this before and I can handle it. I don't love it, but the worst thing is..." She splayed her hands emphatically. "Evan doesn't say anything. It's like, you know, he could at least acknowledge, 'My parents are a tad, a smidge, just a wee bit racist, and that's how they roll,' which would have been offensive for sure, but—nothing. He looks at the floor every time they ask me if it feels weird, hiring Mexicans to work in the restaurant, or in the fields because, you know, *I'm one of them.* They talk to me like I've risen above my station in life, like they can't quite believe my parents could get their act together and buy land. Like every Mexican-American is riding around stoned in low riders holding tallboys. Like we're all supposed to be maids and gardeners, and a world in which a Mexican family owns a winery is just incomprehensible. Evan is one hundred percent quiet. And then it gets worse—"

"Yeah, I sensed that one coming."

"You can't actually call them on it because everything is so passive-aggressive."

"Really? Because I'm not hearing a whole lot of passive."

"I don't know if you talked to them. Peter and Estelle are both terminally boring. Estelle loves talking about golf. Golf! They've been to the most exotic places in the world and it's like, 'And then we ate that rice bowl. What was in that rice bowl? Was it rice? Oh yeah, it was rice. What kind of rice? Jasmine?' Then they talk to each other about every kind of rice in the world. I should have taken a voice memo of them going on and on about the Forbidden City. Use it when I can't sleep. Seriously."

We watched a couple wave riders cutting wakes, listening to the buzz echo off the cliffs. "I'm sorry they're so boring."

"It's okay. I could even take the racist part if Evan would deal with it. Tell them to stop."

"I think he needs to grow the hell up."

Carmen sighed. "I guess I do too. I shouldn't be jealous of my best friend. That's so junior high."

"You're allowed. Some parts of us never get past junior high."

"I'm glad my skin got over it." Carmen patted her smooth, previously acne-plagued, skin.

"Remember when we highlighted my hair with that cap where you pulled the hair through with the little hook?"

Carmen nodded. "You looked like a skunk."

"With over-processed hair."

"Yeah, that was my bad." She crossed her arms. "Look, I'm over being jealous. Mostly. Honestly, that ring makes me backslide a little."

I lifted my hand. Low light sparkled on the stones. "I called my mom." I let that little bomb settle.

"What?"

"Yeah. Told her about the wedding. Kind of. I left a message saying, 'Hi, how are you,' in a very robotic, awkward way. Anyway, I *intended* to tell her about the wedding, which is sort of like telling her, right?"

"You guys are the worst."

"You think? We put the fun in dysfunctional."

"Is that why you came here?"

"Oh, right." We studied a speedboat sailing across the water, releasing a hornet buzz into the quiet dusk.

There was exactly one person in the world who knew about me returning here. Who understood that it drew me like a magnet. "Everyone should have a best friend to figure them out."

Carmen took my hand, placing her head on my shoulder. "Agreed. So listen, about that wedding."

"Yeah. I'm still not sure about marriage, but I'm going ahead with the wedding. That makes sense, right?"

"Totally."

"I'm not crazy."

"Not a bit."

"Obviously I can't function without you."

"Me neither. And here's the thing. I am going to plan the wedding with you. We can't let that witch Rosalia do everything."

"Too late."

"Give me her number. I'll set her straight."

We called her an hour later. After I drove Carmen to Orchard House, she'd invited me in for a glass of wine.

"Okay, I'm sorry. I didn't know it was two o'clock in the morning. I'm very sorry. I was caught up in the moment."

Rosalia was cranky on the other end of the line. Carmen put the phone on speaker, letting us hear Rosalia run up one side of her and down the other, furious at having her beauty sleep interrupted.

"You don't have any consideration for anyone else. So typical of Americans. To not think of anyone! So unthinking. Uncaring. Very selfish!"

Carmen, Lola and I were on the back patio of Orchard House, sharing a bottle of wine. There was a slight chill in the air. Carmen had turned on one of the space heaters. It glowed in the creeping dusk. Faint laughter and the clatter of dishes came from the front patio of the wine bar, on the other side of the house.

"I'm sorry, Rosalia, I'll call you tomorrow."

"It is tomorrow!" Rosalia snapped. "What do you want?"

"To talk about the wedding."

"What about the wedding? It's all set. Paolo and Stella chose October seventeenth. Before the weather cools. Four o'clock wedding. Two hundred people, a string quartet and the best caterer in the region. Hopefully the priest won't die before it happens. Father Angelli is close to a hundred."

Carmen tapped the piece of paper on the table scrawled with some of her ideas: a DJ after dinner so we could dance, wine from Blue Hills on the table with a custom label with my favorite photo of Paolo and me and making Adella's kids part of the wedding processional. I nodded. "I see. That all sounds lovely, but some of that is going to have to be adjusted."

Rosalia didn't beat around the bush. "Nothing will be adjusted."

"Yes, it will."

Rosalia didn't respond for a minute. "Do you have me on speaker phone?"

Carmen's eyes went wide as she mouthed, *How did she know?* She pressed the button, taking it off speaker, and began to speak to her. "No. I see. Okay. Yes, Rosalia, I realize that the wedding is taking place on your property, but here's the thing. It's not your wedding. I'm going to help you make sure that we will be having the wedding that Stella wants, not the wedding you want."

Carmen took the phone away from her ear. "Okay then."

"What happened?" Lola asked.

"She hung up." Carmen handed me back the phone. "Don't worry. I'll book the tickets."

*

When I got back home, Paolo was on the couch, engrossed in his computer, purchasing wine bottles. I bent down to kiss him on the cheek. "Hey. Carmen talked to your mom about the wedding."

He looked up, raising his eyebrows. "I heard. Mamma called me."

"Yeah, she's not loving the idea of sharing the spotlight."

He shrugged. "Are you sure you don't want to get married here? In our front yard? Have some ducks and a couple of gooses as guests?"

"That sounds lovely, but no." Because if I backed down now, Rosalia would win.


"Nothing works for Evan until November," Carmen said, dropping her sandwich onto her plate in exasperation. "He said it's terrible timing. There's no way both he and Paolo can leave at the same time in October."

Carmen and I were at the Vogue café, two doors down from Twig. A narrow room with dark brown walls, a homey atmosphere and a small stage where musicians played nightly for tips. For the longest time, we met here once a week, splitting a turkey and Swiss and a piece of pie. It was reassuring to be here with Carmen. The Vogue was a Chelan institution. It was also a signal that we were back on track.

"That's okay, isn't it? This is all so rushed." I knew it would irritate Carmen if I took Evan's side, but I liked Evan. I loved Carmen with all my heart, but she was a type A perfectionist. Dating her wouldn't be so much an activity as an endurance sport. The problem was,

Evan was the same way. When they got into an argument, it was a rock meeting a boulder. Neither one knew how to give. And right now, Evan was on thin ice with Carmen. He needed all the friends he could get after his performance with his parents. He still hadn't talked to Carmen about their behavior. But glossing over things wasn't an option with Carmen. I'd built a life around avoiding the uncomfortable. Carmen was different.

Carmen shook her head so violently, hair flew in her face. "No, it's not okay. You're my best friend and not only that, Paolo is one of his best friends. When I pointed it out, he said he couldn't even spare Paolo, but he was letting him go."

"He said 'letting him go?'"

"Yes! Do you see what I'm dealing with here? I told him that what he saw as his sacrifice was, in reality, treating his friend and colleague like an indentured servant." She used air quotes to emphasize the words. "And that Paolo was giving up an entire winery to stay in Chelan with you."

I wasn't sure I liked the way it sounded, spoken out loud. "What did he say?"

"He said it was a big mistake. We got into a huge fight. I asked him if he thought you should give up things in a relationship. You know what he said?"

I stared at my sandwich, suddenly not hungry. "No." I'd already heard enough but she was on a roll.

"He said 'not real estate.' It makes me wonder what exactly he'd give up for me. I think what Paolo is doing is romantic."

"Or stupid."

"Well, I'm going with or without him, and so's my family." She reached across the table to squeeze my hand. "It's going to be the best wedding ever."

When I first woke up, I thought Paolo had been talking in my dream, but then realized he was on the phone. Through the window, early morning sun shone on the green hills across the lake, barely touching the top of the willow tree, which meant it must be early. Paolo's boat bobbed in the water. He'd moored it to a buoy. The reddish-orange wood caught the morning light. I lay in bed, gazing at the lake, listening to the voices down the hall. There was a second voice. A woman's voice. I recognized it, but couldn't quite place it. Slipping out of bed, I winced at the cool wood floor, creeping into the hallway on bare feet. I paused before entering the living room. Froze, when I finally placed the other voice.

Paolo was talking to my mother. On speaker phone. Paolo used speaker phone more than any person I'd ever met. His hands always had to be busy: baking, gardening, working on the boat. In the morning, he'd put the phone down and make his breakfast, drink his coffee or, sometimes, simply talk with his hands. The man hated having a phone stuck to the side of his head, and he could never find his AirPods.

"No, that's okay, let her sleep. Stella loves to sleep. Who is this?" My mother sounded different, talking to Paolo. Less guarded. Friendly. Warm. All the things she wasn't with me.

The smell of coffee drifted from the living room and I badly wanted a cup. But not enough to miss this opportunity. I remembered that Paolo was going into work earlier than usual to meet a delivery of new barrels. He wanted to inspect them personally and didn't trust Evan to recognize the cherry wood he'd ordered for the red wine. "Paolo. Her boyfriend."

"Oh, nice to meet you, Pablo."

"Paolo."

"So nice to meet you, Pablo. I hope we can meet in person someday."

"Yes, October seventeenth. We will be meeting soon enough."

My mother wanted to meet my boyfriend in person? What? She'd never met anyone I dated. Since she'd moved to Arizona, our conversations consisted of her sharing tidbits of her life, her friends, her water aerobics class, my dad's newfound passion for painting. When she gently probed, asking what I was up to, I always shared a bit about the salon before making an excuse to get off the phone. I knew I should step into the living room, pour myself a cup of coffee and not spy on Paolo, but it was irresistible to listen in on this conversation. Hear it unfolding without my presence. An alternate universe, in which my mother was charismatic and engaging. The kind of mother I'd wanted, after Rosie died. It was so strange to hear my mother's voice in this context. Like some crazy, worlds-colliding experiment. What happens when you put your boyfriend on the phone with your estranged mother? I'd never actually thought of my mother as estranged; we just weren't particularly close. But in this context, the word fit. The thought made me uncomfortable, but not enough to show myself. I couldn't resist hearing what they'd say.

Paolo must have heard my phone ringing from the kitchen where I'd left it to charge overnight. I couldn't sleep in the same room with my phone; if I did, I lay in bed scrolling until my eyes were bloodshot with fatigue. If I woke up in the middle of the night, I'd pick it up and never go back to sleep. Most of my clients texted me for appointments. I rarely turned off my ringer. Paolo must have answered it so I wouldn't wake up.

"October seventeenth?" Mom sounded confused.

Paolo didn't answer right away. He was weighing his answer. I wanted to run out and grab the phone and stop this from happening. "Yes, did Stella not tell you?"

"Tell me what? She called and left a message but she just said she wanted to say hello, which isn't really like her. Is there something she was going to share?"

"I think maybe I should let Stella tell you herself."

"Okay. That's fine."

"It's better that way. She'd probably want to."

"Okie dokie. If you think so." Mom sounded disappointed. It probably took a lot for her to be this friendly with a stranger. The woman I knew was guarded.

Paolo cleared his throat uncomfortably, as if stalling. "I look forward to meeting you." He seemed to be searching for the right word. "When we, uh, get together. Either here or another place."

My mom was quiet for a moment. "Okay, Pablo."

"Paolo."

"Yes, Pablo. I'm looking forward to it. Please tell Stella I called." She added on another "Pablo" for good measure.

Paolo chuckled to himself. "I guess I'm Pablo now."

"Excuse me?" asked my mother.

"A pleasure to meet you, Mrs. Gallagher."

"And you as well." Mom hung up.

Paolo must have stayed on the couch. Weighing my options, I decided, in classic Gallagher style, to creep back to the bedroom and pretend nothing had happened.

Sitting on the bed, I stared out the window, thinking about the phone call, imagining my mom in some neat trailer home with the clear desert sun overhead. A small yard, with cacti surrounded by white pebbles. Her lean face webbed with a few wrinkles, her skin tan. She'd be drinking coffee out of a mug with a Chelan apple packing company label. I'd bought the set at an end of season sale from the hardware store where my dad used to work. Sent it for Christmas one year. She'd written a thank you note, saying she drank her coffee from one of them every morning and thought of me. I still had the note in my purse. We occasionally lobbed kindnesses at one another, but our hits were returned in such a desultory fashion we lost momentum. Love requires work.

Outside, the sun bathed the weeping willow golden green. Nature kept on with the business of being reliably gorgeous, oblivious to human drama. Maybe that was what was so magical about living on the lake. Reliable access to beauty.

Part of me hoped Paolo would walk out of the house. We'd pretend like I hadn't heard his conversation. We never shut our bedroom door and I was a snoop. He knew I couldn't resist eavesdropping. People interested me. Paolo, however, hadn't mastered the art of pretending everything was okay. It took a minute, but he appeared in the doorway with a penetrating look. As if he'd opened me a crack, and was curious about what would spill out. Good luck, buddy. I'm Irish. Magically delicious and stubborn as hell.

There was no doubt that he knew I'd eavesdropped. He stood in the doorway, leaning on the frame with his arms crossed.

"Hi, Pablo."

"*Buenos días.*"

"I guess she thinks you're a nice Hispanic boy."

"*Sí.*"

"Sounds like you had a good conversation."

"Very interesting. Especially when I know you're in the hallway and I am talking to her."

"How did you know?"

"The floorboards. It's an old house. Why didn't you tell her about the wedding?" There it was.

My shoulders bunched up. "I was going to. I will."

Paolo sighed. "When?"

"When I'm ready." My voice had a sharp edge to it.

"My mother knows."

"Not all families live in each other's pockets, Paolo."

He pulled the lining of his pocket out. "You see there? Look, no mother."

"It's a figure of speech." I got up to brush my teeth.

He followed me, looking at me in the mirror through the doorway, rolling his eyes. "I know it's a figure of speech. I have a mother who meddles, and where I come from, that's normal. The mother asks too many questions. Always tries to be closer than you want her. It's irritating, but it means she cares. What's not normal is to have the mother that doesn't even know her daughter is getting married!"

"I have my own timeline!" I spoke through a foam of minty toothpaste, spitting in the sink.

He patted his chest. "Your *timeline*—" he did air quotes " —is a little off. Where I come from, when someone asks you to marry, you say, yes, please, thank you very much. Not you. You say, maybe I think about it. Then you say yes, but you don't tell anyone. You keep it a secret."

I rinsed my mouth. "Says the guy who didn't tell me that his visa was denied."

"I was thinking!"

"Which is exactly what I'm doing." I brushed my hair as if it had personally insulted me, opting for a high ponytail, an aggressively bitchy hairstyle.

"Thinking if you still want to get married?"

I pushed past him, glaring evenly as I passed. "I'm wondering about it now."

He matched my malevolent glare. "That makes two of us." He pointed down the hallway. "I was waiting for your mother to say congratulations and I'm so happy for you, and she doesn't even know that October seventeenth might be a day to remember. And you don't even think it's strange."

I flicked through my closet, randomly extracting a light cowl-necked dress that I knew I'd regret later, but was easy to pull on. "Our family isn't like yours, Paolo." The way it came out sounded like a warning.

"How would I know? I haven't even met them."

My head popped out of the dress. I adjusted it in the closet mirror, pretending like my appearance mattered. "You didn't give me much time, did you?" Crouching, I grabbed my wedge heels, purchased in a simpler time when I'd religiously followed Kate Middleton's fashion lead, thinking her shine could rub off.

Paolo's fists clenched and released. "That's not my fault."

"Don't make fun of my timeline."

He lifted his hands. "Ah, the sacred timeline." He sighed. I was on the bed, jamming my feet into the espadrilles. "Stella, I understand that this is a lot. And I also know that families can be very complicated. But my mother, for all her faults, she came here. She visited us, and she is throwing herself into this wedding."

I stood up and he joined me. Thanks to Kate Middleton, we were nose to nose. "And by that, you mean taking over this wedding."

His voice rose a notch. "Have the wedding here. I keep telling you."

"No." I was at the dresser, jabbing hoops into my ears.

He stood behind me, his nostrils flared, taking deep breaths like a boxer before entering the ring. Paolo hated losing his temper. Liked being seen as an easygoing guy when, in fact, he really preferred things in boxes. Like family. "You are making it so much harder on yourself."

"It's fine." Even to myself it was laughable. All my life I'd said this to myself. When exactly did it stop working?

Paolo's laugh was short and hard. Didn't sound like him at all. "Very funny, Stella. Look at you. Fighting with your best friend. Hiding the wedding from your own mother."

"Would you please stop saying that? I'm not hiding anything." I spun to face him. "I'm omitting certain details."

"Stella, you and I…" His hands sliced the air between us. "We are different. I am the dog and you are the cat."

"Dogs and cats do not get along." I marched into the kitchen, pouring myself a cup of coffee. We were out of half and half; I drank it black, leaning on the counter, wincing at the bitterness.

"Let me finish." He noticed my tapping toe, shaking his head. "You see, the cat does what it wants. Follows its own desires. The dog just wants to be loved."

"Are you doubting my love?"

He ran a hand through his hair before shaking his head. "No. That's not it."

I looked up, accidentally meeting his gaze. Those familiar eyes had never looked so distant. "Please, Paolo, just talk to me."

He nodded. "I am nervous and a little scared because, Stella, my love, I know…" He clutched his heart. "That someone who really wants to get married doesn't hide it from her family." The last part he whispered.

My heart clenched.

I wrapped my hands around the mug. Like everything else in this house, it was tasteful and earth toned. A symbol of everything I aspired to be. Someone who fit in. "I do want to get married. Just let me do it my way."

He threw up his hands. "Okay. I give up. I do everything, I came to talk to you and…" He flicked his fingers. I followed them, as if I could see the effervescence in the air. "Phhhhht, nothing. If you were excited and happy about marrying me, you'd be telling everyone because when people are happy, they want to share their joy." He grabbed his phone, his eyes full of pain. "I love you, but I don't understand you."

The door shut. His Jeep growled to life, crunching on the gravel as he backed up with unusual speed. Paolo didn't understand me. *Well, I thought, rinsing my coffee mug in the sink, welcome to the club.*

# CHAPTER FOURTEEN

## Bigger Fish

"Wow, Stella, he's rich," Carmen said. We were in the living room of Orchard House, side-by-side on the couch, scrutinizing the Google Earth satellite view of Gentillo Vineyard on Carmen's laptop. On the coffee table in front of us were two glasses of wine, although I'd hardly touched mine. I was too tired. Standing on my feet all day was taking its toll. My argument with Paolo hadn't helped. I'd surgically removed my wedge heels after I sat down. My feet were curled up under me, wiggly little sausages.

"His mother is." The vineyard stretched for miles, or kilometers, since it was Italy. Rolling hills of neatly terraced vines, undulating across the countryside. The house, if you could even call it a house, was baronial, with formal gardens and a large fountain at the entrance. They had a pool tucked into a patio, surrounded by stone walls staged with potted urns. The winery was far from the house with multiple barn-shaped modern buildings with stacks of casks and several forklifts. Colin Firth would look perfectly at home in an ascot and riding boots.

"That means he is," Carmen insisted.

"Not if he marries me."

"I thought you said Paolo wasn't worried about being disinherited."

"Who knows what that woman will do? Paolo doesn't worry about it. He literally throws himself at each day without worrying about one thing." Except me.

"What's that like?"

"I'll tell you. It's blissful. It's like being a teenager with your own apartment, income and bar tab. Adulting without the responsibility. It's like waking up and realizing that you're finally free of your childhood, until some handsome, amazing, funny, sweet guy proposes and every neurotic thought you've ever had comes bubbling to the surface like scum."

Carmen turned toward me. She looked so sad. "Stella, I'm sorry. This should be a happy time for you. How can I make it better?"

I reached my arm around her and squeezed. "Paolo and I got into a fight because I haven't told my mom."

"That makes sense, though. You and your mom aren't close."

"Right? He doesn't get that. And it bothers him."

"It's okay. Don't worry about it. We've got bigger fish to fry." She opened a window to a bakery website. "Look at this cake. I mean seriously." It was a confection piled with flowers and a delicate webbing of spun sugar.

"It doesn't look real. In a weird way, none of this seems real."

She squeezed my arm. "I know. It's because it's in Italy. It's all so fast." She clicked on another image. A cake decorated with sugared berries and mint leaves. "This is cake porn. I love it."

Peering into the computer, I tried to get excited. "They're pretty, but maybe we should get something simpler."

Carmen turned to me. "Ah, no. The girl I know would be picking the fanciest cake, the most fabulous dress. You aren't going to dim your shine, my friend. As your maid of honor—wait, that's what I am, right?"

"Yes, you're hired."

She clutched her throat. "As if there was another option. Anyhoo, as your maid of honor, I'm here to make sure that everything, and I do mean everything, is to your liking. Weddings," she said, warming to her theme, "are the one day that you can embrace the fantasy and say yeah, I'm a feminist but I want a frilly dress and flower girls that are definitely going to cry and you, sir, are going to take off those cargo shorts and put on a tux. You get to wear this epic dress that makes absolutely no sense in any other context. And you, my bestest friend, are going to have the works."

"I'm glad that one of us is into it."

Carmen willfully ignored my Debbie Downer comment. Returning to her browsing, she clicked closer to one spot on the screen. She was on the Gentillo Vineyard website. Maybe she'd found Hugh Grant. "There it is!" She lifted her wineglass and took a sip. "That's it!"

Frowning, I bent closer to look at whatever it was she'd zeroed in on. "It's a field."

"Look at that." She pointed to a blue spot. "It's perfect. You can get married there. Look. There's even a little church with windows overlooking the lake. We can have drinks outside first, and then everyone goes in; we have a little ceremony and then walk to the house for the reception." Her delivery was very sing-songy Disney princess. God help me when it came time for her to get married.

"Hold up." I squinted into the screen. "Is that the church?"

"Yep." She zoomed the camera in for a better look. "Right there."

The crumbling stone structure perched on a bluff was probably the most romantic thing I'd ever seen. White stone, with a pitched roof and soaring steeple. Arched windows embedded with leaded glass. A small garden in front contained lilac trees and blossoming purple lavender. You could practically hear the bees buzzing. There wasn't a more picturesque place on earth to get married.

"It's beautiful. And much bigger than I thought. It's a real church, not just some roadside chapel. You could fit a small village in there."

"Rosalia didn't strike me as the religious type."

"Before her time, by the looks of it. It looks ancient."

"Right?"

"This isn't making it seem more real." I pointed at the scenery from someone else's life. Someone richer, prettier and from the right kind of family. "Maybe Emma Stone should be getting married here. Not me."

"Nope, it's you."

This was all happening so fast. There was a date, place and a man. A gorgeous ring that I double-checked to make sure it was still on my hand. "I'm getting married."

"In Italy. You are getting married in Italy. Remember when going to Seattle was the big time? That time Adella dropped us off to shop. Took us a half an hour to get up the nerve to ask for a table at that restaurant in Nordstrom!"

"The Grill. So fancy! Sat there like idiots, trying to figure out how to tip until you looked it up on your phone."

"Small-town girls." Carmen did a little whistle, shaking her head. "Now you're getting married in Italy. And I'm going to be right by your side, with or without Evan Hollister."

I dropped Carmen off at Orchard House after a morning of wedding dress shopping in Wenatchee. Arriving early, we'd looked through two stores and settled on the third, Bella Bride. They focused on glittery confections that reminded me of prom dresses. Not one had the simplicity I wanted, but we barely had time for this trip. Seattle was out of the question. Lucy, the store owner, found a dress that worked. It was sleeveless with a full skirt. Simple enough. My waist looked smaller. After moving around to make sure my breasts wouldn't make a surprise appearance, I bought it, wishing I could get married in my favorite sundress.

Carmen leaned into the car after she got out. "The dress is nice."

I shrugged, eager to get to Twig. "It works."

"What if we hemmed it a few inches?"

"Go to work. I'll call you later."

I was halfway down the hill when Evan called. I put him on speaker phone. "She's pretty mad. Right?"

"Hi, Evan. I found a wedding dress."

"I saw your car at Orchard House. I've been meaning to call you. How's the wedding planning going?"

I took a left at Pat and Mike's gas station. "Carmen's planning it. So, great."

"I'm still trying to work out how I can make it to the wedding. Paolo's making me a list of what needs to be done in his absence. He runs this place."

"You might have something to do with it." I was tempted to fish for hints about how he thought the visit with his parents went, but decided not to do it on the phone. That was a conversation for another time. Between Carmen and Evan.

"If I can't make it, we'll do something to celebrate when you're back here, okay? If Carmen doesn't run off with an Italian."

"I'll keep an eye on her."

"Thanks, that makes me feel better. Okay, your fiancé tells me it's time to get off the phone and get some real work done. Bye, Stella."

During a break at Twig, my phone lit up with a call from Mom. Even though I was cutting Izzy's hair, not a paying customer, I let it go to voicemail. Like a coward. Izzy saw the word "Mom" flashing on my screen, raised her eyebrows with a disapproving Izzy glare.

Izzy had gone to high school with my mom. Knew her when she played volleyball on the girls' championship team, when she was yearbook editor and an accomplished seamstress who copied dresses from magazines. Izzy was at my parents' wedding, heard all the jokes about how you could see my mother's baby bump before she came around the corner. Twins! Izzy had chuckled at the double stroller taking up most of the sidewalk. She'd known my mom before Rosie died.

Every once in a while, Izzy gave me a nudge, asked if I'd heard from Mom. We both knew it was her way of saying it wouldn't kill

me to call her. I offered vague answers and she gave me The Look.
Izzy's Look is an eloquent arrangement of facial and eye coordination
meant to convey that although she loves you like her own daughter,
you could do better. That life is about human connection and
although you're currently sucking at it, she will always have your
back. But do better.

Izzy could say all this without uttering a single word.

Today, she chose words.

"This is me not saying anything," Izzy said.

"Thanks."

Izzy sighed. "I know that y'all have a very complicated past,
but that's the thing about weddings, darling. It's a chance for new
beginnings." Another thing Izzy was big on. New beginnings. Rehab
was a big turning point in her life. While Mom grieved, Izzy lived,
she said, at the bottom of a bottle.

I played with Izzy's bangs, adjusting. Snip, snip, snip. "That was
a very wordy way of staying silent."

Rachel, busy sweeping up after her last client, snickered. Sometimes I thought the bulk of what Izzy and I did was keep Rachel
entertained. Haircuts were secondary.

"That's enough out of you, Rachel Craw."

Rachel knew better than to get between us. She kept her blue
eyes on the piles of hair under her broom.

"Also, I looked online. We can afford tickets to Milan," Izzy added.

I screamed and dropped the scissors, jumping around the salon
like a flea on fire. "You're kidding me?!"

Izzy frowned, talking to Rachel. "Just look at her. Like she's never
heard of maxing out a credit card."

I couldn't help it. I'd sprung a leak.

"Sweet baby Jesus, the girl's bawling. Come on, finish my haircut so we can make happy hour at Señor's. And pay attention to what you're doing. At my age, I cannot afford a bad haircut."

"As if," I quipped. But I did what she asked.

Later, when I was in the supply room, I took a moment to listen to my mom's message. "Hey, hon, your boyfriend Pablo and I had the nicest conversation. He was talking like you two were going to visit or something. I don't really understand but if you could just give me a call, I'd appreciate it. I know you're really busy, sweetheart, and you don't have time to call much but I'd sure love to hear from you. Love you, honey."

Hitting delete was almost a reflex, like cleaning up a mess. Once the message had disappeared, I felt much better.


"Lemme fix you up a bit," said Rachel, as we were readying to leave the salon.

I'd done a little extra on Izzy's hair, blowing it out into a sleek shiny bob, using the flattening iron. She was freshening her make-up, cursing under her breath at the difficulty of attempting a cat eye with liquid eyeliner. Although she'd never managed a proper cat eye, it was on Izzy's bucket list, even if a mortician had to be the one to apply it.

Rachel smoothed a styling serum on both hands, running it down the strands of my hair, pursing her lips as she worked. Coconut and lavender filled the salon. Izzy peered into the mirror, muttering darkly as liner leaked into her crow's feet. The salon was half dark.

Slanting beams of late-day sunlight worked their way in, alive with floating dust motes, illuminating the window plants, casting spidery shadows on the polished concrete floor.

"This is as good as it gets, girls, isn't it?" Izzy turned to us, her marine blue eyes ringed red.

"You don't need the cat eye," said Rachel. "Your eyes are so pretty without it."

"That's not what I meant," said Izzy, fixing her sock before slipping her cowboy boot back on. She gestured to the three of us. "This. Us. We got something to celebrate. Our girl is getting married. We got this business. This town. I'm telling you. This is it. These are the good old days."

Rachel shrugged, like she didn't understand. "Okay." She sniffed her pits. "Lemme change my shirt."

She ducked into the back room.

"I get it," I said, hugging Izzy.

"I know you do."

Señor Frog's was the shaggy dog bar attached to a Mexican restaurant across the street from Campbell's resort, less than a block from the lake. It was a rumpled, friendly hangout for tourists and locals alike. A dark, cool cave-like atmosphere in summer and the one place everyone could agree upon for winter meet ups. Old timers liked the bar. Adults enjoyed a margarita while their kids munched tacos. It was our after-work favorite.

Our little trio crossed the street in high spirits, end-of-day fatigue tempered by the anticipation of food we'd regret eating and drinks we'd thoroughly enjoy. We entered the bar, blinked a few times in the dark and scouted for tables. A long bar ran the length of the large, open room. Clusters of small tables were surrounded by booths.

"The back's quieter." Izzy grabbed my arm with surprising strength.

We made our way back into the wilderness of neon signs and two pool tables. It took a minute to focus on a table of beaming faces, extraordinarily pleased that they'd gotten the jump on me. A large banner strung over their heads proclaimed: CONGRATULATIONS! White paper bells were taped to the wall. The table was strewn with silver and white confetti.

"Surprise!" yelled everybody.

Izzy grabbed my arm, handing me a drink. "Your wedding shower, kiddo." She kissed me on the cheek. "Not much, but you kinda sprung this one on us."

My recently reapplied mascara smeared into my tears. "Aww, you guys. This is perfect."

Rachel looked inordinately proud of herself, placing her hand on her heart. "I kept the secret."

"You did." I hugged her.

"You don't know how hard it is for me to keep secrets," Rachel gushed.

I did.

Not a great quality in a hairdresser, but whatever.

"Come on now, Rachel." Izzy dragged me toward the table. "Let the girl have her party."

They'd pushed three tables together to accommodate everyone. All the Alvarez girls, including Adella, got up for a hug. Wading around that table was a journey through my life. Women I'd known since high school sat beside clients who'd been there since day one. They patted my arms and back, sharing my happiness. From the flushed cheeks around the table, it appeared they'd started drinking a bit earlier.

"I'm sorry I can't go to the wedding." Esther grabbed my hand.

I explained to everyone that I didn't expect anyone to go to the wedding.

"I'll host a reception at Blue Hills when we get back," Carmen said. I shot her a look.

"Come on, it'll be fun!" This was magnanimous Carmen. She appeared after two glasses of wine and did things like offer to sit in dunk tanks for carnivals and try water skiing, despite an earlier attempt that had led to a broken nose. After three glasses of wine she turned into festive Carmen. On second thought, maybe this was festive Carmen. Only festive Carmen would sign up to host another party.

"Thanks so much for coming, everyone. This is amazing," I said, hoping to divert everyone's attention from a Blue Hills reception.

Lola clapped her hands. "Yay, a wedding party."

Didn't they realize that their entire life was hosting parties? How long had this bridal shower been going on before we got here?

Two waitresses arrived with trays filled with champagne. "The first round is on us," said Lucy, the waitress. "You been coming in here a whole lot less since you met Paolo, but you're still a regular. Congratulations."

I put my first drink down and took a sip of champagne. Señor Frog's, as the name suggested, was not typically a champagne joint. I took a sip, to be polite. It was surprisingly good, but shockingly, for the first time in this particular establishment, and every other one in town, I didn't feel like drinking. Instead, I sat down to chat with Carmen, who, like every other person in the history of surprise parties, wanted to share the details of how she and Izzy had conspired to make this night happen. After that, I dove in, letting the well wishes and congratulations wash over me like warm rain. Everyone was delighted that I'd been ambushed. Rachel, who confessed that the last two days had been "sheer agony," seemed to think she deserved an Academy Award.

Carmen and I giggled at her recounting, second by second, the torture of almost slipping up.

"She thinks this party is for her. As a reward," I pointed out.

Carmen lifted her glass. "Who knows, maybe it is."

Two hours into the festivities, Juan stopped by, hugging my shoulders, kissing the top of my head. "Stellita, I know this is for the ladies, but I just wanted to say that I am very happy for you and—" he stood up, pointing at himself "—I'm finally going to Italy."

Everyone at the table cheered.

"Sit down, old man," said Izzy, offering him a chair.

"No, this is for the ladies," Juan insisted.

A great chorus of protest rose up, affirming my opinion that Juan Alvarez was the most beloved man in Lake Chelan. After a weak protest, he sat down, ordering himself a glass of beer, pleasing everyone at the table.

The drunken toasts began shortly after, with Carmen holding her glass aloft, chin trembling. "We've been through so much. Remember when we borrowed Mr. Hale's speedboat and ran out of gas?" I nodded. "What about when Elise Partner threw up on my dress in the girls' third grade bathroom?" I nodded. "Remember when my mom died, and you sang Spice Girls songs to me until I could fall asleep?"

I sang the chorus to "Wannabe" softly, tears dripping down my face. Carmen wiped her face. "Three months. She sang Spice Girls songs to me every night for three months. By phone and next to me."

I shrugged. "Almost turned me off of them. Almost."

Carmen sniffed, lifting her glass. "To you, Stell."

My throat choked with emotion. "I know I should say something wonderful back, but all that comes to mind is 'hoes before bros.'"

Carmen laughed. "So touching."

I tapped my heart twice with my fist before pointing at her. She made a heart shape with her fingers. We were a sloppy, emotional mess. I loved it. Every second. Contrary to everything I believed, surprise parties could be fun. Provided that they were this one.

The bar crowd thinned out. The party wound down to the core group: me, the Alvarez family and Izzy. While everyone else chatted excitedly about the trip to Italy, Carmen leaned into me. "I'm so happy for you. Paolo is exactly the guy I would have picked for you. He's kind of perfect, you know?"

"Thanks, Car. That's really sweet."

Carmen hiccupped drunkenly. "I'm a sweet person." She lifted my untouched champagne. "What's up? You're not drinking at your own party?"

I sighed. "You know, it's weird, but lately I haven't felt like drinking. Booze just tastes kind of, I don't know, off." I didn't realize, until the words came out, that it was true.

Juan was beside us, idly watching a football game on a large screen over the bar. He took a sip of his beer. "Mercedes was like that sometimes. Couldn't drink the wine." He cocked his head, watching the action on television. Carmen and I turned to him, always interested in stories about Carmen's mother. "There was something funny about it." His brow furrowed as the game went to commercials. On the screen, a dad chased a toddler across a green lawn. "That's right." He lifted a finger. "I remember now. It was when she was pregnant." He ate a few chips from a bowl on the table, dropping salsa on his pants, making a big production of cleaning up.

Carmen's eyes met mine. Her eyebrows shot up. "Not a thing, right?" she whispered.

I did some quick math in my head, chewing on the inside of my lip. My routine had been so disrupted when I'd moved into Paolo's house. I'd skipped pills, taken them the next day. Multiple times. "I don't know."

"It can't be."

"Probably not, right?"

Carmen shook her head. "Nooooooo, because you—" she pointed at me "—don't want children."

"Shhhhh."

Carmen mimicked me, putting her finger over her lips. "Shhhhhh."

I grabbed my purse. "Come on."

"Where are we going?"

Thus began the difficult task of extracting my drunken friend from my own bridal shower to locate an open pharmacy in Chelan. Because if we got there after all the stores had closed, it would be the longest night of my life.

# CHAPTER FIFTEEN

## Pregmate

It is a universally held truth that when you want to remain utterly anonymous, you will run into local gossips. Walmart pharmacy was still open. Tipsy Carmen and I stood before a wall of pregnancy tests, stunned by the harsh white light, the vast refrigerated cold and, as usual, the overwhelming variety. Twenty-three ways to determine if guests had checked into the Airbnb of your womb. Twenty-three.

"Which one is better?" I asked Carmen.

She put her hand on her heart. "Why me? Am I a connoisseur? No. Do they all involve urine and a stick? Probably. What if you're pregnant?"

"Is there such a thing as false positives?"

"No." She read a package. "They're looking for hGC. The knocked-up hormone."

"Pregmate," I said, picking up the box. "Sounds friendly enough. Although I don't want a pregmate. I want the kind of mate that will give me good news."

Carmen's fist went to her nose. Her eyes expanded. "Oh my god, Stella, what if you're pregnant?"

A deep, cleansing breath did absolutely nothing to calm me. So much for every single wellness expert in the world and their stupid advice. Instead of feeling centered, I had visions of a squalling infant turning pink with indignation while I cowered in the corner, unable to muster a thimbleful of motherly instinct. Of being alone in a room, whispering, "Somebody do something!" knowing full well that help would never arrive. A human being incapable of fending for itself. It was enough to knock me to the floor. But the floor of a Walmart wasn't the place to be.

Grabbing Carmen's shirt, I drew her to me as if I was a gangster, threatening her. "Look, Car, I know you're still a little drunk, but since we left the restaurant you've asked that question nine hundred times. Please stop."

Carmen nodded obediently, then whispered in the tiniest voice possible, "But seriously, what if you are?"

"Not helping."

"I want to be godmother."

I spun toward her, waving the box so close to her face, she blinked. "This isn't a joke. I'm terrified. I cannot be a mother, Car. I can't. I realize that this is impossible for you to understand because you have always known you wanted a family, but I'm different. What I can't do is face this without your help, so can you please, please, please take this seriously?"

Scientifically, according to every presentation from the Washington State Patrol at Chelan High School, instant sobriety isn't possible. Nonetheless, that night I witnessed Carmen Alvarez sober up in a moment in the Personal Intimacy aisle of Walmart. Her shoulders squared. The idiotic grin was wiped from her face. Her focus realigned. "All right. I'm sorry."

Perhaps it wasn't a miracle, but it was precisely what I needed. Nothing is lonelier than sobriety with a drunk best friend.

At the checkout area, Carmen grabbed random items from the end cap displays. A cellophane-wrapped eight pack of Hershey bars. Whitening toothpaste. A pumpkin-scented candle. A four pack of ChapStick. "What are you doing?" I hissed.

"We can't check out with just a pregnancy test. Someone will see us."

"Nobody will see us."

Naturally, at that exact moment, a mini high school reunion formed before our eyes.

"No. No. No. It's Celia Diaz. And Honore Sullivan. What are they doing here?" Carmen hissed, backing away.

Although there were fifteen checking stands in the Walmart, most of them were closed. Honore and Celia were in the line closest to us. I dragged Carmen into the aisles of men's shorts to hide out, but Honore spotted us, waving.

"Look, Celia, it's Carmen and Stella. Hey there! How's it going?"

Carmen plastered on a fake smile as we shuffled forward. "Hey."

Celia offered a warm smile. "Nice to see you two. We're doing some last-minute shopping for our conference on Monday."

Honore sneered. "Celia works for me now."

Celia had a pained, prisoner-of-war look. "Yes. Since June."

"Oh, wow. I did not know that." Carmen raised her brows, glancing between the two women. I could tell she'd be in touch with Celia later to hear the whole story.

"Campbell's. She made it to the big-time," Honore said.

"But is it?" I had to add. Honore's narcissism always annoyed me.

Honore winced. "We won the regional Best Breakfast Service Hospitality Award in the resort category at the Washington State Hospitality convention in 2018."

Celia, Carmen and I exchanged pained looks. *Breakfast?*

"What? It's a big deal." Honore had the same indignant look she'd worn throughout high school, bearing the burden of convincing the entire school that she was, officially, superior.

Honore and Celia placed their items on the conveyor belt. Celia slid the divider down the belt toward us. "Well, go ahead," Honore said testily when Carmen tightly clutched her random items. I was holding the pregnancy test behind my back. Celia and Honore both stared, as if they knew I was hiding something.

"Congratulations," Celia smiled. "I heard you were getting married."

Attempting to hold both their eyes by chatting in an overly loud voice, I casually tossed the Pregmate box, an unfortunate attention-grabbing neon pink, onto the conveyor belt. "Yes, to Paolo. We're having the wedding in Italy."

Honore, attuned like a truffle-hunting pig to sniffing out others' misfortunes, saw the box. Her eyes lit up with greedy delight.

Celia had seen it too. As she paid for their items, her voice went up a notch. "Nice bumping into you two." She grabbed the plastic shopping bags, valiantly attempting to extract Honore. "It's late. Come on, Hon—"

"Goodness!" Honore crowed, ignoring poor Celia, who looked mortified. We all knew Honore well enough to brace ourselves.

Honore picked up the Pregmate box, waving it. "Who is the lucky girl?"

Carmen's face went sheet white. "Put it down, Honore."

"Touched a nerve?" She studied both our faces, her ferret eyes darting between us. "I'm guessing it's yours, Stella."

"That'll be twenty-eight sixteen," said the clerk, snapping her gum, studying Honore as she tossed the pregnancy test between her hands.

Carmen gave the clerk her credit card. I snatched the Pregmate box mid-toss. "Honore, what do you love so much about seeing people in pain?"

Honore looked surprised. "Well, I hope you're not pregnant because—"

Celia grabbed her arm. "Honore, that's enough."

"I'm your boss!" Honore squealed as Celia escorted her toward the exit.

Carmen grabbed the Walmart bag from the carousel. "Honore is so much fun."

"A peach."

"That's one word for her."

"Shall we do this?" Carmen asked.

My knees went a little weak. Carmen took my hand. "Seriously. You've got this."

She headed for the bathroom, but I stopped her. "How well do you know me?"

She furrowed her brow. "Um, I can guess exactly what kind of underwear you're wearing right now. You wear granny panties if you're feeling fat. A thong if you woke up feeling sexy." She pressed a finger to her forehead, closing her eyes as if reading my mind. Her eyes popped open. "You're wearing a thong."

"Very impressive. Now, given that you know me right down to my unmentionables, do you honestly think I'm the kind of person who is going to take a pregnancy test in a Walmart bathroom?"

She narrowed her eyes. "Hmmmmm. Interesting question. Is it because you're worried that Honore will follow you in, stand on a toilet and start a Facebook Live broadcast?"

"Stop it. I'm never going to laugh. Not here. Not now."

Carmen lifted a finger. "Okay, right. Where are we going?"

"Do you want me to sing you a Spice Girls song?" She sang the first few verses of "Viva Forever," humming the rest of the song to herself because I wasn't responding.

She didn't like her voice, which was always slightly off key and wobbly. She could carry a tune, but just barely. But her mother thought she was a good singer, always encouraging her to join the church choir, which she never did. That's what I was thinking about as I stood in the bathroom of Twig, not staring at the stick on the counter, which was nestled on a carefully folded paper towel, looking more like a thermometer than something that might forever change my life.

Carmen's mother had thought she did nearly everything well. One time, Carmen made Mother's Day muffins and mixed up the measurements for the salt and sugar. Nobody else had tried one beforehand, but Mrs. Alvarez, who had received the breakfast in bed, took a bite and then slathered it with jam, eating the whole thing. Never said a word, while all three daughters sat on her bed, watching her eat. Carmen had only realized afterwards, when she had taken a bite of another one and spat it out instantly.

Mother's Day at our house was a silent affair in the years after Rosie's death. I'd hand my mom a homemade card. She'd smile and give me a hug, before retreating to her bedroom with a closed door. Another day when Rosie's absence was more acutely felt. Sometimes I wondered if Rosie and I would have been friends as adults. We hadn't agreed on everything as kids.

"Are you okay?" Carmen asked from her perch on the supply room stool in the hallway between the salon and the back room.

"Yeah." The door was shut because the moment felt unusually private. I didn't want anyone to look at my reaction. Not even Carmen. I couldn't share this one thing with her, because unlike her, if I was pregnant, I wouldn't be happy. "I can't look at it."

"Do you want me to?"

"No, I thought we could just stay in here all night." I'd already pulled up my pants and washed my hands.

"What if I have to go to the bathroom?"

"Good point."

"I do have to go. A little."

"All right, I'll look."

"I can go, and I won't look."

Her comment highlighted the perversity of avoiding reality. My fear wouldn't change whatever waited for me on that paper. Avoidance wouldn't make the last part of the evening rewind. Picking the pregnancy test up, I stared at it, blinking as if to reset my eyes. The floor went out from under me. I dropped the stick and opened the door.

Carmen reached for me, holding me up while I shook.

"Two lines." Who knew that such a little line could mean so much?

"Shhhhh. It's okay. It's okay. We'll get through this. We'll figure this out."

"This shouldn't be happening. I was on the pill," I whispered, thinking that our roles should be reversed. Why not have the friend who was built for motherhood and matrimony be the one who got the tiny little pink line? Why couldn't life be just a little bit tidier? Just once.

"I know."

"You can't tell Paolo." It rushed from my mouth before the thought was fully formed.

She stood back from me. "Wait, what?"

Pushing the hair back from my face, I scrambled to come up with a plan. My mind was blank. "I can't deal with his reaction. I don't want anyone to take ownership of this until I've accepted it."

"Okay…" She looked uncomfortable. If Carmen got this news, she would be doing handsprings down the narrow hallway of the salon. She'd be on her phone, sharing the happy news with Evan. They'd start arguing about baby names. "But when will you tell him?"

It was clear: breathing room was the answer. "I need some time."

Carmen, to her credit, nodded, as if this made total sense. "Okay. It's our secret."

"I need to process."

Carmen sighed, clearly unhappy with my decision. "Right. But you're going to tell him, right?"

"Maybe when the baby graduates from college."

"Right, hit him up for tuition."

I took a deep breath, wanting her to believe my reasoning was sound. "Car, I know telling him is the right thing. I know that. But for someone who grew up the way I did and who never wanted to get married or have children, this is like falling off a cliff."

She nodded. "I'm really trying to understand but it's hard."

"I'll tell him. I promise. Let me get used to the idea. I need to rethink everything and I can't do it when there is an us. For right now, I need it to be me."

Carmen's face relaxed. "Stella, there is no right way. There is no *What to Expect When You're Accidentally Expecting*. And I know it's scary. I get that. But you have to forget all the people like Honore. Ignore those bitches. Their judgments mean nothing. You have to look out for you. Not Paolo and not whatever people in this town are going to say. Make your own rules. You always have, so it's not time to start second guessing now. You've got this. We've got this." She hugged me long and hard. "I'm like cellulite. I'll always be here."

"I know." I did a weird snort that was half cry, half giggle.

We hugged so closely, I felt her heartbeat. Somewhere, inside of me, was a growing heart that would change everything.


"Are you okay to drive?" Carmen asked. We were at my car, which was adjacent to the city park. Pale orange lights shone across the rippling water, traveling toward the Columbia River. Skateboarders jumped off the rails, scraping cement with their wheels, carving sound from the quiet night. Green mineral richness hung in the air, mingling with the smell of cooking food and backyard fires.

I was a whole new kind of exhausted, but I nodded. "Yes."

"Do you want to come over? Maybe spend the night?"

"Yes."

"Good, I'm—"

"I do, but I can't. I can't run away from Paolo and pretend this isn't happening."

"Sure you can. It's what you do."

I grinned, wanting to cling to her like a favorite sweatshirt. "There's an old saying. Getting accidentally knocked up is nature's way of telling you to grow the hell up."

"Right. I think my *abuela* said that." She gave me another hug. "Call me tomorrow."

She wobbled slightly as she walked away from me and I followed her. "Car, hey, let me give you a ride."

She waved a hand without looking back. "I'm fine."

Catching up with her, I grabbed her arm. "Maybe so, but I'm going to drive you, okay?"

She shrugged. "Sure."

We strolled arm in arm up Emerson Street toward my car. Abruptly, she stopped, lifting a finger into the night air. "Drive carefully because—" She waited for my response.

"The loaf you save may be your own." I grinned. When we were little, there had been a grinning loaf of bread with arms and legs, waving from the back of bakery delivery trucks, advising people to drive cautiously. Carmen and I became slight obsessed, naming him Larry the Loaf, fabricating countless adventures. Larry goes to space. Larry runs for president. Larry fights off a hungry bear who wants to toast him over a fire and slather him in honey. In grade school we'd whisper, "Drive carefully!" to each other, giggling at our secret world of Larry the Loaf. It was a comforting memory. One of the million common threads knit into the fabric of our friendship.

When I dropped Carmen off at Orchard House, she leaned over, giving me a hug. "You do know what Larry the Loaf would say to you right now, don't you?" I shook my head.

She climbed out of the car, leaning down. "You've got a bun in the oven."

"That was truly a horrible joke."

She grinned. "One of my worst. Good night."

She'd made her way to the patio when I called out to her from my open window. "Hey, Carmen, the wedding shower was wonderful. Thank you."

Batting away a moth flitting around her face, she beamed. "That was nothing. Wait until you see your wedding."

"The party was fun?" Paolo asked, as I bent down to kiss him. He was curled up on the sectional, his hair damp from his evening swim, smelling of cold mineral-tinged water. He'd swim until there was frost on the ground. Until the lake was so cold it gave him a headache. In some ways, we were so different. What Rosalia failed to see was the Venn diagram meeting spot of our relationship. The overlapping points. The house that smelled of garlic and baked bread. This was more of a home than any place I'd ever lived in my life. Because I was safe here.

Paolo's bare feet were propped on the coffee table. An empty wineglass tinged with burgundy residue sat next to winemaking trade journals.

"You knew." I curled under his arm.

"Yes. They invite me, but it was your night."

I kissed his cheek. "It was."

Shutting his computer, he reached over to turn off the light. Sometimes we watched the lake at night. The light dancing on the water. The comforting dark space. Our lake. I began to drift off to sleep. Curled up inside of me was a secret. An acorn waiting to sprout. I told myself that it was forgivable. My life was hurtling through space at uncontrollable speed. Keeping this quiet was an attempt at control. Slowing things down. He'd forgive me.

That's what I was thinking when he kissed the side of my head and said something that came as a surprise.

"*Bella* Stella?" he whispered.

"Mmmmm? I'm falling asleep." *Please let me sleep. Pretty please.*

"I have to go."

"Where?" I was slipping away. Dozing.

"Back to Italy. My visa has run out. I leave day after tomorrow."

I'd known this was coming, but I'd pushed it to the furthest corners of my brain. I'd lost track of time. A door opened, and reality came crashing down. I burst into tears.

Paolo wouldn't let me drive him to the Wenatchee airport. He was taking a shuttle flight out of Wenatchee, insisting that I keep my salon schedule. I'd already rebooked clients during the block when I'd be in Italy. There'd been a bit of an uproar about the entire salon being shut, but when I'd told people the reason, most of them had calmed down.

I enjoyed driving with Paolo. The highway to Wenatchee bordered the Columbia River, snaking through red canyons and orchards. He'd sing famous arias along with the Three Tenors, hamming it up as the songs reached their dramatic crescendo. But I was secretly glad we wouldn't be spending the forty-minute drive together. I needed to be alone with my secret. In a strange but lovely way, tinged by more than a little guilt, I was enjoying the privacy. I'd grown accustomed to keeping so much inside. It felt comfortable allowing myself the freedom to adjust, panic or accept this pregnancy as I saw fit. And it would be a relief to stop worrying every time Paolo walked into the room, overwhelmed by a nauseating cocktail of emotions. Two parts guilt mixed with one part fear. The voice of my Sunday school teacher, Mrs. Marsden, haunted me. "Now, Stella, share with the class the worst lie you have ever told." (My example had been a lie, of course. There was no way I would answer her question truthfully. Dream on, old gal.)

We said goodbye at the door with much kissing and hugging and waterworks on my part. Paolo was amused by my prolific tears. "I see you in a week, Stella. A week. Not such a heavy deal."

"I know," I said, through the Niagara Falls streaming down my cheeks.

I'd left a list on the counter: *wedding cake, band or DJ?, hair, menu, call Mom*. On the flip side of the list were the books I planned on buying. *What to Expect When You're Expecting, The Girlfriend's Guide to Pregnancy* and *The Expectant Father: The Ultimate Guide for Dads-to-Be*. The last book, I'd decided, was a firm step towards telling Paolo. At the big moment, if I lost the ability to speak, I'd simply hand him the book. It felt very efficient. We're having a child, here's the manual, now let's talk about something else. There was no book called *What to Expect When You're Freaking Terrified*, but I'd order the rest.

Making breakfast, I watched a growing storm ripple across the water. Ominous clouds hung low, growing darker by the second. My phone rang and I answered, thinking it was him.

"Stella, darling, it's your mother. I'm so happy about Pablo. He's such a nice man."

She was acting like we were a normal chatty mother-daughter duo, so I went with it. "Yeah. By the way, his name's Paolo. He's Italian."

"I know." Was this my mother? She sounded genuinely enthusiastic. Even buoyant. "I'm just so happy about everything."

A flare went off in my brain. "Everything?"

"The wedding. The marriage. Italy. Stella, I'm overjoyed for you. Honestly. Your father is ecstatic. He actually jumped up and down. Your father. As you can imagine, it was quite a sight. He had his coffee mug in his hand. It went all over the picnic table. Well, honey, we're just thrilled. Truly."

With each word, my throat constricted tighter and tighter until I was gasping for air. "What?" The piece of toast I was eating lodged firmly in my throat. I coughed violently. "Who told you?"

"Pablo, of course. He called just now on his way to the airport. Told me everything. It's such a romantic story. You're getting married on his parents' vineyard."

"It's Paolo, Mom, and it's his mother's vineyard," I said weakly. How did Paolo get her number?

"Your father and I are just delighted."

"Thanks."

"Well, don't you want to know?"

"Know what?" I checked my watch, hoping I could catch Paolo before he got on the plane.

"If we can come or not?"

That got my attention. I was genuinely interested. "Um, yeah?" Why not throw my parents into the mix?

"Well, I told Pablo we'd love to come. It was so nice of him."

Apparently, Mom was never going to get his name right. "What was so nice? Calling you?"

"No, silly, that he paid for our plane tickets. I can't believe that your father and I are going to Italy to see you get married."

# CHAPTER SIXTEEN

## Hating Kittens

"You had no right to do that!" I screamed into the phone. In the background, someone told Paolo he had to put his phone away. "Did you get her phone number off my phone?"

"Stella, can this conversation happen when I am in Seattle? I have to go through security and my phone battery is nearly dead."

"No, it's happening now, Paolo. You had no right to tell my mother about the wedding."

"She called me, said she left you a message. Asked why you weren't calling. I don't know how she got my phone number. I didn't mean to tell her, but when I am happy, sometimes the information slips out. I'm not good at secrets. Excuse me." He stopped to explain to someone, in great detail, that he had to talk to his fiancée and why. Paolo always thought people were interested in the minutiae of his life. Usually I found it endearing. Not today.

"Paolo, I swear to god you'd better learn to keep secrets, because you took this one away from me."

"What did I take?"

I thumped my chest self-righteously. "I wanted to tell my mother."

"You do not act the one."

"What does that even mean?" I was jumping up and down in the kitchen, which felt incredibly stupid but I needed to express my anger. My first choice, dashing my phone against the wall, wasn't going to happen.

"Don't make issue of my English."

"I'll make issue of your English if I want to." This wasn't fair. I was punishing him, deflecting from the real issue. How many voicemails had I deleted without ever bothering to listen over the last few years? Hundreds? "You got the chance to tell your mother and your sister about the wedding. You took that away from me! I can't go back and say, hey, Mom, forget what Paolo blabbed and let me have the honor."

"You don't care. Someone who cares about getting married tells their family."

"What do you know about my family?!"

"Nothing, because you don't tell me! We are getting married and I don't even meet your parents. Your mother thinks I am Pablo."

"Then maybe we shouldn't get married."

"Why is this the reaction?"

"Because I'm mad."

"Then maybe we shouldn't!"

I didn't know whether his phone battery died, or he hung up. Either way, we were cut off.


On my way to work, I tried to deep breathe my way into serenity, enjoying the steely waves lashing the shore, the trees waving in the wind and the anchored boats bobbing.

My phone rang, shattering the silence.

"Oh my god, your future mother-in-law is a piece of work."

"I already hit her for you."

"Thank you. It took me a solid twenty-five minutes to negotiate her out of a harp at the wedding. A harp. We hate harps, right?"

"Nobody hates harps. That's like hating kittens."

"Well, the harp is out. We won the cake. I got the one we liked. You can't even believe how much she's spending on champagne. Seriously. I'm so freaking excited about the wine, my toes curl every time I think about it."

"Thank you. I can't drink."

"One little sip?"

"With all the stress this kid is undergoing, I'll be lucky if it isn't born with hooves."

"That would be so cute."

"Shut up." I drove around my favorite curve of the lake. On the left was a rocky wall of luminous grey slate. Clumps of green sedum sprouted from cracks. To the right, the road passed close enough to the lake for me to peer into the sandy bottom, a clear turquoise on sunny days. Today it was sea-glass blue.

"How does pear-glazed mini lamb chops, chèvre potatoes with rosemary, roasted honey-glazed turnips, purple carrots and a salad of microgreens from the estate sound? Let me emphasize that when I say estate, I mean Paolo's estate, because you're marrying someone with an estate. I feel like I need all new clothes. I do, right?"

"We just got into a fight."

"Perfect, because I'm not talking to Evan. We're in this massive chicken fight and I'm not going to blink."

"He left for Italy this morning."

"Oh, I'm sorry."

"Yeah. But I'm kind of glad he's gone. You're the only person in the world I can actually say that sentence to."

"I get it. What with the whole having his baby but not telling him thing."

"I'm going to tell him."

"What did you think of the menu?"

Poor Carmen. She was more excited for my wedding than I was.

"What's wrong?" Izzy was a human lie detector. Tell her a fib and she'd pretend she believed you out of courtesy, but she knew better. She was attuned to a frequency I didn't recognize and had zero fear of confrontation.

Usually, I loved this about her. Today, it was annoying. One step inside the salon and her radar went off.

"Good morning, Izzy. How are you today?"

Her eyes narrowed, lips pursed. "You look like something the cat dragged in."

"I'm fine, thank you. Nice of you to ask."

Izzy crossed her scrawny arms, then opened them wide, as if she was a game show host and I was the prize. "Rachel, is that what fine looks like to you?"

Rachel glanced nervously between us both, trapped between being honest and being nice. Always a hard choice for her. She was as sweet, pretty and uncomplicated as sunshine. She'd make someone a wonderful grandmother. "Um, well, that's um…"

"Oh, good Lord, child." Izzy shook her head with disgust. "You got a spine. Use it."

Rachel's eyes welled with tears. Izzy went to hug her. "I'm sorry. Don't cry." Kissing the side of Rachel's head, she winked at me. "Like shooting Bambi."

Hanging up my coat, I whispered to Rachel, "Ignore her. Someone put decaf in her mug."

Rachel managed a weak smile.

All this, and it wasn't even noon.

Once Rachel was mollified, Izzy motioned for me to come closer. "Spit it out. Now. Before clients get here, as we actually have to work."

When Izzy had first started working for me, I'd tried avoiding confrontation. The month we'd opened, Gary Hartley had kept dropping into the salon in full uniform, checking and rechecking his gun, reminding us that he was licensed to kill (as if every man within spitting distance didn't have a hunting license) to make sure we were safe. When we'd asked him if there was a murderer on the loose, he'd soberly told us no, but that there could be.

Izzy had forced me to give him the friend zone speech. "Put him out of his misery. That man could be eaten alive and he'd still try to reason with the crocodile. Make like a Nike commercial and just do it."

Another time I'd pointed out to Izzy, quite reasonably, that Twig was our place or work and we didn't need to discuss our personal lives. "That is just pathetic," was her rejoinder. Twig was a hair-salon-shaped confessional and Izzy was the high priestess.

So.

I shared the whole sad story of my fight with Paolo, omitting my pregnancy. Izzy nodded and threw in an, "Uh-huh. Yes. Well. I see," as she saw fit. Izzy listened with her whole body. Every muscle taut with anticipation. Every molecule attuned.

I relaxed as I talked. In another life, Izzy would have made a fabulous therapist. Maybe that's what she was. We heard other people's life stories and she heard ours. When I was finished, I felt lighter. "I'm not even sure we're engaged anymore."

There was no hesitation. "Honey, of course you are. I've seen the way that man looks at you. Do you honestly think he's weak enough to let one little bump derail him?" She lifted a finger to my face. "Don't answer. That was rhetorical. It's a wedding. You've styled enough brides and bridesmaids to know that a wedding is one part ritual and two parts drama. Nobody gets hitched without a bucket of tears. Half the time it's the groom because he wants the girl, not the ceremony."

She nodded sagely, glancing at Rachel as if this was a quorum and they'd come to an agreement. "Well now, there's only one thing to do."

I raised my eyebrows expectantly. "What? Tell me!" She needed me to ask. Such a drama queen.

"Call your mother. Give her the pleasure of talking to a daughter bubbling over with enthusiasm and not one who is upset with her fiancé."

"Pablo." Izzy and Rachel gave me questioning looks. "I don't know. It's what she calls him."

"That's adorable," Izzy said.

"It's weird." My mother and I might be estranged, but she still bugged me.

Izzy shook her finger at me. "Stop it. Just stop. After you talk to your mother, you call Paolo. You tell him that when you walk down the aisle it's going to be the best day of your life."

"I don't know what kind of day it's going to be. We've got issues."

"Sweetheart, welcome to adulthood. Everyone's got issues."

"Yeah, but I never wanted to be married in the first place."

"Come here."

I obeyed, taking her hand.

"I have known you your entire life. I've seen you through bad perms and braces. I've dragged you out of Señor Frog's when your hair smelled like a deep fryer and you thought some scary old leatherhead was The One. I know you never wanted to get married, but if you want to keep this guy in the U S of A, you've got to get hitched. Here is what you do. You lie. Because that's what you do when you're in love."

I laughed. "Are you serious?"

"Damn straight. You're scared. Fear is a healthy reaction to stress. But it's not what Paolo needs to hear right now. He is in another country, feeling all the same things: scared, lonely and worried."

Rachel gave me the shifty look of a dog trying to avoid eye contact. I turned back to Izzy. "I cannot believe you're telling me to lie."

"If you say the words out loud, it will happen. 'I love you, Paolo, and the day we get married is going to be the happiest day of my life.' Go home tonight and practice. Because here's the thing, kiddo: happiness isn't passive. You can't sit around looking for that bluebird. It will pass you by. Happiness isn't the common cold. It's not going to spread unless you do something about it. You got to choose it every day. You got to wake up and be grateful. Choose a life full of joy. Now, I think Paolo was put on this earth to teach you this lesson. You spend a lot of time pretending to be happy and it's about damn time you give yourself permission to do the real thing."

I stared at her a long time, putting the pieces together. "You gave my mother Paolo's phone number, didn't you?"

She lifted her chin, nodding. "She's my friend too."

"You shouldn't have, Izzy."

"Maybe. But she wasn't going to give up until she got his phone number and she was going to call Carmen next, so I gave it to her. What you have to understand is that I love you with all my heart and I might be wrong but I really do think I know what's best for you. I'm so convinced of it that I'm going to travel all the way to Italy just so I can see if I am wrong or right."

# CHAPTER SEVENTEEN

## That Foreign Fella

The wispy clouds hanging over the hills had a feathery, tropical glow. After an afternoon thunderstorm, the lake had settled into a dark gloss. Our weeping willow spilled into the water. Sunset leaked into the house, making the hardwoods glow. Nestled on the couch, I was enjoying the view, trying to stop thinking. Wishing my brain had a pause button. Evening was the hardest time without Paolo. Had I not been reading my pregnancy books, I would have eaten cereal for dinner. Instead, I'd dutifully shopped at Safeway after work, loading my cart in the produce aisle. I'd cooked fish for the first time. It had exploded in the microwave.

My phone sat on the coffee table, daring me to lift it. To call my mother or Paolo. Wedding plans marched forward, regardless of my mood, thanks to Carmen, who was channeling her anxiety about Evan's refusal to attend the wedding into planning. Every night I received an update about a fresh quarrel she'd had with Rosalia. The latest iteration was about table centerpieces. There was a battle royal over lilies (Carmen) versus roses (Rosalia). God help us when they got to the wine. Rosalia didn't know that Carmen had shipped two cases of a special label Blue Hills Vineyard vintage to the Gentillo Estate. Rosalia, Carmen gleefully informed me on her way back from the FedEx office, was going to have a heart attack when it arrived.

My phone rang. An unfamiliar, foreign number. FaceTime.

Who FaceTimes a stranger?

Curious, I pressed the button, holding it up to my face, panicking for a second when I realized that I was in my fuzzy pink Victoria's Secret bathrobe.

Emilia, Paolo's sister, smiled at me. "Hello, Stella. Is this bothering you? The FaceTime?" She was wrapped in a colorful zigzag blanket, a mug cradled in one hand. "I have the insomnia and I think to call you. Are you so excited for the wedding? Is my mother driving you absolutely insane?"

I winced. "Did you hear about our little incident?"

Emilia rolled her eyes dramatically. "The way she tells it, you picked her up and tossed her from a cliff. Then she was pursued by wolves." She lifted her slender palm. "But please. My mother can take the tiniest incident and make the insult. I know this. We know this. Mamma should have really been an actress."

It was a relief, knowing that Emilia understood her mother so well. "It was kind of horrifying."

"If there is one woman you don't want to have that happen with, it's Rosalia Gentillo." Emilia leaned into her phone, her tawny skin surrounded with luxuriant auburn curls. "Ah! I see Nonna's ring. So perfect on your hand. And the wedding plans? Mamma isn't too much?"

"My best friend, Carmen—you'll meet her—is doing a lot of the planning. She's um, dealing with Rosalia."

Emilia's face broke into a grin. "*Perfetto!* You're very clever. Unfortunately, I do not have this person. Mamma wants me to come early. I have the classes I teach and every day she calls me, telling me that nothing is more important than this wedding." She rolled her eyes, playing with a thin gold bracelet.

"I'm really sorry."

She waved her hand, running a slender finger across one thick eyebrow. "Ah, no. This is how she is. When she doesn't get her way, she finds another avenue. Don't worry." She glanced away from the phone, frowning. "I have reason to call."

It felt like the other shoe dropping with Rosalia. There was a certain inevitability. "Okay."

Emilia bit her lip. "My mother…" She really didn't want to say this. "My mother is seeming like she wants this wedding to happen, but, Stella, she's got something up her sweater."

I laughed, despite myself. "It's something up her sleeve."

Emilia looked confused. "What?"

I shook my head, grateful that Emilia was like her brother, who I missed more now that I noticed they shared the same mannerisms, warmth and charisma. The bright flash of a grin. "Nothing. What's going on with Rosalia?"

"That's the problem. She doesn't tell me."

"Oh." Great. Thanks, Emilia. Now I'd just be paranoid. And emotional. And occasionally nauseous. Here comes the bride.

"I feel terrible. I don't know if I should call you. I just want you to know."

"Thanks, Emilia."

"Is there anything I can do?"

Lock her mother in a shipping container until after the wedding? "No, that's okay. Thanks for the heads up."

"Paolo, marrying you will be the happiest day of my life." No, that was wrong. I needed to emphasize the word "marrying." I tried again. And again, trying to believe the girl in the mirror. Who looked tired. Maybe because she was growing another person. Acting like it was no big whoop, this creation.

I was sitting in my salon chair at the end of the day, holding my phone and practicing. Occasionally I stayed after work, enjoying the peace of an empty business. I'd water the plants huddled in their silver pots in the white frame I'd constructed in the large storefront window. In a weird way, the plants were my children. Little growing beings that depended on me for life. Once, when I'd had the flu, Izzy had neglected them. When I'd returned, they'd been shriveled. It had made me surprisingly sad, and later, elated, when they'd unfurled themselves back to their former splendor.

If the plants could make a comeback, and if Izzy was right, maybe I could throw myself into a wedding and a life I wasn't sure I wanted. Maybe life was about making the best out of what you were given, not what you wanted. Izzy had scraped a life together out of the wreckage of what she blithely called her "pickled phase." She'd totaled two cars and three marriages, one of which had been a complete train wreck from the beginning. She'd alienated both her children, who had grown tired of the embarrassment and pain. Fed up with their mother showing up drunk at family gatherings. Of getting the wee hour phone calls with drunken tears and apologies.

After rehab, Izzy had popped up like a prairie dog all over town: apologizing, making amends, knitting her life back together, one heartfelt word at a time.

If Izzy, who everyone knew had been drinking herself into an early grave, could become the sage of Woodin Avenue, maybe I could allow myself to enjoy my own wedding and step into the life I'd been given, instead of the one I had planned.

I met my own eyes in the mirror, my chin firm with resolve. "Paolo, marrying you is—"

There was a loud knock on the glass door. Gary, in his sheriff's uniform, peered into the semi-dark salon. Geez. The last person I wanted to see.

Hopping off the salon chair, I waved. Pointedly not unlocking the door. "Hey, Gary."

"Oh, hi, Stella." He acted surprised, as if he wasn't the one knocking. "Just checking to make sure everything's okay."

I gave him a thumbs up, hoping he'd leave. "All good. Thanks. Just getting some work done." Had he seen me chatting up a storm at my reflection? Leave it to Gary to stick his nose into my business after hours when I was behind a locked door.

He rattled the door. "Do you mind?"

*Yes, very much.* If Gary hadn't become a sheriff he'd be a peeping Tom.

Sighing, I turned the dead bolt. Outside, a few people drove down Main Street, whipping up the first yellow-tinted leaves of fall with their tires. I raised my eyebrows at Gary as he stepped in, bringing the cool air inside. Hot chocolate weather was on its way.

Gary made a big deal of wiping his perfectly clean boots on the mat. "Thanks." He looked around. "It looks really good in here, Stella. Really stylish."

"Thanks, Gary." Seriously? That was it?

He took off his Smoky the Bear hat, which, unlike every other sheriff, he wore every day. As if the point of the job was the hat. His cheeks flushed a hectic red. He examined his feet. "I just wanted to tell you that, uh, I'm happy, you know. For you."

"Why?"

He glanced up with cautious optimism. "Wait, you're getting married, right?"

"Yes."

"To that foreign fella."

"Affirmative."

"Well, I for one, just want to say that I'm real happy for you."

"Thank you, that's very sweet, Gary. Means a lot." I took a step toward the door, which anyone else would have interpreted correctly. But no. Not Gary.

"We—" he motioned between us "—we have a history, you know. And I just wanted to tell you that there's no hard feelings. I hope you have a real nice time." He put his hand on his chest. "I can't make it to the wedding. I'm sorry."

I bit my lip to stop from laughing. A history? Sorry he couldn't make it to the wedding? The layers of wrongness stacked up like a French pastry. I was dying to tell Carmen, but then again, maybe I wouldn't. Gary could have his vision of how things went, and I'd have mine.

"Thank you so much."

The tips of his ears went crimson. "Do you mind?"

"Mind what?"

"I just wanted to give you a hug. To say, goodbye, you know."

Instead of inquiring what, exactly, we were saying goodbye to, I stepped forward and hugged him. He smelled like peanut butter and Barbasol shaving cream. He whispered into my ear, "Good luck, Stella."

Nodding, I tried to keep my face solemn. Clearly, this meant a lot to Gary. When we drew back, I thought for one horrifying second that he was going to kiss me. Thankfully, he didn't.

"He's one lucky foreigner," Gary said, with a two-finger salute off his hat brim. He walked out the door, shoulders sagging, leaving me bemused and grateful. For the first time I realized that with Paolo, I'd chosen the opposite of settling. I'd fallen in love with my equal. A man who knew my flaws and accepted every part of me. We were already partners. Our marriage was the absolute right thing. Something I wanted.

I picked up the phone.


"Mom, I'm so excited that you're coming to the wedding!" Studying my reflection in the mirror, I gave myself an A plus for enthusiasm.

"Honey, your father and I are just over the moon." Mom was breathless with joy. "I bought a new dress at the Fairview Mall. It's really pale pink, but I don't think it's close enough to white to be an issue. Do you think that will be a problem?"

Apparently tonight was my night for utter confusion. "Why would your dress be an issue?"

"Only the bride is supposed to wear white, silly."

I couldn't believe that my mom still used the word "silly." It made her sound like a bible school preschool teacher—which she had been, eons ago. When Rosie and I were little she'd called us her itty bitty sillies. "Time to get the itty bitty sillies into the bath!" she'd sing, chasing us around the house after a day at the beach. I'd loved our beach days. For picnics, she'd always packed potato chips in margarine tubs, something I'd thought everyone did until I found out that there was a rich-people thing called a Ziploc bag. It must have been hard for my parents, seeing the uber-wealthy flood Chelan, hogging the sidewalk as if they owned it, knocking down the charming old homes they'd once dreamed of owning. Erecting sprawling faux-rustic palaces, stomping out old Chelan like a sandcastle.

My throat choked up and I had to swallow, staring down my reflection, remembering Izzy's exhortation to give my mom the pleasure of an enthusiastic daughter.

There was a pause in the conversation. Not long. Just a hitch, space enough to feel the faint shadow of Rosie. Her memory walked beside us, always present. Except this time, instead of a rough punch to the gut, it felt more like a gentle nudge. A reminder.

Mom was worried about tradition. Trying to do the right thing. "I'm sure you'll look amazing. I don't think anyone worries much about stuff like that anymore."

"Oh. I see. That's good. I do like the dress." She sounded relieved. "Isn't it nice that they don't?"

Had I been part of the reason my parents had left Chelan? Had I inadvertently caused this anxiety in my mother? Worrying about always doing the right thing. Fitting in. Because I'd thrived in the new Chelan. I'd spun out onto the lake, hair flying, on those rich kids' boats in high school. Carmen's dad would never let her go but if I was invited, I hung on for dear life, threw myself into the party. Studied their girlfriends. Their hair and nails. Their simple but expensive clothes. I'd painted, hammered and styled Twig to draw those kind of people in and transfer their wealth. And it had worked. I was even marrying a newcomer.

"Yes," I said. "Although I think if someone showed up in a long white dress with a veil, some people might object."

"That's funny. Should your father wear a tux?"

"It's not that kind of wedding, Mom."

"He was all ready to charge out there and buy one. Can you imagine, buying a tuxedo? Do you know what he said? 'Our daughter is getting married. What are we saving our money for?'"

Again, with the constricted throat. The singular daughter. "That's really sweet."

"Pablo insisted we stay with his mother. Are you sure we won't be imposing? Does she really have room?"

I thought about telling her everything—about how massive the Gentillo Estate was—but decided she'd stress less if it were a surprise. She'd feel like she'd stepped into an episode of *The Bachelor*. "She has room, Mom. Don't worry."

"What about a hostess gift? I can't go to this wedding with my arms swinging. Pablo said they didn't want us to pay anything for the wedding. Said his mother wanted to do it all. I don't know, Stella. It seems like a lot."

"Why don't you bring her one of those cute stuffed cactus pillows, like the one you sent me?" I thought about the pillow stuffed somewhere in a closet. A sombrero-wearing saguaro.

"You think?"

It made me happy, thinking of chic Rosalia unwrapping the world's tackiest pillow. Rosalia, who at this moment was probably berating her cleaning lady for leaving coffee grounds in the sink.

"Absolutely. And tell Dad any suit would be perfect. If he wants to dress it up, have him get a pocket square."

I thought this would befuddle Mom, but she sounded delighted. "Oooooh. I can get him one the same shade as my dress."

"Perfect."

"Honey, are you doing okay? Planning a wedding in another country, even if Carmen is doing most of it, well… That sounds like a lot of work."

This was the longest conversation we'd had in years. That simple question—was I okay, expressed with genuine concern, felt like a warm fuzzy blanket thrown around me on a cold day. "I'm okay. It's a lot. And it's confusing, I guess. I didn't really expect any of this to happen, but I'm excited."

"I can't wait to see you." Mom took a deep breath and her words came out with ferocity, as if they'd been pent up for years. "I love you, honey."

I didn't realize how badly, how desperately I'd yearned to hear those words. It had been so long. Had we both been holding each other at a polite distance, assuming the other didn't want more? Had I been punishing her for collapsing when Rosie died? Angry with her for not being the same person she'd been before? She'd fought so hard to rescue Rosie in the icy water that she'd spent five days in the hospital treated for hypothermia-related pneumonia. Suffering had changed us both. Why had I expected her to stay the same? Every deleted message was distancing a woman who'd already lost so much. I was treading on the surface of so much pain, terrified that if I looked down, it would swallow me whole. Mom had offered her hand and said, *I've got you.* Tears streamed down my face. My reflection looked like a girl who'd just finished a marathon. "I love you too, Mom."

"We'll see you in Italy," she whispered. I thought it sounded as though she too was weeping.

"See you in Italy." I hung up, feeling like Paolo had given me the most important gift I'd ever received in my life.

I kissed my hand, touching my face in the mirror. "Go home," I whispered.


"I cannot find a quiet place to think here," Paolo said. "The entire house is in, how do you say, uproar? Very chaos. Chaotic." It was an early morning phone call. From my bed, I studied the streams of light punching through the clouds, illuminating the lake in random spots of indigo.

"Why?" I glanced at my watch. Six o'clock. Only people with children should be awake at this hour. The thought was a dash of cold water. I was a person with child. Literally, with child. I'd be one of those wild-haired women, with bags under my eyes smeared with not-quite-blended concealer, clutching a wailing infant, shouting orders for a triple vanilla latte with extra syrup, because Lord knew I'd need the sugar. Then I'd tack on a coffee cake to my order, subconsciously rubbing my post-pregnancy belly. Paolo would insist the belly was a badge of honor, but would it stop him from checking out nymphets at the beach?

*Tell him!* screamed the troll living under the bridge of my subconscious. *Tell him.*

Instead, I wrapped the sheet around my head, thinking that this view, my beloved weeping willow, my tidy, audaciously green lawn, the gardener, the cleaning lady, would all vanish, sucked into the spaceship of toddlerhood. Who had the energy to chase down a toddler on the dock? Who wanted to sit in the Adirondacks at sunset, hollering "Stay in the middle of the dock! No. Too close! Sit down. Mommy does not want to jump in the water while she's pleasantly buzzed. A sliver? Where do we keep the tweezers?"

Paolo interrupted my thoughts. "My mother is running around the house, screaming at the builders—"

"The builders?"

"*Sì*, the builders. Working on the place to get married outside. Like a little porch with a, how do you say, root?"

His English had deteriorated in a matter of days. "Roof. Yes, they have them in the garden. But we're getting married in the little church."

"Ah, but the church is too small, my mother said. We have many friends here. Or maybe she does. I don't know." He groaned, conveying this information was a burden. I could well imagine that living under the reign of Rosalia while she planned a wedding would be slightly terrifying. Maybe we should just get out of her way and go find a justice of the peace, or the Italian equivalent? The idea of leaving Rosalia stranded was balm to my panicked soul. "It's looking very nice, I think. She's having many flowers planted."

"But I love that church."

Paolo sighed. "Me too. It's very beautiful."

A better person would have let the old witch have her way. She was a widow, losing her only son to a country she despised. However, my better person was MIA. If I was going to stand up for this little person growing inside of me, it had to start with standing up for myself. "Don't you want to get married in the church?"

"*Sì.*"

"Talk to your mother. Tell her."

There was a long pause.

"Paolo, I know you just want to get married and come back to our life here, but I've been realizing a few things… I spoke to my mother. You were right, about talking to her. It felt like a piece of me clicked back into place. And the thing was that I realized that this wedding isn't just about me. It's about my family. It feels like a fresh start. Carmen's been talking to me about the importance of the ceremony. It's special. And I want it to be what we both want. Not what your mother wants."

"*Sì.*" So much fatigue was conveyed in one syllable. I knew that Rosalia was keeping him up at night chattering about details which Paolo, who only wanted to immerse himself in all things viticulture, cared so little about. He'd told me that out of politeness he'd nod, while pondering the acidity, the bouquet, the tasting notes of the wine they were drinking, how they lingered on the palate and felt in his mouth. How the Hollister Estate could adapt more European winemaking methods.

"Paolo, I want our wedding to be like one of your wines. To leave a lasting impression of beauty." I was inordinately proud of this image. I had a vision of our wedding. In a church. The night I arrived, I'd tell him about the baby. The three of us would walk down the aisle. We'd keep it secret until after the wedding. Then we'd share our happy news. We were three.

"*Sì,*" Paolo replied, a grim note of resignation in his voice.

"You can't wait, Paolo. I'm leaving tomorrow. Promise me you'll talk to her now."

"For you, *bella* Stella, anything."

He would face down La Tempesta. It wouldn't be easy.


The morning of the next day, I was blissfully dreaming. Paolo was in his Jeep, repeatedly blasting the horn. What did he want? I was in a bathing suit I hadn't seen since high school, which made me happy. In the dream, I'd missed the bathing suit. All the fun I'd had while wearing it...

A second later, I awoke with a start. Someone was pounding on the front door. Sleeping more soundly than I had in my life, I'd somehow missed my alarm. We were supposed to be headed for Seattle to catch a plane.

Carmen popped up outside my bedroom window, dancing around on the wet grass, making me scream.

"Oh my god! You forgot to set an alarm!?" she yelled through the glass.

I was shucking off my nightgown, changing into jeans and a T-shirt, thanking my lucky stars that I'd packed the night before. Not left anything to the last minute. "I slept through it!"

"You are literally going to be late for your own wedding."

"You are literally going to wake up our neighbors."

Carmen glared. "Don't care."

Waving her away, I promised to be at the front door in two minutes. Squirting toothpaste into my mouth, I rinsed and spit, inspecting my bleary eyes. Despite slight under-eye shadows, I had the calmness of a happy person. "You're getting married in Italy," I told my reflection. Would this all vanish, or was I going to be allowed to have a fabulous life?

# CHAPTER EIGHTEEN

## Packing Light

The Blue Hills Vineyards van felt like a clown car. We'd crammed in the three Alvarez sisters, Juan, and Adella's five-year-old twins, Angel and Connor. The baby had stayed home with Bob but when I'd said it was too bad Bob couldn't come, Adella had laughed. "Are you kidding me? The baby goes to bed at seven. Bob's the one having the vacation."

That used to be the type of comment that had confirmed my decision not to have kids. Now it made me uneasy, wondering how I'd do compared to women like Adella, who'd always known they'd be mothers.

Angel and Connor were arguing over who got to carry the ring and who was carrying the flowers. Lola, who'd insisted that Adella not wedge them into traditional roles, had told them to choose for themselves. They were pale, serious kids with dark hair. Like miniature vampires. I wondered how they'd managed to stay so pale throughout the summer. They made me think of Rosie. How we'd learned to swim in Manson Bay in group lessons, the sun hot on our heads, sunscreen scented, eager to jump in the water.

"Connor, do you want to carry the flowers or the ring?" Lola asked.

"Flowers," Connor said solemnly.

"Sounds good," Lola said. "Angel, you get the ring."

Angel shook her head. "I don't want it."

Lola smiled. "But it's the wedding ring. It has real diamonds."

Angel, whose hair was in two dark plaits on either side of her face, frowned at Lola. "I like flowers."

Connor nodded. "Me too."

Lola lifted her hands. "What about flowers and the ring?"

"I want to be the only one with flowers," said Connor. "She gets the ring."

"No." Angel was quite firm.

I was in the passenger seat beside Adella, who snickered at her sister, raising her eyebrows in glee while her kids bickered about their roles. Adella had chosen driving over sitting with her children, steeling herself for the long flight. "Carmen said you found a nice dress. What does it look like?"

I inhaled so sharply that Adella glanced over. The van swerved into the other lane, nearly nicking the highway barrier. Everyone in the car groaned or shouted.

"What?" Adella asked, looking at me for too long, as if in a movie, driving against a green screen and not pavement.

"The road!" Lola hollered from the back.

Adella turned her head to glare at her sister. "What?"

"Oh my god, pay attention to the road!" Carmen shrieked.

Juan rolled his eyes, making the sign of the cross.

"That's enough," Adella said. "It's fine."

"My mother is a terrible driver." Angel shook her head like an eighty-year-old pensioner.

"Out of the mouths of babes," sniped Lola.

A deer was grazing near the road at the next turn, which helped release tension in the car. Adella turned back to me. "Okay, the dress. What does it look like?"

I glanced at Carmen in the rearview mirror. Her eyes drilled into mine with dawning awareness. We both started laughing.

"What's so funny?" asked Adella.

"The dress," Carmen said.

"The dress!" I howled, wiping tears from my eyes.

"Can you let us in on the secret? What about the dress?" Adella asked.

"It's in the hall closet of Stella's house!" Carmen said, slapping her knee.

"We forgot it." Something about forgetting my wedding dress was hysterical.

Lola accepted it as a thing that happens. Adella looked as though we'd said the wedding had a nudist theme. "You forgot the wedding dress?"

Adella counted things off on one hand, keeping the other on the wheel, which made everyone concerned about her driving. "Your suitcase, your ticket, your passport and your wedding dress. How hard is it?"

Carmen shrugged. "Let's just agree that we're *not* telling Rosalia."

Crossing the 520 bridge across Lake Washington was one of my favorite views. On clear days, Mt. Rainier appeared to the south.

Ahead was the skyline of Seattle, propped up like a movie set, with the Space Needle pointing to the clouds. Further along the bridge to the right were gracious lakefront mansions. The Cascade Mountains lingered in the distance. Approaching land, you could see the University of Washington Husky Stadium with canoes paddling from the Husky boathouse.

Everyone in the van was chatting with excitement, except the twins, who had finally tired of arguing over their roles in the wedding. They gazed out the windows with morbid detachment. Maybe it had been a mistake asking them to walk in the wedding processional, but then again, since they both looked like they'd stepped out of a Victorian daguerreotype photo, they'd add to the old-fashioned church setting.

Those were the random thoughts passing through my head when Adella, who had, under duress, given up the wheel to Lola, looked up from sorting passports. She'd gathered all of them earlier during our stop at Dairy Queen, stashing them in a Ziploc bag. When I'd pointed out that I was, in fact, a fully functioning adult (nearly, minus a secret pregnancy), she'd pointed out that when she and Bob had gone to Quebec for a friend's wedding, it had been easier to have everyone's passports together, to hand them to TSA. I'd forgotten how much of a busybody Adella was. Also, I did not want to hear about the friend or his wedding. I'd surrendered my passport like a murder suspect in an Agatha Christie novel. Adella's bossiness did yield a crucial issue with our travel plans. Her next sentence nearly made me upchuck my peanut buster parfait onto the bug-spattered windshield.

"Daddy, your passport is expired!" She said this as though her father was a jet-setting retiree and not a man who suffered from moderate dementia.

"Is that a problem?" Juan asked, which made me love him all the more.

*No problem, Juan. For you, they will make an exception.*

Carmen repeatedly muttered the same scatological expletive. Adella pointed out that her children were only five.

Carmen snapped, "Oh please, they've heard it all."

"We have, Mommy," agreed Connor.

"I know," Adella said. "I just don't need to hear that right now."

We'd merged onto I-5 in downtown Seattle, a veritable Amazon river of traffic with six southbound congested lanes. Lake Union was a brilliant sea of tranquility dotted with sailboats at the foot of Queen Anne and Capitol Hills. South Lake Union started low with the Google complex, growing as it progressed south into skyscrapers dotting the skyline. The Space Needle vied for attention like a shrunken but beloved maiden aunt.

Lola, a goofball who had a charming way of pulling through in a pinch, shouted, "Shut up, everyone. No freaking out allowed."

"We're not freaking out!" Adella shrieked, holding her hands to the seat as if a crash was imminent.

Lola snorted, driving across five lanes of I-5 traffic as if escaping a heist. "Someone google the passport offices! I went there once with a friend so I know about where it is, but I need directions."

"We don't have time to go to the passport offices," Carmen objected.

Juan watched his daughters volleying back and forth as if it wasn't his concern, occasionally glancing out the window at the city and lake.

"Oh, so you just want to drop Papi off with a skycap?" Lola snarked. "Is that your plan?"

The twins excitedly demanded to know the role of a skycap. My first instinct was to ignore them, but my second thought was, *Oh yeah, I'm going to own one of these little things so I'd better familiarize myself with their make and model.* After explaining that a skycap helped you check your luggage, I thought they'd thank me or look happy, but they both had the glazed look of teenagers at a family reunion.

"Oh," Angel said, looking very sad and disappointed, like I'd just informed her that the tooth fairy had run into a lawnmower. "Sounds boring."

"It's not." I explained that skycaps had important jobs helping people travel.

"When do we get there?" was Connor's next volley.

I felt like telling him that he was a cliché.

Seattle traffic morphed us into the metal orb in a pinball game. Forces beyond our control conspired to send us in a different direction. We drove up a one-way hill, fighting traffic rather than have Lola back down. "I'm going for it!" she screamed, as irate drivers yelled out of their windows and honked.

Lola finally found us a parking spot at the top of a hill near an Asian senior center. We hiked over a freeway overpass that sloped toward Elliott Bay. The twins asked if they could roll down the patchy grass bordering the sidewalk. Adella glanced at the broken liquor bottles and empty syringes littering the broken pavement, before grabbing the children firmly by their hands. "No. Stop talking."

The passport office was housed in a turn-of-the-century building adjacent to the steep hill we'd just descended. The building appeared fused to a cement retaining wall holding back the hill. Seattle was a giant Lego table made of concrete, slanting up from the water.

After passing through security and riding the elevator, we wandered down a dim corridor that hadn't been updated since Barry Manilow ruled the charts. The passport office was strictly 1970s: a human hamster cage. A row of divided office slots was protected by a sheer wall of bulletproof Plexiglas. Some of the slots were empty, leaving bored-looking functionaries to process paperwork. They faced an austere waiting room droning with fans.

Adella took a number and we sat in the waiting room. Our fellow citizens had the aggressively bored look of people who'd been waiting a long time. Having caught up on their social media feeds hours ago, they now tracked bloated flies for entertainment.

Adella briskly trotted up to a window. The middle-aged black woman in cornrows behind it studiously ignored her, tapping away on her computer.

"Excuse me."

The woman didn't look up. She pointed to the ticket machine.

Adella held up the flimsy ticket. "I did get one. Thank you. It's just that my father has a plane to catch and we just realized that his passport is expired."

"You don't say?" The woman still didn't turn her head, although she'd stopped typing to inspect her carefully manicured nails. I admired her attitude. She was fully embracing the stereotype of a government employee. Had it down cold.

"We're going to miss our flight."

The woman glanced toward our party, sprawled out on the molded bucket seats designed for the comfort of another species. She pointed at Mr. Alvarez. "That your dad?"

Adella nodded, visibly relieved that this delay was going to be resolved posthaste. "Yes."

The woman winced. "Ma'am, I'm very sorry but this isn't a vending machine type of situation. You don't pay your money and get the passport. These things take time."

Adella's body lost its tautness, a helium balloon with a pinprick leak. "But we're going to a wedding." She saw the woman's spark of interest and pointed to me. I tried to look adorable and sad at the same time. "Her fiancé was going to be deported, so they—"

The woman's squint morphed into a severe frown. "Is this like a green card marriage type of situation? Because there are people in this building that would looooove to know about that."

Adella shook her head while Carmen muttered under her breath about Adella's stupidity. "No! God no! Of course not. They're totally in love. And we're going to miss our flight."

The woman gave us one last look and, with a grumpy sigh, heaved herself from her chair, hiking up her uniform pants as she strode into the hinterlands of the paper-strewn office.

Carmen glanced at her phone. "Our plane boards in one hour."

I'd checked Waze. We were at least, with no traffic, forty-five minutes from Sea-Tac Airport. And Seattle traffic was an anaconda that could strike at any time. "Are we going to miss our flight? Paolo says it takes a long time to get through security for international flights."

Lola dashed over to Adella, grabbed the Ziploc bag, extracted two passports and thrust them into Carmen's hands. "You go. We'll meet you there."

"We'll meet you in Italy?" Carmen said. "That's it?"

Lola looked up at heaven as if asking someone, *Can you believe this?* "Yes, that's it. You're the maid of honor; she's the bride. You don't want to miss the wedding. Run! Go!"

Adella lit up. "They can take the twins."

"No way," Carmen spat out, looking at me for confirmation. "Sound okay?"

"Yes! Let's go." We dashed down out of the passport office, stabbing the elevator button multiple times as I envisioned our jet taxiing down the runway without us.

"Should we take the stairs?" Carmen asked.

Nodding, I took off at a sprint, looking in vain through the dark hallway for an exit sign. Behind us, the elevator dinged. We raced back just as the elevator door had almost closed. Carmen pushed her arm inside, muscling the door open with a groan. She threw her body against the opening, forcing it wide.

"Get in!"

I slipped into the elevator where I noticed a tall elderly woman with round eyeglasses and a neat grey bun. "You girls sure are in a hurry. Where you headed to?"

Carmen was leaning on a railing, catching her breath. "Hopefully, a wedding."

On the next floor down, the elevator opened to let in three more people. Two of them pressed different floors. At this pace, we were going to miss our flight. The elevator stopped again. The old woman passed us on her way out. "Good luck, you two. Hopefully you don't have far to go."

When the elevator opened onto the main floor, we sprinted through the lobby past security as if the place were on fire.

# CHAPTER NINETEEN

## By Appointment Only

The cheery reservations agent had lipstick on one overly whitened tooth. It was the only thing that stopped me from wanting to jump across the desk and strangle her with her ridiculously pert silk necktie thing. "I'm sorry, your flight is currently taxiing down the runway." Her nametag read "MARGARITA."

"Oh goodie," I snapped.

"Excuse me?" Although I should have felt a solidarity with Margarita (we were both in customer service jobs and knew that even bad news should be delivered with a smile), I couldn't muster up anything but furious resentment. We'd missed our flight. She didn't have to be thrilled.

"She was being sarcastic," Carmen said soothingly to Margarita, as if speaking to a customer who'd found an insect in their wine. She explained the whole wedding and expired visa situation. Margarita had probably heard a million lies from people who'd overslept, and remained stony-faced. "Can you possibly get us on another flight?"

"No, sorry," said Margarita, motioning for the next passengers, who stepped forward to take our place.

Carmen leaned into the counter, whispering, *"Disculpe, señora. Podría mirarlo de nuevo, por favor?"*

Margarita cracked a tiny smile. "Okay. *Solo una vez más.*" She glanced at me. "I'll try, but it's probably not going…" Frowning while she studied her computer, she traced her finger down the screen. "Oh, wow." She glanced at her watch. "There is a British Airways flight that boards in twenty minutes. There is a six-hour layover in Heathrow." She raised her eyebrows. "We'd have to put you in first class. That's…" She did some calculations. "Yikes. Okay. That's a lot."

Fumbling for my credit card, I passed it to her. "See if that works."

Carmen had done the same thing. Margarita stared at both credit cards and the line behind us, before pushing the cards back. "Complimentary upgrade." Printing our boarding passes, she handed them to us as quickly as possible before the people behind us missed their flight.

In keeping with our dignified world traveler ethos, Carmen and I jumped around like fleas, clapping and making complete fools of ourselves, singing "First class," like hayseed ninnies until Margarita leaned forward and hissed, "If you don't stop doing that, the rest of the passengers are going to know that I did this and it won't be good for anyone."

Carmen clapped her hand over her mouth, pretending to zip her lips and throw away the key. Margarita grimaced. "You'd better get going or you're going to miss your second flight." We were still falling all over ourselves to thank her when she signaled for the next customer.

"Next!"

*

Forty minutes later, as we passed over Chelan, the vast lake reduced to a shining blue ribbon. Carmen was lightly toasted.

"Look at us! Just look at us!" she chortled as a flight attendant topped off her champagne flute. The only thing wrong with flying to Italy to marry the love of my life, besides my misgivings about the institution itself and the tiny human I'd smuggled on board, was that my best friend was getting gloriously tipsy without me on French champagne. She babbled on about the flowery aroma and light finish, pink-cheeked and expansive. Her enthusiasm was kind of infectious.

When I said to the lovely flight attendant that no, I still didn't want any champagne, Carmen leaned into the aisle across our cushy, wide, first-class leather seats, blurting, "She's not drinking right now!" with a wink.

Subtle.

"Oh. Ooooh!" The flight attendant, Deirdre, went wide-eyed. Apparently, she approved. She accepted my pregnancy much more readily that I had, showing up seconds later with a glass of sparkling apple juice, whispering, "Congratulations!" in a singing tone that, although supremely cheesy, made me, in my own way, drunkenly happy. I'd gotten myself knocked up by accident and people were going to congratulate me. Nobody would ask, "Did you really want kids?" or "Are you happy about it?" They'd get all glassy-eyed with joy, like Deirdre, attaching their own significance to my situation.

Who knew?

It was better to let things go, I decided. My body was flitting from despondency to sheer joy like a darting hummingbird. Perhaps losing control of my emotions was preparation for the terror of being handed a baby in the hospital and then pushed out the door with a cheery, "Good luck!"

Carmen and I had decided, after snuggling into our plush blankets and soothing ourselves with warm towels, that we'd act cool. Like we weren't rubbernecking first-class tourists. This lasted until we gazed down on the undulating wheat fields of the Palouse Prairie. "It's even prettier from first class, right?" Carmen whispered.

"You're joking, right?" I asked.

The glossy woman across the aisle flipping through *Town and Country* was eavesdropping, likely memorizing titbits to share with her cronies at the tennis club over skinny margaritas.

"Nope. It's situational. Like how food tastes better when you're camping."

"Right." Carmen knew perfectly well that I'd throw myself out of this plane rather than set one foot in a tent. Furthermore, she was aware that this was the second flight out of Chelan in my entire life.

Somewhere over Kansas, I dropped off while staring at the patchwork of corn and alfalfa fields. I dreamt of Paolo descending a tall staircase at his mother's house, which weirdly resembled Tara from *Gone with the Wind*. He was angry, threatening to cancel the wedding. He stormed out the door while I looked everywhere for my parents, who seemed to have gotten lost on the way to the wedding.

I woke up to the smell of something delicious and Carmen lifting her wineglass for the flight attendant to fill. "I'm drinking for two,"

Carmen giggled. A plate of garlic roast chicken, whipped potatoes and glazed carrots lay on my lowered seat tray.

"How far are we from Heathrow?" I asked Deirdre groggily, wiping my eyes.

"Two hours," she said. "Fresh ground pepper?"

The smell of garlic and chicken morphed into eau de garbage, prompting me to push my seat tray back up onto the seat in front of me and dash away to christen the first-class bathroom toilet with the contents of my stomach. On the way back to my seat, I apologized to the unlucky soul seated in front of me, who glared at me spitefully. Deirdre, who'd already wiped off most of the food smashed into the nooks and crannies of the seat back, was much kinder, graciously accepting my thanks, saying it happened all the time.

She was professionally kind until I uttered, "I have one more favor to ask."

Her smile was strained. "Sure."

"Can you please stop serving my friend alcohol?"

This time her grin was genuine as her guard came down. "No problem. Would you like a cheese and cracker platter and some sparkling water?"

"That would be amazing." God bless all the Deirdres of the world.

Navigating Heathrow Airport was hard. Weaving through a multicultural mass while towing a half-crocked Carmen was my own personal Super Bowl. Oddly, the tiny human inside of me seemed to be saying, "Feed me." Ironic, since my digestive system was in full revolt. We were fish-fighting our way upstream. One fish was drunk, despite the heroic efforts of Deirdre, who'd said that coffee, although unlikely to sober anyone up, was "better than nothing." Carmen had refused to drink water, saying she didn't want to lose her "first class buzz."

So much for playing it cool.

I followed signs, consulting with Carmen, as if we were both in a play called *Sober Carmen*, searching for the shopping and dining concourse.

Carmen's eyes zeroed in on one of the signs and she stopped walking, stiffening like a hunting dog who'd caught the scent. "Shopping!"

"Yes, but we're eating. Or at least I am." I dragged her forward, mentally tallying our bags, making sure nothing had been left hooked to a bathroom stall.

She refused to budge. "You just ate."

Swarms of people surged around us. "We're not going to have a discussion right now."

Carmen crossed her arms. "Yes, we are."

"We're going to eat."

Carmen lifted one finger. "Darling." Apparently, she had become an aging vixen on a soap opera. "We are in London."

"True enough."

She unfurled another finger. "You forgot your wedding dress."

"Two points, Carmen. I'm also hungry."

She showed me three fingers. "Three, we're going shopping. Because you are going to be the only woman in Chelan, Washington who will be able to say, 'I bought my wedding dress in London.'" She widened her stance as if anticipating that I might try to drag her into a restaurant. "I'm not taking no for an answer."

"We're staying here."

"We have six hours."

"Not that long."

She pointed to the blue-lettered sign: SHOPPING AND DINING. "Look, it's a sign."

"Yes, it is a sign, Carmen, but not the kind that says, 'Take a cab into London during your layover.'"

Carmen's finger nearly hit my nose as she pointed at me. "That's where you're wrong."


"I want the kind that Lady Mary takes when she's in London," said Carmen, referencing *Downton Abbey* as we stood in the ground transportation area amid honking cars. Travelers wheeled luggage like obedient pets. Outside Heathrow, there was a crush of traffic and people, with police blowing their whistles and waving their arms. The tar-scented air was making me ill.

"We have to take the first one in the queue," I said primly, very proud of myself for knowing that it wasn't called a line.

A classic black cab broke free of the congested traffic, ready to pass us three lanes away. Carmen's arm shot out like a seasoned New Yorker, followed by a three-fingered whistle so loud the people next to us muttered "Americans," as if they'd spotted rats.

Seconds later those same people watched us with jealousy as the driver opened the door. "Quick now. I could get reported for queue-snatching." He winked happily. "Perfect—no bags."

"What are you two ladies up to in London?" our ruddy-cheeked driver asked, after we'd told him that the city, in general, was our destination. "Maybe that'll help me narrow down where I should drop you."

Carmen gazed lovingly at me. "Wedding dress shopping." Which was fine, until she tacked on, "She's pregnant."

The driver chuckled, glancing at me in the mirror. "Nothing wrong with that. The missus and I might have had a similar circumstance a while back. Worked out just fine. The missus might tell a different tale, but I'm happy."

I shot him a grateful look.

"There's quite a range of shopping districts, from Mayfair to Notting Hill to Hatton Garden."

"I loved the movie *Notting Hill*," Carmen enthused. "Julia Roberts and Hugh Grant." She slid down the seat, closing her eyes. The cab driver glanced kindly at me from under his tweed cap. Why not buy a ruinously expensive dress for an event that would potentially happen the day after tomorrow? We'd already left the airport during our layover—what was one more questionable decision? Decisions abroad, like the local currency, didn't have to make sense.

"Notting Hill, please," I said.


Our drive into the district was colorful. Carmen gazed out the window, exclaiming, "Oh my god, is that Big Ben?"

"That's a watch shop, love, with an old clock," our driver replied.

"We should see Buckingham Palace!" Carmen said. "Say hello to the queen!"

I leaned closer to our saintly driver and said, "No."

He mimicked the universal drinking sign of, Is Your Friend Two Sheets to the Wind? "Did your friend perhaps partake during the flight?"

"She partook and partook some more."

"Six hours isn't much time to find a wedding dress and get back to Heathrow, so perhaps save the sightseeing for another time, love," he said, glancing at Carmen in the rearview mirror.

Carmen slumped back into her seat. "Aww. You're harshing my mellow."

The driver didn't bat an eye. "I'm sure I didn't mean to harsh anyone's mellow," he said. "Just want to ensure you'll make it to the wedding."

Carmen sat up, brightening visibly. "Oh right, the wedding."

I patted her on her back. "Yes, my wedding. The reason we flew across a huge chunk of the world."

Carmen leaned toward the front, proudly patting her chest. "I'm the maid of honor."

"That's lovely. Just lovely. Make me very happy, weddings do."

Carmen's face had drooped. "She's got hot Paolo, and my boyfriend isn't even coming to the wedding."

"That's a pity," said the driver. "I'm sure he has his reasons."

Carmen blew a raspberry. While I wiped her spittle off my face, she continued, "Fear of bloody matrimony." She twirled her hand in a flowery gesture, leaning over to whisper, "Did you hear that? I said 'bloody.' I'm practically a Londoner."

"Want me to try another shop?" said the driver, checking his watch.

But Carmen was already out of the taxi, knocking on the door of a quaint shop called Fairest with the words, BY APPOINTMENT ONLY in the window. A beautifully dressed girl opened the door and engaged in what looked like a spirited debate with Carmen. I said a regretful goodbye to our lovely driver and went to drag Carmen away from the prettiest shop in the world.

# CHAPTER TWENTY

## Say Yes to the Dress

The interior of Fairest was modern and stylish with sanded hardwoods, bright white walls and a marble vase filled with peacock feathers beside an antique gold floor-length mirror. Wedding dresses billowed like clouds from the high racks.

Carmen had managed to talk our way through the door against the wishes of the annoyed saleswoman. Carmen simply would not take no for an answer. The saleswoman was tiny, dressed in elegant heels and a silk slip dress. A china doll facing two bullish Americans. We were utterly out of place in her gleaming salon. Her luxuriant Kate Middleton waves spilling down her shoulders made me feel greasy and unkempt.

"As I said before, we're by appointment only." She crossed her arms, keeping her manners, despite what she obviously viewed as a rude interruption.

"Yes," said Carmen, upping the warmth factor with grit and style. "We've traveled from the west coast of the United States of America and my friend, Stella, is getting married and—" she waved both arms at me like a game show hostess "—forgot her wedding dress."

The woman's eyes went wide. As if we'd admitted to forgetting a person, not a dress.

Feeling the tires of the proverbial bus crushing me, I pointed to Carmen. "She was supposed to remind me."

Carmen's grin stayed firmly in place. "We were in a hurry. It was in the hall closet." As if this was an adorable anecdote.

The woman gulped. "I see. So. When is the wedding?"

"Day after tomorrow." Carmen kept it crisp and matter-of-fact, tacking on, "If my dad makes it."

"Did you forget your father too?" the woman asked, pointedly not laughing, as if a person dumb enough to stash a wedding dress in a coat closet could forget just about anything.

"No. Long story. Anyway, our driver said that this was the best bridal store in London, and we thought we'd give it a shot," Carmen said.

"Hmmmm." The woman frowned, clearly unmoved by our plight.

I silently prayed that Carmen was sober enough to omit my pregnancy.

"Tiny detail." Carmen pinched her thumb and forefinger together to demonstrate. *Here we go*, I thought. "We have to be back at the airport in two hours."

The woman's elegantly shaped eyebrows shot up. "This keeps getting better and better, doesn't it?"

Carmen didn't miss a beat. "Yes, if you like a challenge."

Bam. There was my best friend. Back in battle gear. The woman glanced at her watch again, just to let us know that she was fully booked and very busy. "Typically," she said, slowly, "selecting one of our dresses is an involved process. We take into consideration the wedding's theme, what the groom is wearing…" She paused. "What's your price range?"

"No limit," said Carmen, with a flourish.

When I turned to her, she grinned contentedly. "I talked to Paolo when you were in the bathroom at Heathrow. It's supposed to be a surprise. So. Surprise!"

"Paolo?" said the girl, warming to us. Or Paolo.

"She's getting married in Italy." Carmen scrolled through her phone. She found a photo that had been taken of us during a dinner on Evan's patio. Paolo's linen shirt was just the right amount of rumpled; one of his tan arms lay over my bare shoulder. Lake Chelan spread below us in all its glory, the hills across the water verdant with vineyards. Looking at the photo, I could practically smell summer, feel the lingering rays warm upon my skin. It was a beautiful photo of a wonderful night. One of many that stacked up against each other in glorious succession. Carmen showed the girl the photo. "To that guy."

The assistant studied me with newfound respect, extending her hand. "I'm Sophia, by the way. Let's find you a gorgeous wedding dress."

Once Sophia signed on, she was a pro. I was installed in a dressing room composed of lush brocade curtains. Inside was a velvet settee and a glass table with water in a carafe. Undressing, I donned a white robe while Sophia located a dress based on what I'd described. Simple. Elegant. Modern. She didn't want us pawing through her dresses without looking at their website. Every dress was zipped into plastic mesh.

"We have to keep the lace and beading protected. You'd be surprised what can wreck delicate fabric. Moths. Sunlight. Once, a lady brought a coffee in and tripped. It was awful."

While Sophia was in the salon, I poked my head out to find Carmen napping in a chair. "Carmen, pssst!"

Her head popped up, eyes bright, as if she thought she could fool me. "Yep?"

"What's taking her so long?"

Carmen looked over and frowned, whispering, "She's standing in the middle of the room with her eyes closed."

"Great. She's a narcoleptic." As if on cue, Sophia's heels clicked on the hardwoods. A moment later, she appeared.

"Here we are," Sophia said, holding one limp dress bag.

"That's it?" I moved aside. "That bag looks empty."

"Not at all." She hung it up, brushing aside my concern. "Bear with me. I have a talent, if you will. I can match the girl with the dress." I must have looked skeptical because she added, "I have a ninety percent hit rate."

"We'll see," Carmen trilled.

Once out of the bag, the dress was a puddle of soft fabric in my arms. A featherweight fabric with a slight sheen. "Is that cream or yellow?"

"Try it on," Sophia said, putting a hard stop to my dithering by closing the curtain with a muscular tug.

There was a reason why girls like Sophia belonged in a bridal shop. The unpromising-looking dress slid onto me as if it were made for my body. A sweetheart bodice curved over my breasts, leaving my décolletage and shoulders exposed except for a barest whisper of fitted cap-sleeved lace that was modern, yet classic. As if someone had sketched drawings of lilies on stems and programmed them into a sewing machine—which was, I supposed, how it worked. The high-waisted satin skirt was straight and long, hitting the ankle with a graceful flare.

"Look at these," I heard Sophia say to Carmen.

Carmen squealed. "Oh my! I want to get married." I couldn't see her behind the curtain, but her voice fell. "Actually, I do."

"You will," Sophia said confidently as she swept open the curtain. I could have hugged her. But I didn't, because she was holding a whimsical work of art in the form of footwear. Meant to be worn by fairy princesses as they led unicorns into the woods. So utterly impractical, I might as well have taken a match to a pile of money. Sophia quoted the price, which was, of course, astronomical. It didn't quite register. I'd left the world where such things as car insurance existed, entering the magical realm that retail executives count on. The money-is-no-object, you-only-marry-once, slippery slope of rationalizing indulgence.

The shoes were the perfect heel. High enough to be elegant, low enough to last through a day standing. Wide ribbons of gossamer wrapped around the foot, crossing over the arch and winding up to tie above the ankle in a bow.

"Some people tie them in the front. Some like the back. Your dress is very simple, so it's really up to you."

When I stood up, Carmen had tears in her eyes. "That is so much more you than the dress in your hall closet."

Sophia beamed, waiting for my approval.

I hugged her. As one does. When a total stranger transforms you into a bride.


After we'd promised to send Sophia wedding photos and follow each other on Instagram, she showed us to the door. We said stupid things like, "Drop by if you're ever in Seattle." As if Seattle was near Chelan. As if the Pacific Northwest was near anything. Carmen promised Sophia that when she got married, she "wouldn't think of getting the gown any place but here!"

Right.

Because we were totally those people.

Spending four months' rent on a dress was a thing we did.

The traveling gods shone upon us. Our sweetheart of a cab driver had waited for us. He climbed out, tipped his hat, and expressed great satisfaction that we'd found a dress, acting as though he hadn't been worried a bit that on our ride to Notting Hill, Carmen would redecorate his backseat.

"So then, ladies. Remind me, if you would, of your departure time?"

Carmen studied her phone. I was busy smoothing the garment bag across my lap. I hadn't trusted myself to leave it in the trunk. Or the boot, apparently, which made about as much sense as calling it the trunk.

"At three ten," Carmen said, losing volume with each syllable.

"Oh my," said the driver, his bushy brows descending as he glanced in the rearview mirror. "Time to hop to it, I suppose. Can't have you ladies missing another flight, can we?"

The doubt in his voice was unmistakable.

# CHAPTER TWENTY-ONE

## Cranky

Our jovial cabbie must, in another life, have been a Formula One driver. "I'll lose my license," he kept muttering, as he inserted his cab into the snarled traffic with a friendly wave. "We represent London, you see," was another utterance. Weaving in and out of the long lines of vehicles on the M4 like a mad genius, he kept us utterly silent, white-knuckling the door grips.

"Trips takes a solid hour normally but I shaved off a few minutes," the cabbie said. Brilliant blue signs for Heathrow loomed over our heads. "British Airways, isn't it?"

"Yes!" said Carmen.

"Are you sure?" I asked, unwilling to dig out my phone and risk the dress sliding off my lap.

"I'm completely sober and sure."

"You can nap on the plane."

"Thank god."

"And what's your one job?"

Carmen rolled her puffy eyes. "I won't forget the shoes."

*

We were running in through the automatic doors at Heathrow Airport when someone yelled.

"The shoes!"

We turned to see the cabbie. Detached from his quaint cab he looked like a walrus, whiskers and all. By the time he reached us, he was out of breath. "I heard you talking about them. They sound lovely."

I glared at Carmen as she snatched the box from his hands, thanking him profusely as he waved her on, exhorting us to run.

"Good luck!" the cabbie yelled, waving like our long-lost uncle.

"We'll talk about it later," I threatened Carmen as we sprinted into the expansive lobby of Heathrow Airport. Two madwomen on a mission to get it right. Clumps of travelers gazed idly as we dashed past. We'd become those dreaded, irritating humans. Feckless losers who can't seem to read a watch or a phone. Who neglect the details of life's important moments like, say, catching a plane to their own wedding. A cautionary tale, with a rapidly growing layer of flop sweat.

Rounding the corner, my heart sank at the security line. It wove around tightly onto itself, intent on stomping out lingering optimism.

"Are you kidding me?" Carmen said to nobody.

"Living the dream," said a black man in a bow tie with braces.

"This isn't happening." I covered my eyes.

"Oh, it's on," said bow-tie man.

We were telling bow-tie man and another woman our tale of woe when a bystander in her sixties with the authority of a school principal waved down security. "Hello, yoo-hoo. Young man? Over here. That's it." The security officer trotted over like a good student. "This lovely American lady is about to miss her flight. You don't want her to miss her flight, now, do you?" Security man shook his head.

Carmen pursed her lips, whispering, "What am I, chopped liver?"

Security man asked us what flight we were on, checking his device. "That flight is now boarding. Very sorry."

A uniformed security woman peered over his shoulder, tapping the screen with a bedazzled nail. "Boarded."

Principal lady straightened her already ramrod-straight spine, supporting her considerable bosom. "Dearest man. You must have some authority here. The lady in question is getting married." She pointed out the window in an arcing motion. "In Italy."

"Congratulations," said security man.

Security woman gave us a tight smile, getting on her walkie-talkie. "You should be doing this," she snarled at security man.

He gave us a little nod, speaking softly. "So cranky, that one." The line moved forward. He leaned in to speak confidentially. "I'm going to set her up with my brother."

"Excellent," said principal lady, although I wasn't sure if she was referring to our progress or the budding matchmaker.

"All right," said security woman, moving the cordon to the side. She beckoned us forward. "This way." We followed like children. "They're holding the flight for the bride."


We boarded the plane to applause. Almost everyone loved a bride. One couple, however, wasn't thrilled. They'd been upgraded into our seats. They were crabby, making a big production of gathering their stashed belongings as if being evicted.

"You know what? It's fine," I said to the flight attendant. She clearly wanted this airplane in flight. "We'll sit in their seats."

We had a weird little exchange with the people near us, who insisted that we should retain our first-class seats. We were "entitled." We were one of them. But we weren't. Despite delaying their departure, the passengers in the general seating section appeared delighted to see us.

"Congratulations! All the best! Where are you getting married?"

I wanted to be a fiancée on the cusp of matrimony for the rest of my life.

When I shared this sentiment with Carmen, she took out a bottle of water, struggling to open the cap, and glared at me. "You cannot be serious."

I wrinkled my nose. "I kind of am."

"Our whole lives you're the one that didn't want to get married," she hissed. "And now you're blissed out on matrimony."

"I'm allowed to enjoy this."

She glanced around, as if our fellow passengers were eavesdropping, which they clearly were. "I never said you weren't."

"A wedding is nothing but a beautiful party." I blinked innocently. I did enjoy winding her up.

"Don't kid yourself, Stella. A wedding is about families and families are always complicated. Enjoy yourself but remember, we're going to be on Rosalia's turf."

I leaned my head back on the headrest, closing my eyes. "I know. I know."

"Look, I know I said, a while ago, that you could marry or not marry, but I have dealt with Rosalia, okay? La Tempesta is a little too picturesque a term for that control freak. You know *The Devil Wears Prada*? She's the devil."

"I'm really glad I hit her."

"I thought it was an accident!"

The plane had taxied and turned at the end of the runway. Engines roared to life. I settled back, bracing for take-off. "Honestly, I'm not sure anymore."


Malpensa Airport was bright white and glass, a lovely portal into mountain-fringed Northern Italy. We wove our way through the shining halls, lined with kiosks selling things nobody needed. Airports, I was beginning to realize, blurred together on long trips. My arm was sweaty where the garment bag hung limply over it, but I refused to drape it over my shoulder or allow Carmen to help. This wasn't a dress, it was an incentive.

Locating our luggage, we wandered into the massive main lobby.

When the double doors hissed open, the honking, exhaust-filled scene overwhelmed us. Beyond the overhang, the blue sky faded to pale lilac. Dusk. I imagined our dock at home. Swallows swooping atop the lake, so close their wing tips skimmed the water as the sun dipped behind the dark hills.

"Stella?" Carmen tugged on my arm. "We need to find the rental car place. Do you see any signs?" She repeated my name. "Stella? Maybe we should ask someone."

A tooting car pulled up, stuffed with passengers. I wandered away from it, to ask a woman if she knew where to rent cars. She shrugged. "No English."

"Stella!" Carmen shouted.

I whirled around. The car was overflowing with cheering Alvarezes.

# CHAPTER TWENTY-TWO

## Legoland

"We caught a direct flight!" Adella crowed.

Lola navigated the Opel rental car through the airport freeway system. "That lady at the passport office was awesome. We were out of there in an hour." She paid fierce attention to the clogged lanes.

Italians took the rules of the road casually. As if sticking to one lane was a quaintly outdated custom. Cars raced up, slammed on the brakes and acted as if the car in front of them had no right to be on the road, let alone the planet. Darting vehicles. Honking. Fists shaking. Arms thrusting.

"Left. No wait, there's the sign, right!" said Adella.

Lola swerved our car across three lanes of traffic. Drivers (and passengers) went ballistic, shouting in Italian. A man in a convertible saw Lola's pretty face, waggled his eyebrows and blew her a kiss, guiding her into his lane with a gallant gesture.

"Why thank you, kind sir," Lola said.

Juan kept trying to climb into the back to get out his new passport, forgetting that we'd decided I'd look later. "My first stamp is nice. Italians seem very official."

"Daddy, it might just be the ones in the airport," said Lola as we left the airport, traveling north to join the freeway that would take us toward the Italian Alps. The car settled into a pleasant quiet as we passed the red-tile-roofed buildings with painted shutters and lush gardens, a landscape so unfamiliar to our American eyes.

*We're in Italy*, I kept thinking. *Paolo's home.*

The children woke up after sunset. We were wandering lost through the mountainous Lombardy region. Traveling down narrow dark roads that did not appear on Google Maps. It didn't help that Lola was exhausted. She'd surrendered the wheel to Adella. Carmen was the designated map reader. Nobody asked me to help. Another bridal perk, perhaps.

"When do we get to Lego?" Angel asked, peering sadly out the window at the distant lights coming from far off houses and farms.

Adella turned around, nearly hitting a postal box. "I told you on the plane. It's not Lego. It's Lecco."

"But they have a Legoland, right?" Connor asked, as if his life depended upon it.

Lola took his hand. "Hey, pal, they don't have a Legoland, but they might have pigs."

Adella turned again, but Carmen blocked her view into the back seat with her hand. "She said 'might.' Doesn't mean they have them."

"They'd better have pigs!" Angel said, arms crossed. A tiny terrorist.

Carmen glanced at me with wide eyes. "Isn't having kids the most fun ever?"

"Shut up and see if you have any coverage," Adella snapped.

"You're not supposed to say 'shut up,'" said both the twins at exactly the same time, arms crossed, brows furrowed. Kitschy salt and pepper shakers.

Everyone in the car was slightly freaked out except for Juan, who messed up Connor's hair, avoiding Angel, who didn't like anyone touching her unless explicitly invited. "Aren't they fun!"

"Loads," Lola snorted, holding her phone aloft. "One lousy bar."

"Is that it?" Lola asked, craning her neck forward to peer out the windshield. An impressive carved wooden sign built into a stone wall read: AZIENDA AGRICOLO GENTILLO.

Everyone looked at me. "This must be it. That's his name."

"Gentillo. Could be *español*," mused Juan, turning to me. "Are you going to take his name?"

I frowned. "I—"

Adella took her eyes off the road. "Don't tell me you haven't discussed—"

A coyote-sized animal darted across the road. Everyone screamed. Adella patted her chest. "Don't scare me like that. You're all a bunch of nervous nellies."

"That's name-calling," Angel said, glancing at her twin for confirmation.

"What kind of an animal do you think that was?" Juan asked the twins, but they pursued their persecution of their mother, saying she'd now committed two offenses.

"First one to spot the house wins," Lola said.

"We're not babies," said Connor, whining with exhaustion.

"She didn't say that!" said Angel, igniting a bickering match.

If I hadn't been eager to surprise Paolo, who didn't know we'd made the connecting flight, and also if I hadn't been concerned about whatever had run across the road, I would have opted to walk. It was a good thing I didn't, though, because we kept driving through acres of dense vineyards, rolling up and down hills, until we saw two signs in Italian. TENUTA GENTILLO to the right. To the left: AZIENDA AGRICOLA.

"Right," said Lola, thanking her new best friend, Google Translate.

"Is this a hotel?" Adella smoothed her hair as she pulled around the marble fountain under the portico. Urns of potted flowers flanked the stairs. Google Earth did many things well, but scale wasn't one of them. I'd seen pictures of houses like this in old copies of *Architectural Digest*, classic beauties that had been restored. No wonder Rosalia had thought I needed to see this place. However, I opted to save my panic about Paolo losing his inheritance until tomorrow. Because somewhere in this magnificent pile was the love of my life.

"There isn't a doorbell," Angel said as we got out of the car and huddled on the curved stone steps of the Mediterranean-style mansion. The enormous double-sided door was arched and flanked by shimmering glass windows. The tiny panes reflected the coach lights under the portico. Perplexed, we stood, waiting.

After a few befuddled moments, Carmen lifted the heavy iron knocker in the shape of a wolf's head, dropping it against the door. We waited again, listening to the breeze rustle the grape leaves. It

was much quieter than Chelan. No street noises. No boats. Silence.
The ultimate luxury.

"Evan is an idiot for not coming," Carmen stated.

"You miss him," said Angel.

Carmen winked at her niece. "You're way too smart."

By making us wait, Rosalia couldn't have evoked more insecurity
if she'd rolled out a red carpet and produced the Queen of England.
As I stood on the step, I realized that Paolo had played as a child
in hallways bigger than our entire house. Sailed with the children
of the Lombardy elite. From the moment he'd followed his dad
around the cave, he'd been trained to take over this estate. Rosalia,
in her own twisted way, had been trying to spare me. I'd sat across
from her in Campbell's, a restaurant that couldn't match a snack
kiosk in Milan, and had heard her say, "Paolo will never be happy
in a town like this."

She was right. The blood drained from my head. I felt weak.

"Knock again," said Juan, lifting up and down on his heels.
"They must not hear us. It's a big house."

"Can you call a place like this a house?" asked Lola.

*Paolo calls it home*, I thought, studying my distorted reflection
in the tiny panes of glass.

The door opened. I straightened. Standing at the threshold was
small woman in her sixties in a white shirt and pressed black pants.
She had a disgruntled look, as if we'd gotten her out of bed. *"Sì?"*

I didn't feel like talking, but everyone deferred to me. "We're
here for the wedding."

"*Sì*, to stay?"

I frowned. Why else would we be knocking on the door? "Yes, I'm Paolo's fiancée."

She beamed, ushering us into a foyer with roughly plastered white walls, crossed by dark beams. The flooring was terracotta with decorative tile patterns in blues, corals, yellow and bright white. Arched insets in the walls held urns of flowers. A small marble Virgin Mary was bright white against a vast wooden table. The whole place had a solemn, hushed beauty.

The woman opened her arms, hugging me fiercely. "So pretty. Oh, the Americans! So happy to have Paolo here and—" she magnanimously threw out her arms "—his wedding." Clasping her hands together, she shook them in the air. "To this, we owe you." She rubbed my arm. "*Mille grazie.* Thank you." Bending down, she whispered to the twins, "Welcome, *bambini!*"

The twin *bambini* scowled in unison. Connor looked tempted to break rank until Angel gave him a glance that clearly said, *They could be cannibals.*

"I show you to your rooms." The woman scooted us toward the sweeping staircase, hung with handsomely framed portraits. "Please, leave the bags. We have a little food, some wine." She glanced at her toughest audience, the *bambini.* "The cook made a *torta bertolina.*" She tapped her chin, thinking. "Hmmm. A cake. With the little fruit."

Adella rubbed Connor's head, accidentally covering his eyes. "That's so kind of you. Or the cook. Anyway, thank you."

"Where's Paolo?" I asked.

"Ah, I don't know." She picked up a phone on the table, pressed a few buttons, then some others, speaking in rapid-fire Italian. As she spoke, she lifted her eyebrows at me. "He's at the winery. He'll be here pronto." She clasped a hand to her cheek. "Ah, I forget my manners. My name is Lucia."

The bed. Where to start with the bed?

The mattress, cradled in a four poster with swirled spindles, soothed my aching spine. The sheets Lucia had turned down were composed of a million perfectly woven threads. The high ceilings felt cozy with the heavy curtains drawn. A glowing bedside lamp burnished the pale walls, which were hung with vivid lake scenes that reminded me of Chelan. Although I'd always cherish my sloping Alvarez room with the orchard view, this was a beautiful bedroom. Couldn't I just hand my life over to Lucia while I took a week-long nap? *Let the world keep spinning, I'm sleeping.*

"Paolo is trying to fix the many things before the wedding." At the foot of the bed, Lucia watched me sigh with contentment. It should have felt strange, but didn't. "He wants to be here now. He talks about you all the time." Her smile shone like the sun. "I know you are someone special because Paolo, he is." She tapped her chest. "In here. For me." She turned to go. "You rest." She paused. "You know, things are not easy for him after the papa die. He takes care of very much." She nodded. "He deserves this happiness." Another warm smile, tempered by something else. "You rest. Soon he'll be here."

# CHAPTER TWENTY-THREE

## Stella Gallagher, This is Your Life

I awoke in the morning to the grinning face of the most handsome man in the world. How could I forget those golden topaz shards in his eyes?

"Someone wants to see you, *bella* Stella."

I wrapped my arms around him, luxuriating in the smooth skin of his back, his muscular arms. We kissed for a long time, curling our bodies around one another, feeling the irresistible tug.

"Whoever it is, they can wait."

He ran his hands through my hair with a groan. "These people cannot."

"Who is it?"

He ignored my question, shaking his head, jumping up from the bed, already halfway dressed. "The coffee, you will love."

*Yes, but is there decaf?* I collapsed on the pillow. "When are we going to have time to talk?"

His face broke into a happy grin. "The rest of our lives."

\*

Stella Gallagher, this is your life.

That's what it felt like, strolling outside onto a stone patio near a rectangular pool. Under a trellis heavy with blooming white wisteria stood all the most important people in my life—including my parents. My body floated somewhere overhead, observing me stopping, turning dead white because I was thunderstruck, nearly knocked senseless by the momentousness of this occasion. My life was changing so rapidly that my brain raced to catch up. My parents were here. They'd traveled thousands of miles to share in my happiness.

But of course, there was one person who wasn't present.

The Alvarez twins, I thought, looking at them now, would always have each other. That link, that ineffable experience of being matched at birth. Rosie's death had left a gaping hole that flapped and tore in my life. From the moment she'd slipped from my grasp, I'd felt raw and exposed.

Half.

Until this moment, I'd fooled myself. Pretended it wasn't the case. But it was.

How could I get married? Or have a baby? Or do any of the things that Rosie would never do? The shock waves rolled off me. The breakfast party waited, uncomprehending. Faces bright with expectation and growing confusion.

But I was plunging headlong into a chasm of despair so deep that I was never coming back. The worst thing was that I would take my child with me.

Paolo's face flickered. "Stella?"

But I'd fled from the patio, back into the cool house.

*

I marched through the house, through the living room, unsure of what to do. Carmen called to me from the back of the house, but I needed time to think. I'd clear my head with a walk. When I pulled open the heavy front door, I'd planned on rushing down the long drive through the vineyards. *Away. Get away. Run.* The world, being a deeply imperfect place, had instead presented me with the following scenario: Rosalia, in a golf cart emblazoned with the vineyard logo. She'd taken one look at my face and patted the seat beside her. "Come on."

There wasn't another option. No doubt Paolo would be busy calming down my disappointed parents. I slid into the strange vehicle. Rosalia took off at surprising speed, down the road to the winery where a row of trucks and cars were parked. Pulling smoothly into a parking spot, Rosalia ushered me toward a huge black Range Rover. The engine roared to life and she continued down the road off the estate though the vineyards.

"You need the coffee," Rosalia stated. I didn't bother nodding, letting the beauty of her estate in daylight wash over me. Sun-warmed grapes sent their fruity aroma into the air.

I was expecting Rosalia to lecture me on everything her precious son was going to lose if I went ahead with my evil plan to marry him. Instead she continued driving her posh vehicle down the world's longest driveway.

"You're really rich," I acknowledged.

Rosalia nodded. "Yes. I am."

*

"Pick one," Rosalia ordered, as I faced an array of decadent pastries topped with glazed berries, glistening apricots, half-moons of wafer-thin lemons and sprigs of fresh mint.

I picked three, just to spite her. When I asked for decaf, Rosalia's face remained impassive. She translated with a shrug, likely adding some comment about fat Americans. She ushered us to a small marble-topped table on the sidewalk of the cobblestone street. The residents of Lecco were waking up. Stylish Italians downed shots of espresso from tiny white cups. Glimpses of the turquoise lake beckoned between the tiled roofs. Lakefront hotels alternated with boxy white mansions, fronted by verdant gardens. Red and white umbrellas stood at attention, awaiting sunbathers.

A picturesque setting in which to feel miserable. Rosalia remained silent, lighting a cigarette. The smoke drifted in my direction.

I stopped eating. "Please put it out."

"Excuse me?" Rosalia lowered the cigarette, away from my face. "It calms me." She took another drag, turning to release the smoke in an elegant thread.

"I'm pregnant."

A spark of joy shot through my misery, observing the panoply of reactions cross Rosalia's face like a slideshow. The Hermès veil was lifted. Rosalia flitted through anger, vulnerability, helplessness and, ultimately, fear. She dropped the cigarette, grinding it under her heel. Standing, she pushed her sunglasses down. "Eat."

My taste buds started working after Rosalia left. Each flaky layer was a symphony. The lemony tang with the bright blueberry cream provided a welcome distraction. Further down the flower-bedecked street, Rosalia appeared to be an ordinary window shopper on her phone, out for a morning walk. By the time she'd returned to the table my blood sugar was restored, but I wasn't ready to face Paolo or my family. Not yet.

Rosalia's manner was brisk. "I'm taking you to see someone."

I opened my mouth to protest, then clamped it shut. I'd lost control from the moment I'd seen those two pink lines. It was useless to pretend otherwise.

"Are you kidding me?"

Rosalia had delivered me to a Catholic church, pulling over at the curb, blocking the entire narrow road. She climbed out onto the cobblestones in front of a crumbling white church, waiting for me to follow. The flowering vines winding around one side appeared to be holding the corner up.

"Rosalia—" I was going to ask her about leaving the car.

"Stop!" Rosalia was a new level of terrifying. Righteous.

Yikes.

"You got your little surprise in. My turn." She turned, heading not into the church but behind it, down a flagstone path shot through with flowering lime-green moss. At the end of the path, a faded blue cottage with potted lemon trees was surrounded by an effusive flower garden. Sunflowers, phlox, lilacs, lilies of every sort: a veritable encyclopedia of flowers. I obediently followed while Rosalia marched up the steps and pushed open the door, speaking to someone in Italian before stepping back, indicating that I should enter alone.

I hesitated. "Aren't you coming in?"

She pursed her lips, shaking her head. "No. This is a conversation for you."

Puzzled, I stepped across the threshold, surprised but not shocked when I saw who was waiting.

# CHAPTER TWENTY-FOUR

## Car Talk

Father Navone reminded me of Yoda. Which was an unkind thought about a man serving me tea made from his own chamomile flowers. He chatted about his garden while I wondered how much of a payoff his church would get toward renovations if he spouted the Gentillo party line.

*Maybe Rosalia is right*, I thought. *Maybe Paolo belongs here.* Chelan was the place I wanted to raise our child. I wanted to recreate the world I'd known for nine lovely years before Rosie died. Overflowing with love expressed in hugs, cuddles and shared dinners.

While my mind wandered, Father Navone waxed poetic about migrating birds who visited every October for his sunflower seeds.

"Rosalia was my sweetheart," Father Navone then said, casually, as if my arch nemesis dating a priest was a known thing. Seeing my shocked look, he nodded. "Before I was a priest."

"Gotcha." My witty rejoinder.

"I have been a friend to her these many years. I counselled her after her husband died. A very dark time in her life. What most people don't know, not even Paolo, was that her husband left Gentillo in debt. It was very tough for many years. Rosalia thought she was going to lose her home. She had to fire people who'd worked their entire lives on the estate. She had help from her brother but Paolo, he was her great hope. The one to continue the family legacy."

Here we go. "She's told me this. Not about the debt, but everything else."

He nodded. "She went to see you in America."

"To scare me off."

Father Navone shook his head. "No." He took a deep breath. "Not to scare you. To save you from the pain of being married to an unhappy man. She believes that her son shares her connection with the land." He placed a gnarled hand over his heart, patting his chest twice. "A deep connection that is rooted in her soul. Many people raised on the land they farm feel this way."

"And what do you think?"

The priest shook his head. "It is not for me to decide God's will."

I rubbed my eyes tiredly. "Maybe it's up to Paolo."

"Maybe I speak as the priest now?"

"Yes. Please. I'm not Catholic."

He waved his hand. "A lot of good people aren't Catholic."

I looked out the window at his mammoth sunflowers. "I would like all the answers, please."

"What are the questions?"

"Should I take Paolo away from his family home, make him raise his child in another county, speaking a different language, possibly lose his family business?"

The priest raised his finger. "The business?"

"Rosalia said she'd disinherit him if he married me and stayed in Chelan."

He laughed as though I'd told a joke. "She's funny, that one. Very passionate."

"Totally. A laugh a minute." I pushed the hair off my face. "I just…" I lifted a finger. "One second." I exhaled slowly. Counted to five, but it didn't work. Tears ran down my face.

The old priest took my clammy hand in his dry ones, tenderly folding my fingers inside his. "I'm listening."

The two most beautiful words in the English language.

Inside the baby blue cottage, surrounded by its riot of flowers, with a priest so still it felt as though he would listen forever, I relived those last minutes on the icy road. The wet touch of snowflakes on my face, the bite of wind on my cheeks. The terrifying moment of impact as we hit the icy depths. My mother's failing arms reaching. Our bond severed as my sister's hand slipped from mine. Losing the girl who I'd still see every day of my life in the mirror as I passed milestones she'd never reach. Sweet sixteen. High school graduation. First kiss. First job. The gorgeous ring on my hand.

Missing her, every step of the way.

The ring shone in the light streaming through the cottage windows. "It's nice," said the priest, clearly unmoved by gemstones.

"I don't understand how I'm supposed to walk down the aisle when she never will." It stuck me with singular clarity, this was the reason I'd never wanted to get married. Not because I was worried about becoming my parents or because I didn't want to be tied down but this… I'd survived. And I felt guilty about living my life when Rosie could not.

The priest stood, opening the window to allow a breeze into the room. "My child…" He moved his chair closer to mine, taking both my hands. "My child, your sister is here." He took a deep breath. "Do this." I obeyed, familiar with how to calm myself. "Now do it again."

As I exhaled my second breath, the priest swirled his hands around the room. "There, do you feel it?"

"Feel what?"

"She's here." He gazed around the room. "Your sister is in every oxygen molecule that enters your body every single day." He gently tapped my temple. "She is in here, locked in your memories, walking with you, shoulder to shoulder. Your children will know her through your memories. You cannot deny yourself life because of your sister's death. Her death demands that you live a full and rich life."

"You think I owe it to her?" Dust motes danced in a sunbeam.

Father Navone shook his head. "No. To yourself. You owe it to yourself."


Rosalia smelled of cigarettes when she picked me up in the town car. Smoothing her linen pants, she waited for me to speak. The car traveled the narrow streets of Lecco, climbing the hills toward the Lombardy vineyards. Low stone fences ran along olive orchards. Lake Como came into view as we drove up vertiginous switchbacks, through neighborhoods of impressive mountainside homes topped with scalloped tile roofs.

I turned to her after carefully, composing my single query. "Rosalia, will you really disinherit Paolo if he marries me?"

Rosalia snorted, waving the question away like a gnat. "No. I will disinherit him if he chooses to spend the rest of his life in America."

"Because you will be lonely?"

She pursed her lips. "Don't be absurd. I have spoken to Paolo, told him the truth, and he is willing to give everything up for you. I tell him that I want you to get married outside, so all my friends can participate in the ceremony, and he says, no, Stella and I want the old, ruined church where the mice live. He says let your friends stay outside and wait for us. I tell him that a girl like you can get used to life in Lombardy and he says you need to stay with your friends. My son is willing to give up everything for you. Everything."

We wound our way back up the hills, passing vineyards and farms tucked into the mountainside. It really was beautiful country. "And you want to know what I'll give up for him?"

She turned to me, her hooded eyes sharp before she turned them back to the road. "I was married to Paolo's father for twenty years. We worked hard at the winery and our marriage because we loved each other. And not once in all those years did I think about what I was giving up for my husband's happiness. I thought about what I was giving him."

# CHAPTER TWENTY-FIVE

## Twinning

My parents brightened when they saw me in the vast Gentillo living room. They stood up from the couch, dwarfed by a fireplace large enough to roast an entire buffalo. We hugged and chatted about their flight, the beautiful countryside and the food.

"Oh my goodness, Stella girl, the food is unbelievable!" said my mom. "Good thing I brought sweatpants for the flight home!"

Rosalia had already hosted them for two days, insisting that they come early and enjoy the pool and lake before the big day.

"You were right, sweetheart," my mom said, pointing to a leather sofa across the room with a gaudy pillow. "She loved the cactus."

I smiled, hugging my father again, who was trying to pretend that he wasn't choked up. "It's okay, Dad. We're all together again." Which of course made Dad weep, because we weren't all together. I whispered in his ear loud enough for Mom to hear, "She's here, Daddy. Breathe in. She's with us."

"Oh, hell's bells," my mom said. "Now I'm gonna have to fix my make-up." She swiped at her tears. "Bob, didn't I say I wasn't going to cry?"

"You did, Lorraine."

Mom ran a finger under her eyes. "Gosh darn it to heck. Look at me now."


Paolo was in the cave, an oblong wooden structure made to look old on the outside. The inside was modern, with rows of barrels receding into the dark. The air was chilled by an air conditioning system humming like a sleeping giant. I dragged Paolo out into the afternoon sun, holding both his hands as he blinked in the light.

We sat on a couple of wooden crates. Chickens pecked at the ground. During our drive back to the estate, I'd noticed the rental company trucks unloading their vans. Unpacking the wedding like a parade. Our parade. Three people, walking down the aisle. I studied Paolo. He looked so much like Rosalia.

"I'm sorry I ran off like that. I had a few things I needed to figure out." A good place to begin.

Paolo tucked a piece of hair behind my ear. "It's fine. Your parents. It's much things."

I nodded, lifting my finger. "But, it's another thing. One tiny little thing."

Paolo smiled. "What?"

"I'm pregnant."

"Really?" A broad grin lit up his face. "A baby?"

I nodded tentatively. "A baby." It came out in a whisper.

Paolo's face clouded and my heart stopped beating. "But I thought you didn't want children."

"I didn't. Until I got pregnant with our child."

*"Sei incinta?"* He jumped up, making the chickens scatter, curving his hand over his belly. I nodded and he jumped into the air, shouting. *"Lei è incinta! Lei è incinta!"* He ran in the direction of the house, cupping his hands around his mouth. *"Lei è incinta!"*

A winery worker strolled past, tipping his baseball hat. *"Congratulazioni!"*

Paolo ran over and hugged the guy, who gave me a thumbs up and kept walking.

When he came to his senses, Paolo returned and lifted me up, holding me tightly. "I'm so happy."

"That's not all."

He pulled back, grinning. "Twins? Is it twins? I'd love twins!"

"What? No. I don't even know if I can handle one kid. Not two."

He hugged me, lifting me off my feet. "We're having the twins."

"Put me down. We are not having the twins."

He complied, stepping back. "Tell me, what else besides this wonderful thing?"

I swallowed. "We can stay here."

Paolo's face went serious. He rubbed his forehead. "What? No. You love your home. Your beautiful lake. Your work."

"And you love yours."

He nodded. "It'll always be here."

"Why don't we stay?"


Utter chaos. Two words that perfectly described a household preparing for a simple wedding that had been hijacked by not one, but two wedding planners. It was the morning of the wedding and Carmen was boycotting Evan, leaving him free to spam text me. Every message started with: *So sorry. Know its ur wedding day.* Carmen, previously at odds with Rosalia, was now high on a potent combination of Rosalia's Visa Platinum and champagne. Rosalia kept dragging up special vintages from her cellar, saying they had been her husband's favorite. She kept everyone tipsy enough to manipulate, yet functionally sober. Carmen had supervised the installation of wooden floor panels on the field. The oak that would "glow" at sunset, according to Carmen. She had a maniacal glint in her eye.

I knew the look. Carmen became a whirling dervish when avoiding pain. My wedding was her wedding. Which was fine. My parents were the cutest tipsy grandparents-to-be. My dad bumped into caterers who spoke limited English, trying to help carry boxes of wineglasses out to the field. Paolo was assigned to track my dad. The fields distantly bordered a cliff. Instead of touring Lecco or taking the twins to looks for actual Lego, my mom (heard shouting to household staff, "Goodness me! Call me Lorraine!" on the hour) surfed the internet for quilt patterns, asking about my nursery theme.

Answer: baby-themed.

*Colors?*

Yes.

*Baby shower?*

Hosted by Amazon. Brought to me by UPS.

*Thank you notes?*

I'm busy forming a human. Also, no belly touching. Ew.

Carmen took my mom aside, whispering. All things baby, besides the work of dividing cells, would be happily outsourced to my BFF. Paolo and I would wait until after the ceremony, when we were safely back in the house, to announce our plans. Manic Carmen shouldn't be anywhere near that cliff when we shared our news.

"Come with me," Paolo said, four hours before the Italian guests would arrive. He wanted to take me for a swim. Show me his lake. We drove down the road I'd traveled with his mother, chatting about nothing and everything. Baby names. Grape varietals. How we'd manage our new living arrangement. I rolled down the window, swooping my hand around in the warm air, enjoying the scenic drive with the man I'd call my husband.

We were lucky, he said. It was unusually warm for October.

Before I'd left, Carmen had a meltdown, stomping her feet while Connor and Angel rolled their eyes at her childish behavior. I agreed with them. "You're a hairdresser, for crying out loud. We have someone coming to do your hair."

I'd shrugged, hugged my parents and winked at Rosalia, who'd raised one perfect eyebrow. Maybe that was her version of a wink.

Paolo took a right where Rosalia had taken a left the day before. He drove to a hidden parking lot wedged between two estates. We parked near some hedges. Paolo opened a tall, wrought-iron gate with a card. Ahead were two docks lined with sleek white boats, trimmed in navy blue, black and shining brightwork. A basket of fresh white towels waited beside a smiling young man in a crisp black shirt and pressed white shorts. He grinned, handing us ice-cold bottles of water.

Paolo shook his head, said something in Italian before asking, "You want him to get the boat?"

My eyes nearly jumped out my head. "Are you serious? A boat concierge?"

Paolo grinned. "Something like this." He ushered me toward the closer dock and said to the kid, *"No grazie."*

The boat had a swim ladder, so I didn't have to jump. I kept delaying, using the gorgeous scenery as my excuse. "This is so gorgeous. Much more sophisticated than little old Chelan."

Paolo finished his water. "More developed." He took off his shirt and I wrapped my arms around his warm skin.

"And sexy."

Paolo kissed me hard. "I hope tonight we're not too tired."

"You mean me?"

He kissed my belly. *"Sì."* Standing up, he swiped the hair off his forehead, bending his back, face up to the sun. "We raise the *bambino* Catholic, right?"

"What?"

Paolo shrugged. "A Catholic priest marry us? Why not?"

I thought of Father Navone. "Let's talk about something else."

Paolo raised his eyebrows and nodded, letting me know that we'd talk about it later. "The wine for tonight is going to be beautiful. A song." He kissed his fingertips. "A symphony!" he yelled into the hills. The echo returned, sweeping across the lake. "I go for a quick swim."

Last night, we'd walked arm in arm through the fields and into the dusty old Gentillo church and had our own private wedding ceremony. Told all the truths. Let the wind sweep through the open windows while we promised to share everything. I finally told him about Rosie. He had been hurt that I hadn't shared it sooner, but was working on understanding. He'd spoken about losing his father. Said how he'd wished they had a smaller house near the village or in Rome, where he could be closer to friends or disappear into the city. Rosalia had vanished into the business. Meeting me, he said, had been like discovering the perfect balance in a wine. "I don't know what I am doing, trying the things and then…" He kissed his fingertips. "Magic."

"Nice to know I'm a glass of wine."

He kissed my cheek. "*Quello perfetto*. The perfect one."

Standing on the seat of the speedboat, he turned when I asked him to stop. I scooted over to the transom, asking him to join me. "*Uno, due, tre,*" I counted. We leapt hand in hand into the deep blue. Sunlight shot into the water, guiding me to the top. Dazzling blue shards of light hit my eyes when I surfaced. Paolo dove under again. A mild panic rose, quickly replaced with the image of my own reflection in the mirror at Twig, giving myself Izzy's pep talk. She'd been right all along. This was the happiest day of my life.

# CHAPTER TWENTY-SIX

## Together

Izzy and Rachel had arrived by the time I'd showered, blow-dried my hair and slipped on my dress. It looked even better now that I wasn't slick with plane sweat and nerves. Carmen sat on the couch in my bedroom, digging through my make-up kit. At home, I was a beauty product junkie, buying the latest Instagram trends. For this trip, I'd kept it basic.

"Mrs. Huttinger the goat lady has more make-up than this," said Carmen.

"What about under-eye concealer, mascara and lip gloss?" I asked, wrapping the gossamer laces around my ankles. "Front bow or back?"

Carmen kept busy with the make-up. "Back. Obvs."

I sat on the couch next to Carmen, taking her hand. "I know you miss Evan."

She grimaced. "Who?"

"He loves you. He's looking after your business so you can be here. Running two wineries is kind of a big deal."

"Running one is a big deal. Two is just showing off."

"You always said Evan was a show-off."

"Totally."

"Why don't you forgive him and help me get hitched?"

She hugged me, wiping her eyes. "Can I at least be jealous? I can't give up all my vices."

"Yes. As long as you hold the barf bag for me on the flight home."

She wrinkled her nose. "How about if I continue the trend and drink for two?"

I did a golf clap. "Tipsy Carmen."

She stood, executing a curtsy. "At your drunken service."

It was my turn to get weepy. "You look beautiful and I love you."

"Till death do us part."

I shook my head. "No. Longer."

She shrugged. "Bit creepy for your wedding day, but okay."

"I'm taking lessons from the twins."

She gave me a high five. "I know, right! Very goth, those two." She pulled me up from the couch. "Okay, nature girl, let's light this candle."

"That's for a rocket launch."

She shook her head. "I just want to get to the drinking part, where I can forget that you bought your dress in London and mine will be from Nordstrom Rack."

"Don't knock The Rack."

As we went down the sweeping staircase lined with portraits of Paolo's relatives, Carmen hooked her pinkie into mine. "Pinkie swear. No trashing discount stores."

A teenager in crisp black shorts and a white Lacoste polo opened the door for us. Our carriage, a flower-festooned golf cart, awaited.

*

The sun had slipped behind San Martino, the sheer granite mountainside that shadowed Lecco. The golf cart pulled up at the back of the wooden platform on the field. To me, it looked like the entire town of Lecco was comfortably chatting on slipcovered chairs, sipping champagne and enjoying a violin quartet and a harp, which Rosalia had apparently hired despite Carmen's wishes. A marquee had been set up for the appetizers and drinks, where legions of wait staff stood to attention, watching us arrive.

My father stepped forward, offering his arm. My dress snagged on the golf cart step.

Emilia, Paolo's sister, stepped out of the crowd, unhooked the delicate satin, and gave me a quick hug and kiss on the cheek. "You make Paolo so happy. *Bella* Stella."

She dashed off to help her husband track down their boys, who, Emilia said, were dead set on hunting rabbits.

My father stood tall in his dashing dove-grey suit and white pocket square, his chin trembling slightly with emotion. His arm felt solid beneath my hand. "Shall we?"

"Did you borrow the suit from George Clooney?" I whispered.

He lifted his brows, nodding as we faced the crowd, who rustled in silks and linen as they rose en masse. "We're the same size."

Carmen pushed Connor and Angel down the aisle. Connor was first, carrying the ring on a tiny pillow that he'd apparently dropped in the dirt. Angel held a bouquet of wildflowers to her chest while scolding her brother about the state of the ring pillow.

The musicians started playing the "Wedding March." Izzy had told me that Felix Mendelssohn wrote the "Wedding March" in 1842 as a piece of incidental music for the Shakespeare play *A Midsummer Night's Dream*. "Get married enough, you learn all kinds of useless garbage," she'd said.

One foot in front of the other. That was all it took. One beautifully shod foot after another. My legs sheathed in a flowing satin skirt topped with elegant lace. A length of white ribbon holding my hair back. Tanned skin. A smile.

Making my way up the aisle past unfamiliar faces, I finally reached Juan, who was weeping while my mother rubbed his back; Adella keeping a close eye on the twins, who stood near the priest; Lola sipping champagne; Izzy and Rachel, the latter of whom was batting her eyelashes at a handsome Italian; and finally, Paolo's family. Emilia, her cheeks flushed from chasing her absentee boys and Rosalia, impeccable in emerald-green lace. Her hooded eyes betrayed nothing, but I glimpsed a flash of white as she crumpled a handkerchief in her fist.

Dad released my arm, whispering into my ear, "Breathe." Paolo stepped forward and gave my father a quick hug. We walked up the aisle toward Father Navone, who appeared to be sleeping.

"Pssst. Padre Navone. *Il matrimonio*," Paolo whispered, leaning forward.

Father Navone opened his eyes. From the front row, Connor and Angel clapped. The crowd tittered. The priest fumbled with his bible. Paolo leaned into me. "I bought you a wedding present," he whispered.

"Oh no. Should I have bought you one?"

He smiled. "It's for us both."

"Well?"

"It's a house."

"Where?"

Father Navone cleared his throat and, without checking with us, began. "*Miei cari amici, siamo qui riuniti...*"

"Lovely wedding," said an elegant woman in a saucer-shaped white hat, standing near the marquee. Emilia had told me she was the mayor of Lecco.

Although not a single aspect of tonight was my choice, I decided I'd take the compliment. "Thank you. Do you live nearby?"

Paolo must have told someone to keep my flute topped up with sparkling lemonade, because it never got below half-full.

The mayor beamed. "Wedding so nice. *Bella.* Beautiful."

Paolo, hunkaliciously at ease in an elegant suit, was chatting with a goateed man in what sounded like fluent French. Go figure. I'd married a polyglot, which was much sexier than it sounded.

Emilia grabbed me from behind, pressing me into a Heimlich maneuver of a hug, then grabbed a flute of champagne from a passing waiter. "This dress! This woman! I love all of it so much." Another embrace. "Paolo finally did something right." After embracing the mayor, who then wandered off, Emilia pointed to a far corner of the field near some fairy lights and potted palms. Four beautifully dressed children knelt in the dusty trampled grass, hunched over what looked like a game console. "The devils have found friends."

"Connor and Angel."

"The angel and three devils," Carmen said, grinning at Emilia. I started to introduce them, but they laughed, telling me they were old friends.

"We talked a lot about the wedding, you know." Emilia winked at Carmen. "How to manage La Tempesta."

I wasn't going to be jealous.

Not. One. Bit.

Emilia was advising Carmen on a tour of Lombardy vineyards when a high buzzing noise invaded the pleasant chatter and soothing quartet. Carmen wrinkled her nose, squinting as she looked up. "Are you kidding me? This is your property; they can't do that!"

Emilia shrugged, sipping her champagne with a secret smile. Paolo was staring with a puzzled look on his face into the indigo air, as were all the guests. A small drone hovered above me, dropping a little robin-egg blue bag from its claw.

"What's that?"

Carmen grabbed it as it fell, thrusting it into my hand. "It's from Tiffany, Stella. I'd know that bag anywhere." She glanced at Paolo. "Well done, Paolo."

Paolo laughed and shook his head. "Not for Stella." He pointed at Carmen. "Is for you."

Of course it was.

Glancing around the fields, I searched for Evan. He was nowhere to be seen. The giggling children, who evidently had the drone controller and not a games console, had directed the drone to pick up the mayor's hat directly off her head. The poor woman pranced around the field, angrily shaking her fist at the hat-stealing drone, screaming in Italian.

Carmen peered inside the bag, her eyes welling with tears.

"Open it! Open it!" Adella and Lola hollered, spilling champagne as they jumped up and down.

Juan Alvarez arrived at his daughter's elbow. She glanced at him, her eyes glistening. He nodded solemnly. *"El tiene mi permiso."*

Carmen pried opened the small white leather box, extracting a perfect one karat sparkler in, naturally, a Tiffany setting.

"Where's my phone?" she wailed, gazing about wildly.

"I can always count on you, in life's vitally important moments, to lose your phone." The crowd cleared a little as Carmen stepped toward Evan, who popped an appetizer in his mouth. "Nice wedding. Very organized."

He nodded at Rosalia, who raised her glass.

"You were here." Carmen sounded like the last kid picked up from soccer practice.

He wiped his mouth with a napkin. "Ye of little faith." He kissed her casually. "Try it on. It's from New York."

She glared at him, tears streaming down her face. "You made me miserable on purpose. You ass."

He sighed, shaking his head a little, then shrugged. "But I'm your ass." He took another sip of his drink. "That sounds all kinds of wrong." He handed his glass to a little boy, who promptly took a furtive sip. Borrowing a napkin from a server, Evan made a production of shaking the linen out, placing it carefully on the dirt. He winked at a little girl, who put one hand over her eye, winking back, in a fashion. "Here goes nothing," he said to the little girl, who solemnly nodded in agreement.

Evan swiftly bent on one knee. "My darling Carmen, thorny rose of my heart. We have had our problems and will assuredly have more. We will fight and we will make up. We will have blissful hours of silence not talking for possibly weeks on end. We are one of those couples. My darling girl, what is so terribly wrong with that? Carmen Mercedes Alvarez, you are the love of my life. Will you do me the honor of spending the rest of your life trying to make me into a better man?"

The entire Alvarez family bawled. Carmen sniffled, rolling her eyes. "So theatrical."

He looked up at her. "Darling, my knee."

"Yes!" Carmen grinned. The crowd burst into cheers and laughter. She helped him up off the grass.

He tilted his head, kissing the tip of her nose. "Well done, by the way."

"Who's running my vineyard?"

He shrugged. "Some guy I found in Señor Frog's. It'll be fine."

She hugged him, admiring her ring. "Gorgeous!"

"You girls and your shiny objects."

Evan went off to find Paolo, leaving me alone with Carmen. We held our hands side-by-side, admiring the twin sparkling gems, reliving the proposal.

I cleared my throat. "Hey, Car, now that you're officially hitched, I want to talk about something."

"I'm engaged. Do you think they'll hold a plane for me and stick me in first class?" Her face glowed with happiness, unable to take her eyes off the ring.

The mayor stomped by on her way to the house to fix her dusty spaceship hat. The drone had been confiscated with promises of flight later this evening, over the vineyards, to spy on foxes.

"We were going to tell you later, together… but Paolo and I have decided we're going to live here."

Carmen's eyes narrowed. "You've officially ruined everything."

"Whoa. Hang on. No, I didn't. Paolo made the mistake of buying the Indigo Bay house for me as a wedding present so we can always have a home in Chelan."

She rolled her eyes. "Excuse me, a mistake?"

"The dock is right there. It's a horrible place for children."

"What a jerk. First you have to get married in a slum, now a waterfront vacation home in another country. The horror."

I lifted both hands. "Don't be like this."

She went back to looking at her ring. "It's amazing, right? I'm fine. Money can replace people."

I sipped my lemonade. "We're spending two weeks in Chelan to see if I can adjust to the idea of having a toddler in a waterfront home."

"Keep going."

"Then, we come back here. I have the baby in Italy so they can have dual citizenship and never have to marry someone for a passport."

"Because that is exactly what happened here."

"We alternate years until the baby is ready to go to school." I let that sink in. "That was Rosalia's idea. Once she found out I was willing to stay here for long periods of time, she insisted she'd never actually have gone through with disinheriting Paolo."

Carmen tapped her toe. "What a liar. So what happens when the zygote goes to school?"

"Then we stay here and spend the summers and holidays in Chelan."

She placed her hand over her chest. "Live here?"

I nodded. "Paolo belongs here. But we'll have the house in Chelan, and I'll visit lots."

"I like the sound of that."

Carmen was startled as Rosalia joined us, pursing her lips. "What? Oh, it's time to head to the house for dinner." Rosalia shook her head, lifting Carmen's hand, studying the brilliant diamond with a practiced eye.

"Not bad," Rosalia pronounced, stepping back, lifting her hands and clapping once. *"La cena è servita in casa."*

Guests wandered toward the house. Stately oaks glowed with hanging lanterns. Flowers floated in the pool. Rows of long linen-draped tables were set with antique china and crystal wineglasses. An extraordinary place that had produced an exceptional man.

Paolo hung back, letting me walk with my best friend. One glance between us, and he knew that I'd talked to Carmen about our plans. Paolo and I had the rest of our lives together. We'd have our *bambino*. Two countries. One home.

Hand in hand, my best friend and I navigated the meadow in our heels, just as we'd navigated life's bumpy path.

Together.

# A Letter from Ellyn

Dear Reader,

A huge thank you for choosing to read *Promises at Indigo Bay*. If you did enjoy it, and want to keep up to date with all my latest releases, sign up at the following link. Your email address will never be shared, and you can unsubscribe at any time.

*www.bookouture.com/ellyn-oaksmith*

When I set out to write the Blue Hills series and *Promises at Indigo Bay*, I chose one of my favorite places on earth. Lake Chelan is a crystal-clear lake fed by the North Cascades mountain range snowmelt. It ranges in color, depending on the time of day, from deep sapphire blue to vibrant turquoise. It's surrounded by sloping hills planted with lush green vineyards. In the summer, flocks of tourists play in the lake by day and visit one of the many vineyards and tasting rooms by night. I've visited Lake Chelan nearly every year of my life since I was a teenager, and my own adult children have visited Chelan since they were babies. As I write, my youngest, now grown, is there with friends. If you google "Stehekin" and

"*Lady of the Lake* boat tour in Chelan" you'll be able to catch a glimpse of this beautiful corner of the world and see where Stella takes her mother-in-law.

In the past two decades, the character of Chelan has changed due to the great amount of wealth flooding in from the tech boom in the Pacific Northwest. Indigo Bay, the little house where Stella and Paolo find their way to each other, represents both sides of Chelan. Stella, who comes from working-class old Chelan, has fallen in love with Paolo, who represents new Chelan. Indigo Bay, the charming little house with the renewed interior, represents the best of both worlds. The owner of Indigo Bay stays true to Chelan's humble beginnings by not tearing down the lovely old place to build yet another mega-mansion, allowing Paolo and Stella to live in harmony with the tech millionaires next door.

I hope you loved *Promises at Indigo Bay* and if you did, I would be very grateful if you could write a review. I'd love to hear what you think, and reviews make such a difference, helping new readers to discover one of my books for the first time. I love hearing from you all—you can get in touch on my Facebook page, through Twitter, Goodreads, Instagram or my website.

Thanks,

Ellyn x

ellynoaksmith

EllynOaksmith

@EllynOaksmith

EllynOaksmith.com

# Acknowledgments

As always thanks to Hannah Bond, my ever-patient editor who is a dream collaborator. Kim Nash, thanks so much for your help with the *Summer at Orchard House* launch. You two have been the very brightest spots during my pandemic writing. Thank you to Oliver Rhodes, whom I've only seen on Zoom, as he departed Bookouture when I was lucky enough to hear about the history of this vibrant company. Oliver, you created a unique and special place for writers that I feel eternally grateful to have stumbled upon. Sarah Hardy, thanks for all your social media wizardry. To my sister Liz, for always listening. To Malissa, for being a rock and a cheerleader. To the Bookouture cover artists for these incredible covers. To AMS/CES/SMS, as ever, for being everything, always.